Lost in Revery
Tales of the Dungeon Crawlers

Volume 1

Matthew Phillion

Lost in Revery – Tales of the Dungeon Crawlers Volume 1

Lost Continuity Press

Contact:

theindestructiblesbook@gmail.com

Originally published as:

The Players Guide to Dungeon Crawling - March 2018

The Dungeoneer's Bestiary - June 2018

The Ghoul Slayer's Guidebook - October 2018

Printed in the United States of America

ISBN-13: 978-0-9979165-2-2

Cover: Sterling Arts & Design

To my fellow adventurers of the mind, who survived the real world long enough for dungeon crawling to become socially acceptable. We made it.

From the Author

The Dungeon Crawlers started off as a bit of an experiment. Born out of *Roll for Initiative*, the novella where the heroes of *the Indestructibles* were trapped in (the then-unnamed land of) Revery, this series was a chance for me to continue exploring a reality I wasn't quit finished with after the Indestructibles found their way home. So I asked: we know how superheroes would react to finding themselves stuck in a tabletop role playing game. What about people like *us?*

I also wanted the world the Dungeon Crawlers would explore to feel like a RPG campaign—start off small, in a village, build up to greater challenges, and, of course, find themselves delving into underground caverns and tunnels where new threats lay in wait, without it feeling like a game module. A lot of writers joke that writing fantasy novels is what happens when you want to DM but can't find any players, so you create your own.

That's sort of what happened here.

I did not expect to get such a positive response to the new series, but because of that response, it just kept going—one game "session" after another. And that's how we end up here in Volume 1, collecting the first three novellas in print for the first time.

So pull up a chair, grab some polyhedral dice, roll up a character, and join us in the land of Revery, where the gang struggles to figure out if they're heroes of the realm or murder hobos, and try to understand why they feel so much more alive in this life of danger, fighting bogeymen and undead than they ever did in the real world, if they can ever go home again… and if they even want to.

I need to thank all the usual suspects who helped make this

i

happen: Stephanie Buck, Colin Carlton, Christian Hegg for being test readers; Christine Geiger for her enthusiastic editing skills; and Sterling Arts & Design for another awesome cover.

And thank you for joining me in this experiment in high fantasy and low humor. And for being part of the big, beautiful tapestry that the gaming world has become. I remember the days when this sort of thing was taboo, and it is a wonder to behold, seeing role playing games bring people together, building bonds through laughter, adventure, and slaying monsters together around the table.

Matthew Phillion
Salem, Massachusetts
May 2019

Book 1:

The Players Guide to Dungeon Crawling

Chapter 1: Game Night

Cordelia sat in her car, watching rain spatter against the glass, shattering the light reflected from Jack's house like bulbs on a Christmas tree. She pulled the hood of her canvas jacket up and took a deep breath, regretting the Chuck Taylors she wore on her feet. I am entirely unprepared for this weather, she thought. Bracing herself, she jumped out of her car, slamming the door behind her, and darted across the street. She ran full speed into Jack's front door, which did not move as she expected it to, hitting it with a heavy thud.

The door opened. Eriko opened it, looking at her sheepishly from beneath her short, black hair, which she'd aggressively parted to one side today in a sort of toppled-over fauxhawk.

"Sorry," she said. "I think I locked it by accident."

Cordelia just sort of groaned an indignant response and stepped inside. She made sure to splash Eriko with the runoff from her coat.

"Thanks, Cordelia," Eriko said.

"I had to repay you for the gift of a concussion you just gave me with the door, pumpkin," Cordelia said. She kicked off her shoes by the front door and stepped inside. She could smell popcorn and what might be one of Tamsin's vegan monstrosities pretending to be cookies. Before she could investigate fully, her vision went completely black.

"What the fuck," she said, reaching up to feel a heavy towel over her head.

"Figured you could use it," Morgan's deep voice said, hinting at laughter. Cordelia pulled the towel off her head and wiped down her face and shoulders.

"Great night for this, huh?" she said, seeing Morgan's shirt and pants were also still showing signs of a wet walk here.

"It'll add to the ambiance," he said.

Together they walked into the dining room, where everyone else had gathered. Jack at the head of the table, looking giddy and anxious—and Cordelia knew exactly why, too, because after years of cajoling, he, Morgan, and Eriko had finally convinced everyone to try out an actual, honest to goodness role playing game, something they'd been doing for years and wanted their whole, tight friendship circle to join in on. Cordelia used to play, before she'd had to take on a second job to make ends meet after the car accident, and if she were being honest with herself, she was excited to get back into it, too. A chance to hang out with her best friends for some cooperative storytelling and forget about the real world for a while? Sounded like a perfect Friday night to her.

The twins were the real newbies, though Eriko was convinced Tamsin and Tobias were going to be instantly addicted. Tamsin never met a story about magic she didn't love, and Tobias, despite talking a big game, was a closet geek of a highly respectable level, though his tastes leaned more toward comics and Star Wars than Dungeons & Dragons or *Lord of the Rings*. True to character, Tobias was absolutely blistering his sister with jokes about bringing vegan cookies to a game night, and she was giving it right back to him.

Morgan handed Cordelia a drink and clinked his own beverage against hers automatically. She shot him a huge smile. I love my friends, she thought. I love these people. And she was so looking forward to this, because she knew they all had worries they needed to escape from. Eriko's mother had passed away recently, though from her playful demeanor, you'd never know it. Morgan was paying off medical bills for his father, and she could always tell when he his mind turned to that when his gaze drifted. Jack, sitting on the back of his chair like a gargoyle, presiding over the table, was on layoff watch at his day job, expecting to be unemployed at any moment. And the twins had some vicious family drama they avoided the details about as much as possible, though whatever was going on there, they'd both been losing weight to an unhealthy degree from worrying, and Tobias always seemed to have something on his mind he couldn't quite put into words.

Money and health; family and jobs. Real world stuff. The real world is cruel and unfair. Give me a fight against a goblin horde and rolling some dice any day instead, Cordelia thought.

"Hey Jack!" Cordelia said. "What game did you decide on? D&D? Pathfinder? Maybe Shadowrun?"

"Oh man, I should've done Shadowrun," Jack said, hoping off his chair. He winked at her. Very few people can wink without looking creepy, and because of this, Jack and Cordelia had spent their entire lives together—classmates since the second grade, friends the entire time—practicing the non-creepy wink. It became a tradition to try to be the first one to wink at the other when they got together, and when possible to make it as creepy as possible. He failed on the creepy part as he tripped over his own feet jumping off his chair and almost face-planted on the table.

"Grace and elegance, as always," Morgan said. "Thank you for not shattering your teeth on the table."

Jack bowed dramatically.

"Thank you, thank you," he said. "That was what we'd call a failed acrobatics check. And to answer your question, Cordie, I've got a new game for us."

"So, what you're saying is we're going to spend the next four hours watching you try to figure out the rules," Eriko said.

"What? No. Well. Maybe?" Jack said. "But there's an upside. No dungeon master. We all get to play."

"Instead of you or Morgan trying to kill us with orcs," Eriko said.

"I have never tried to kill you with orcs," Morgan said.

"No, you prefer things out of forgotten pages of a monster compendium so we don't have any idea what we're fighting," Eriko said.

"True," Morgan said.

"That's why I usually like dragons. You know what you're going to fight, but you know you're going to die anyway," Jack said. "Anyway. This thing's got a sort of… it uses cards and dice roles as an AI."

Jack slid the box onto the table, a big, dense cube of cardboard emblazoned with stereotypical high fantasy art. Morgan pulled it in front of him.

"Where'd you pick this up?" he asked.

"Dragon Forge," Jack said.

"I love how you guys basically speak an entire language of your own," Tobias said, eyeballing the box from opposite Morgan.

"And yet you understand every word we say," Eriko said.

"I am fluent in geek," Tobias said. "I judge not."

"Dragon Forge, huh?" Morgan said.

"Yeah. Lonnie's knocking prices down on everything. Trying to clear out stock so he doesn't have to throw anything out when they close," Jack said.

Cordelia picked up on the wistful tone between Jack and Morgan. The game shop downtown had been there since they were kids, but it had been dying a slow death for years. Lack of interest and online sales were killing the small store.

"Okay, I don't speak geek," Tamsin said. "But I'd like a translation. What's going on with this?"

"Usually one of us directs the game and everyone else plays a character," Cordelia said. "Correction – usually Jack or Morgan directs the game, depending on the campaign. And it's like collaborative storytelling."

"You of all people are going to love this," Tobias said to his sister.

"And you're not?" she said back.

"I am open to the experience," he said. "God knows I've heard you guys talking about it for enough years. Might as well actually participate. I feel like this is some part of your life I've never met before. It's like meeting your Mr. Snuffleupagus."

"So, in this case, everyone picks a type of character," Jack said. "The game sort of tells us how the villains react, so we can all be on the same side. Which is a nice change of pace for us."

"And probably a little better for you since we know how much you love confrontation," Eriko said. The doorbell rang, and she darted off. "Pizza's here."

"I really don't like competitive games," Tamsin said.

"Well, I mean, RPGs really aren't intended to be competitive. We're all on the same side to tell the story. But..." Jack said.

"It'll be nice for everyone to play a character for once," Morgan said.

"You're not going to miss playing the all-powerful game master?" Cordelia said.

"You know how much extra work that is!" Morgan said. "No. I'm not going to miss it."

Eriko re-entered and slid three boxes of pizza onto the table.

"Who ordered?" Eriko said.

"Me," Jack said.

"You hungry when you ordered?" Eriko said.

"Maybe," Jack said.

"Because this is overkill," Eriko said.

"First rule of ordering pizza. Don't order when you're already hungry," he replied, sliding the box open, revealing map pieces, dice, and little plastic miniatures in the shape of monsters and heroes.

"Dibs on the rogue," Eriko said.

"Always," Cordelia said. "Have you ever played anything else?"

"I was that multiclass rogue-sorcerer that one time," Eriko said.

"I sometimes wonder how you didn't end up in a life of crime," Cordelia said.

"Who… do I pick who I play?" Tamsin said, gingerly poking through a pile of gray heroic figurines. "Oh, this one's got a book. This one's mine."

"Least surprising moment of the night, ladies and gentlemen," Eriko said. "Tamsin wants to play the wizard."

"Ravenclaw for life, babe," Tamsin said. "You going to try to convince me I shouldn't play a magician?"

"I was going to suggest it if you didn't figure it out for yourself," Eriko said.

"I am so being the dude with the guitar," Tobias said, holding up a figure, vaguely elven in look, with a sword in one hand and a lute in the other.

"Why are you pretending you don't know that's a bard?" Morgan said.

"Because I keep forgetting I'm in friendly company, among my fellow geeks," Tobias said. "Bard it is. Tell me this means I've got magic songs."

"I think you have magic songs," Jack said, lifting a hand up in the air to catch something Morgan threw at him. His face lit up. "You know me so well, Morgan."

"We have had approximately seven hundred conversations about how you miss playing a ranger in the past year," Morgan said. He picked up another piece and slide it across the table. "Yours even comes with a wolf pet."

"Oh, this is so amazingly stereotypical and I love it," Jack said. "I love playing the stereotypical ranger! It's my favorite overused archetype!"

Tobias took his miniature and put it down next to his sister's.

"Look, Tam. We're even twins in the game. Team pointy ears!"

He held a hand up for a high five. His sister left him hanging there for a full fifteen seconds before begrudgingly slapping his palm with her own.

"Of course you guys are elves," Eriko said.

"What? Why do you say that?" Tamsin said.

"Because elves are pretty, and the two of you are fucking

gorgeous in real life," Eriko said. "You're just staying true to form."

"I am choosing to take that as a compliment," Tobias said. "And I will not be persuaded otherwise."

Eriko turned her figurine over in her hand, scoping out the design.

"These are bizarrely nice for a game I've never heard of," she said. "I'm calling my character Rouge, by the way."

"Rouge the Rogue," Morgan deadpanned.

"Come on, you know that's funny," she said. "The internet spells it that way all the time. I'll be the most famous rogue on the interwebs!"

"Basically your life's goal, in real life or otherwise," Jack said. "Who you got, Cordie?"

Cordelia rummaged through the remaining heroes. There were plenty of options—a heavily armored knight, a druidic priestess, some sort of alchemist, someone who looked like a combination of warrior and magician. Then she found the one she knew she had to play. She set it down on the table proudly.

"That is boss," Eriko said.

"That's terrifying," Tamsin said.

"What is that?" Morgan said, picking the piece up. "Oh dude, you're a barbarian!"

"An orc barbarian, if I'm looking at that correctly," Cordelia said.

"Might be a half-orc," Jack said, sliding a card across the table with her character's stats. The card also had a portrait of the character in full color—green-skinned, with a reddish Mohawk, slightly pointed hears, and fierce fangs visible where her lower canine teeth would be. She carried a battle axe almost as tall as she was.

"I think I love this character already," Cordelia said.

"You're playing a monster then," Tamsin said.

"A good monster," Tobias said. "This is why we love you, Cordelia."

"A badass monster woman with an axe and a Mohawk who is going to slay all the critters that try to get you guys," Cordelia said. "I'm basically *Lord of the Rings* She-Hulk."

"Feeling the need to smash some stuff to blow off some steam?" Tobias said.

"You got it," Cordelia sad.

"What about you, big guy?" Eriko said, punching Morgan in the arm. "Paladin? Deathknight? Necromancer?"

Morgan poked around the pile of figures until he found a solidly built character in heavy armor with a two-handed hammer in his hands.

"Group needs a cleric," he said. "I'll volunteer to be den mother."

"Not every group needs a healer," Jack said. "We've played without one before."

Morgan laughed his infectious laugh.

"This motley group needs a healer," he said. "Trust me, I bet we'll all be glad I'm playing this guy before the first session is over."

"Rogue, cleric, barbarian, wizard, with a ranger and a freakazoid bard thrown in for good measure," Eriko said. "Good group. I like it."

"Do we name them?" Tamsin said.

"Oh, please tell me we get to name them," Tobias said.

Jack was thumbing through the instructions, nodding to himself.

"It's a campaign," he said. "We'll play the same characters through a whole bunch of sessions. Absolutely you should name them. It's part of the story. We already have Rouge already."

"Please tell me that's not canon," Morgan said.

"I picked the game. I say it's canon," Jack said.

Eriko stuck her tongue out at Morgan. Morgan pretended to try to grab it.

"I'm going to name my guy…" Tobias started.

"Please don't be super snarky about it," Cordelia pleaded.

"Oberon the Blue," Tobias said.

"That is… not super snarky," Cordelia said.

"It almost sounds like a bard name," Morgan said.

"Then I'll be Nimue the Silver," Tamsin said.

"Oh, it's like you guys have been doing this your whole lives," Jack said, clutching his hands to his chest. "I am so proud of you."

"Are you serious about Rouge?" Morgan asked Eriko, sounding resigned.

"Can it be my nickname, at least?" Eriko said.

"Fine, I guess," Morgan said.

"Okay, Rouge the Rogue. My given name is Scarlet."

"Oh, come on!" Morgan said, sending Eriko into a belly laugh. "What about you, chief?"

"I'm going all in on the ridiculous stereotypes," Jack said. "I'll just introduce my character as Raven."

Now it was Morgan's turn to roar laughing.

"Man, you are just diving right into the fantasy ranger trope machine, huh?"

"We never do tropes! We try so hard not to do tropes," Jack said. "I say for Tam and Tobias' first game, we just own it."

"Fine," Morgan said. "I'll call my cleric Bastion."

"So melodramatic!" Jack said.

"Hey, you said we're gonna own it," Morgan said. "If you're all in, I'm all in."

"You guys were going to give me a hard time about not coming up with a good name, and you're Raven and Bastion?" Tobias said. "You're like, walking terrible fan fic right now."

"And proud of it," Morgan said. "What about you, Cordelia? Are you the Widowmaker? The Deathdealer?"

"Orchid," Cordelia said.

Everyone went silent for a moment.

"Orchid… the orc," Eriko said. "I just want to go on record that nobody gets to make fun of me for this entire campaign when she's playing Orchid the orc."

Cordelia let a vast smile creep across her face.

"Orchids are ridiculously delicate. They're hard to keep alive. And I'm playing a battle-scarred barbarian warrior. I think it's pretty damned clever, what I just did right there."

"It really is," Tamsin said. She raised her glass in the air. "To Orchid the orc!"

"I love you guys," Cordelia said. "So, we have characters, we have names, we have pizza… how do we start?"

Jack picked up the oddly shaped dice from the box and hefted them in the palm of his hand.

"These look weird to you? They're… They look like they're six-sided, but there's something not right about them. Like they're not balanced correctly."

Eriko took one from him and held it up to her eye.

"Are they melted? You're right, this doesn't look balanced."

Morgan took one as well.

"They aren't plastic," he said. "They don't feel like something that would melt. Like stone?"

"Whatever," Eriko said. She juggled her lone die in her hand. "Let's see how they roll, anyway."

She tossed the die onto the table.

And then everyone disappeared.

Chapter 2: Rude awakenings

The first thing Morgan noticed was the warmth. Light filtering through his closed eyes, a gentle breeze, just the hint of fall on the summer air. The seat beneath him rocked comfortingly, and he could hear the clip-clop of horse hooves nearby.

What a weird dream, he thought. I've never dreamed without pictures before. Sound and warmth? It's like I'm sleeping in my own dream. Hello, meta.

Morgan tried to hold on to the dream, but a hand on his shoulder pulled him away.

"Father Bastion," a gruff, older voice said. "Father Bastion? Sorry to wake you."

Morgan opened his eyes, blinking away the blindness as golden mid-afternoon sun splashed against his face.

"Well, shit," he said.

He sat on a wooden wagon, pulled along by a pair of horses who had seen better days. He looked down at his body, realizing he was far from comfortable, to find he wore solidly built armor that had, like the horses, seen better days as well. A war hammer rested between his knees, massive head on the floor, haft where it could be reached easily.

"I'm sorry, Father," the stranger's voice said again. Morgan looked to his left to find an elderly man, with a long, gray beard that had seen even worse days than Morgan's armor, looking up at him with a worried brow.

"I... Huh. Hm," Morgan said. I wonder what was in that pizza, he thought. If I'm hallucinating, this is legit. Everything felt real. He could smell the stale beer on the man's breath, and the stink of the horses. Cicadas hummed in the distance. This is crazy realistic, he thought.

"You were really out just now," the old man said. "I wanted to let you sleep, but the lady seems to be losing her mind a little bit."

"The lady?" Morgan said.

"The elf," the old man said. "The card reader who's traveling with us. I mean I know most magic users are a bit touched in the head, but she woke up from a nap and just started crying and yelling for people who aren't here."

"The elf," Morgan said, remembering the game session they'd just set up. Tamsin. "Where is she?"

The old man pointed to the back of the wagon, which was a simple wooden structure with a tented roof. He could hear Tamsin crying inside. Struggling in his armor, Morgan moved to slide himself through the cloth doorway behind him leading inside.

"Try to calm her down, Father?" the old man said. "We don't want to attract bandits. You know crying women and children attract bandits."

"What about crying men?"

"Them too, I imagine," the old man said as Morgan disappeared inside. "I prefer to repress my emotions with alcohol, myself."

"Morgan!" Tamsin yelled before Morgan's eyes could adjust to the dark. She slammed into him, throwing her arms around him. "Tell me you guys didn't drug me and kidnap me to a Ren Faire."

"I have no idea where we are," Morgan said.

"Well, it's not Massachusetts," Tamsin said. She wore overly-complex robes with arcane symbols stitched in along the cuffs of the sleeves, as well as along the edge of the hood she had pulled back away from her face—her face, Morgan was relieved to see, looked mostly like herself, which meant he probably still had his own face as well. "I mean it looks a little bit like the Berkshires I guess but… Morgan, what the hell happened? This isn't normal, right? You guys haven't been like, group hallucinating playing these games all these years."

"This is the furthest thing from normal I have ever experienced in my entire life," Morgan said. He lowered his voice, looking over his shoulder toward the front of the wagon. "He called me Father Bastion."

"Yeah, and I heard him talking about how I'm some sort of… tarot reader?" Tamsin said. "I don't know how to do tarot cards. I have no idea what I'm doing. And Morgan…"

"What?"

She brushed the hair back from the side of her head, revealing one perfectly pointed, dainty elven ear.

"What. The fuck. Happened to my ears, Morgan."

"No way," he said.

"Oh, they're both like that. I tried to pull the point off. It hurt. It really hurt."

"Where are we?" Morgan asked, intending for it to be rhetorical. Tamsin did not hear it that way.

"How do I know? This is my first game!" Tamsin said.

"I knew we should've just played a Beginner's Box," Morgan said.

He sat down on a bench along one wall. Tamsin joined her.

"Where is everyone else?" she said. "Where's my brother?"

"I don't know, Tam," Morgan said.

"What do we know?"

"I'm a heavily armored priest, you're an elf, this seems to be real, and this cart is being driven by the Middle Earth equivalent of a hillbilly."

"I want my brother, Morgan," Tamsin said.

"Trust me, I'd be just as happy as you are knowing where he is," Morgan said. "I guess the question is… where are we going?"

Morgan stuck his head back out the front of the wagon.

"I'm sorry, old timer. I'm having a lapse in memory. Where is our next destination again?" he said.

"The village of Moderate Expectations," the driver said.

"Is that... is that like its name, or is that an epitaph, or..."

"That's its name. The founders were very reasonable people who did not believe in excessive optimism."

Morgan opened his mouth to speak, closed it again, blinked a few times, and nodded.

"Great. Okay. Sounds good," Morgan said. "I'm... calming the, um, seer back there down a bit. We're going to chat a bit longer. Can you mind the road on your own?"

"We're near enough to town we should be safe, and we've got a couple of young fellas as outriders," the old man said. "Take your time, Father. Administer to the sick, even if they're just a little sick in the head."

"Thank you, um..."

"Bobrick," the driver said.

"Bobrick. How could I have forgotten," Morgan said.

"Most people do," Bobrick said.

Morgan slipped back inside.

"We are screwed in ways I can't even begin to parse out," Morgan said.

Tamsin sat on the bench across from Morgan. She stared at her hands.

"So, if this is real..." she said.

"It sure feels real," Morgan said.

"I wonder if..." She looked up at him. "You showed up looking just like your character. Does that mean we can do spells?"

"Maybe?"

"I should try," she said. For the first time, the fear in her voice had been overtaken by something that almost sounded like excitement.

"Maybe let's not cast fireball in the back of a wooden wagon," Morgan said.

"Maybe later, then."
"Later is good."
"Yeah, later."

Chapter 3: The High Life

I don't know how this happened, Tobias thought as he strolled down the main street of the medieval-looking town he'd woken up in, but if this is how the gang plays this game, I'm in.

He'd woken up in an expensive bed at the local inn—well, maybe not expensive, but certainly the best the place could offer, possibly the best bed in the entire town. He also had not woken up alone, which he was particularly amused about, even though he had no idea how he got there or how he ended up with the sleeping arrangement he found himself in. Confused and amused, he'd slipped out quietly, somehow knowing instinctually which pair of pants on the floor was his, a vibrant pair of pantaloons cut with different shades of blue. He pulled on a well-worn but clean white shirt that made him feel like a pirate, a shiny pair of boots, and a garish pink vest, slung the lute he knew had to be his over his shoulder, and buckled on a sword belt.

He caught sight of himself in the mirror as he left. The pointed ears were a nice touch, he thought, and his hair here was far more dynamic, shaved underneath with a dramatic swoop on the top that fell roguishly over one eye. I look like an anime heartthrob, he thought. If this is a hallucination, I hope it never ends.

As he stepped downstairs, the burly bartender and a barmaid—

both a bit older than him, but handsome folk in their own way, smiled at him admiringly.

"I gotta say, you little elven scamp, you know how to pull in a good crowd," the bartender said. He set down a plate with eggs and bacon on it and a lumpy roll Tobias was slightly hesitant to taste, but he found himself famished, and dove into the meal anyway.

"I don't know if it's your words or your singing that hooks them more," the barmaid said. She rumpled his hair, then fixed it gently, smoothing it back away from his face. "Tell me you'll set up shop in town and play here every night."

Tobias shot her his most disarming smile. Might as well play along, he thought. No telling when this dream will end.

"I can't stay forever. They'll grow tired of me," he said. "You know the greatest musicians always leave them wanting more."

"Just promise you'll come back through town again, then," the bartender said. "We sell more ale and wine when you play one night here than we ordinarily do in an entire week."

"Then I shall always return," he said, winking at the bartender. "Tell me though—it was a very… very long night. How long is my promised engagement here?"

"You only agreed to three nights when you arrived," the barmaid said. "At least that's how I remember. And last night was to be your farewell performance."

Tobias found his eye drawn to a lone figure seated in the corner of the bar, a stein in his—maybe her?—hand, watching from beneath a heavy, deep red hood.

"Well, let me get some air and think about what songs I haven't performed yet, and I'll let you know if I have enough material to play one more night," he said, not taking his eyes off the stranger.

"Very well," the bartender said. He slid a mug of dark, hefty ale down the counter. Tobias caught it. "Something to fortify you. You left quite a few audience members disappointed you didn't go home with them. Walking the streets of Moderate Expectations might be a lot of work for you today."

Tobias took a deep draught from the mug, fighting off a grimace and a gag. Play the part, play the part, play the part, he thought.

"Well then. To the good health and fortunes of Moderate Expectations," he said, hopping off his stool and head heading out the door with a bow.

"Don't forget your hat," the barmaid yelled. A blue pointed hat with a gargantuan white feathered plume sticking out of it awaited him by the door. He scooped it up, bowed gracefully, and stepped outside into the warm sunlight.

"Now. What the holy hell is going on, and how did I get here," he muttered to himself.

He found the journey down the main drag more than a little alarming. He clearly had made a name for himself in this town, with groups of women, and men, murmuring and pointing just out of earshot. He saw a few faces with the sort of grumpy annoyance that could only indicate a spurned suitor, and a few others that told him perhaps this persona he'd come to inhabit had, possibly, not been entirely honorable in his nocturnal adventures.

Okay, he thought. Maybe staying an extra day is a bad idea. I have no idea where to go from here, but clearly Oberon the Blue has made as many enemies as he's made fans here.

He was suddenly very thankful for the hearty breakfast. And that he'd brought all his belongings with him.

That was when a ham-sized hand reached out from an alleyway and dragged him out of the street.

Tobias made a strangled yipping nose, cut off abruptly as his body slammed into a stone wall behind him.

"Little pointy-eared thief," his attacker said. The man was big, moon-faced, with the look of a farmhand, or possibly a draft horse given the size of him. He had a makeshift club in one hand, and was backed up by another man, who held a butcher's cleaver.

"We don't know what kind of sorcery you're using, but we know you're swindling this whole town," the smaller man said.

"Taking whatever you want, whenever you want it. You're

bleeding people dry," the farmhand said. "And I know my sister stayed behind at the tavern the other night."

"I—you know, it's probably a mistake to say so, but I really don't remember," Tobias said. "Everything's a little fuzzy before this morning. I…"

The farmhand cut him off by swinging the club at Tobias' head. Tobias dodged the blow so easily he started laughing.

"Hey, look at that. I have better reflexes here than I do in real life."

"We'll show you real life," the man with the butcher's blade said. But before he could take a step forward, the man let out a small, sharp whine. He lowered his blade.

"The bard's mine," someone said in a voice just above a whisper. Tobias could see the top of a red cloak poking up from over the butcher's shoulder. The stranger turned their captive toward the mouth of the alley. "Go home. Leave the musician to me."

The butcher started walking away slowly. The farmhand hesitated.

"Why should we let you have all the fun?" he said. "We caught him first."

As if from the ether, a throwing knife landed with a deep, eerie *thunk* in the man's club. The force of the strike knocked the improvised weapon from his hand.

"Oh," the farmhand said.

"Next one goes in your left eye," the stranger said. The farmhand reached down to pick up his club, but the stranger made a soft *tsk-tsk* noise, and the big man left his club, backing up out of the alley until he was out of sight.

"Look, I swear I don't remember anything before this morning," Tobias said, feeling himself break out in a sweat.

"Me either!" the stranger said, abandoning the gravelly aspect to their voice and throwing back their hood.

"Eriko?" Tobias said, seeing his friend beaming in front of him.

"Is this not the best thing ever?" she said, throwing her arms around him. "This is fucking amazing!"

"Do you know where we are?" he said.

"Do you really care?" Eriko said. "This is like time travel mixed with Ren Faire mixed with being on the set of *Lord of the Rings*. I love this. This is the greatest day of my life."

"I… I'm not going to lie, this is the most fun I've ever had, and I've been awake like fifteen minutes," he said. "But you seriously don't know what's going on?"

"Not a clue, buttercup," Eriko said. "Seen the others yet?"

"Nope."

"You know you have a hickey, right?" Eriko said, roughly grabbing Tobias' chin to look at his neck.

"I did not, but that's good information to have," he said. "So, what do we do from here? Find the others?"

"What's that Scouts rule? When you're lost, stay in one place?"

"You were never a Scout. You never participated in anything," Tobias said.

"Neither did you," Eriko said.

"True enough. We're not exactly joiners, are we," he said. "So, I guess we… Explore the town of Moderate Expectations?"

"That's not really the name of the town," Eriko said.

"It is, I swear."

"Well," Eriko said, putting her hood back up over her dark pixie haircut. "I guess that sets the tone for the campaign."

Chapter 4: Archery lessons and the local flavor

Jack didn't remember falling asleep. He certainly didn't remember falling asleep outside. But here he was, leaning against an old tree, a hood up over his head and shielding his eyes from the sun. He listened for a moment, trying to get his bearings. The ground was covered with drying leaves, and the air smelled earthy and fresh, like an orchard.

He rolled ungracefully to his feet, immediately noticing attire he didn't recognize—heavy, high leather boots on his feet, loose-fitting dark pants, the green cloak attached to the green hood obscuring his face. He immediately sensed the weight of two short swords, one on each hip, and a leather strap across his chest attached a bow and quiver over his shoulder. He pulled an arrow from the quiver and examined it.

"Okay," he said. "Fever dream maybe. Or I'm finally losing my mind. Had to happen eventually."

Then he heard yelling in the distance, voices echoing through the forest. Jack paused, stock still, and instinctually cocked his head to listen.

Two men. No, three. Metal on metal. Shouting. Taunting. One woman's voice.

A woman's voice he recognized.

"Cordelia," Jack said. He took off in a run toward the sound of the voices.

The closer he got, the worse it sounded. The men were bragging and laughing; Cordelia was saying nothing.

Jack ran up over a ridge and stopped. Below him, three men, all in cheap, makeshift armor and brandishing beat up weapons that had seen better days, had a woman surrounded. That can't be Cordelia, Jack thought. Taller, far more muscular—he could see her biceps from the ridge, clutching a long battle axe in front of her. Her skin was a pale green, and she wore her hair in a dark red Mohawk. When she bared her teeth at her attackers, Jack could make out the hint of fangs along her lower. But even at this distance, even with green skin and tusks, her face was still clearly that of his friend, familiar despite the cosmetic changes.

And these bandits had her outnumbered.

"Green skin abomination," one of them said, jabbing at her with a spear.

"Bet she can't even talk right," another, holding a rusty two-handed sword, said.

"I heard if you cook an orc, they taste like bacon," the third said. He slashed at Cordelia with a one-handed axe, a nicer weapon than his companions had. Cordelia batted it away with her own axe.

"Creepy nightmare or not, I'm not here to be insulted by a bunch of gap-toothed degenerates," Cordelia said.

One of the bandits turned to the others.

"What's a degenerate?" he said.

"Orc babble," the leader said. "Just kill her and be done with it."

Jack instinctually reached up to unsling his bow and took aim with the arrow he'd examined earlier. Logic sunk in and overtook his autopilot movements drawing the bow—you've literally taken one night of archery lessons, with Eriko that one time, your entire life, and you really weren't that good, he thought. But with his friend in danger, he let loose and hoped for the best.

The whole movement felt perfectly natural, as if he'd been born with a bow in his hand. He let his arrow fly, and with a whistling hiss through the air...

It struck one of the bandits in the left butt cheek.

"Not what I was aiming for," he said, another arrow. He watched as the bandit collapsed unceremoniously to the ground, clutching his backside, screaming.

"I've been shot in the arse!" the bandit screamed. "Someone shot me in the rump!"

"Orc lover," the leader of the bandits said, turning to look at Jack. "Kill him too!"

The bandit leader charged up hill toward Jack, leaving his companions to deal with Cordelia. As the unwounded bandit raised his sword to attack, Jack saw the man's head separate from his body as Cordelia swung her battle axe in a perfect arc.

Jack drew another arrow and fired, but the bandit leader was moving too fast, and the shot went wide. Dropping his bow, Jack drew his short swords—how do I even know how to do this? he thought, but the blades felt perfectly at home in his hands as he raised them up and caught the bandit's sword between them like an X, driving him back.

He parried another blow, then jabbed at the bandit with his left blade, but again, missed his mark. Don't think about it, don't get distracted, he thought, realizing that the more he let his instincts take over, the more his body seemed to know instinctually what to do. He clumsily blocked another slash by the bandit leader, but couldn't quite find his feet to return the strike.

Then he heard a low, angry growl followed by a ferocious bark and the bandit leader's eyes went wide with pain. The man stumbled backward, and Jack saw a wolf—not really a wolf, he thought, more of a fantasy interpretation of one, with dramatic black and gray fur, an exaggerated mouth, and bright green eyes that burned with almost human intelligence—grabbing hold of the man's calf, dragging him away.

The wolf looked Jack directly in the eyes and, without saying a word, conveyed the words silently, but clearly: You know what to do.

Jack knocked the man's sword from his hand with one blade then drove the other into his heart. He found himself face to face with the bandit, whose body went slack as the wolf released his bite.

"That orc is my friend," Jack said. The bandit's eyes went blank, and Jack let him slide sloppily from the end of the short sword.

The bandit leader dead, he turned his attention on Cordelia. Somewhere between beheading the other thug and the wolf's appearance, she'd dispatched the final bandit with a pretty grotesque blow to the head. She cleaned her axe on the dead man's shirt.

"So," Cordelia said. She grinned at him. Her orcish tusks, while bizarre and vaguely threatening, really didn't look so terrible on her face. "I'm a goddamned half-orc, Jack."

"And how do you feel about that?"

"If it's not permanent, it's pretty boss, honestly," she said. She slung her battle axe into a holster on her shoulder. She flexed her arms. "Look at these guns. And I'd have to do Crossfit for three years to get my quads to look like this."

"It's a little intimidating," Jack said. He looked down at the black and gray wolf waiting patiently for his attention and put a hand on the beast's forehead, scratching between his ears.

"You've got some sort of dire wolf that looks at you like you're the center of his universe," Cordelia said. "That's not unintimidating either."

Jack nodded. Cordelia started going through the bandits' pockets.

"What are you doing?"

"I'm looting," Cordelia said. "That's what we do in these situations, right? We loot."

"Got anything?"

Cordelia tossed him a purse that jangled with coins as he caught it.

"I'm not going to feel bad taking that," she said. "From the looks of these guys, they didn't earn it honestly anyway."

Jack examined his belt and found a few leather pouches and tucked the purse inside one.

"So what do you think. Are we hallucinating?" Jack asked.

"Dunno," Cordelia said. "Doesn't feel like it, as weird as that sounds. This feels awfully real, Jack."

"It does," He said. "Have you seen the others?"

"Not a one."

"So, I guess the first order of business is making sure we're all here," he said.

"And that nobody's been killed by bandits," she said. "Where should we go?"

Jack scanned the sky, doing a full circle standing in place, then pointed.

"Smoke," Jack said. "Looks like chimney smoke."

"When in doubt, go to the closest village, huh?"

"That's what I'd suggest you guys do if you got turned around in a game," Jack said.

"Um," Cordelia said. She gestured at her face. "What if, y'know. My kind isn't welcome there?"

"We'll figure that out when we get there," he said.

"I'm not in love with this plan," Cordelia said.

"Me either. But we work with what we have, I guess," Jack said.

Chapter 5: The thief and the bard

Eriko felt lighter on her feet than she ever had in her ordinary life. She wasn't quite sure how to explain it—she felt as if she just knew instinctually where to put her feet, possessing a practiced grace she always wished she'd had ever since she bombed out of her career as a ballerina at age seven. But here, she felt almost catlike, resting on the balls of her feet as if perpetually ready to move. Her hands hovered around the knives on her belt with easy practice, too. She knew it couldn't be real, that she did not possess these abilities in real life, but if they were trapped here, she certainly could get used to being a dexterous thief.

She also realized she was more observant of the people around her, too. Eriko had never been much of a daydreamer, so she had always been more observant than not. But she caught herself noticing little details—ticks and tells in body language; the way someone with money touched their coin purses more often; the way those with money looked at those without and vice versa; and, perhaps most of all, the way the local law enforcement looked at Eriko herself. I must give off a thief-ish air, she thought.

Fortunately, though, most attention remained on Tobias. He winked and grinned at everyone who made eye contact, flirting as boldly with a shop keep's daughter as he did with a gruff guard captain.

"Laying it on a bit thick here, huh, Tobias?" Eriko said softly.

"Are you kidding?" Tobias said. "Look at me! I'm some sort of elven rock star here. I feel like a cross between David Bowie, Prince, and Legolas."

"I mean, y'know," Eriko said, nodding her head back at the guard captain as they walked away. "We're in a medieval setting. Don't they burn people who..."

"It's a *fantasy* setting, and I don't think they mind," Tobias said. "In fact, I feel a hell of a lot less judged for being myself here than I am in the real world."

"So there's an upside to this whole adventure," Eriko said. "For you at least."

"You're telling me this isn't your life's dream," Tobias said. "You've wanted to escape into a fantasy world since the first time you read *Wizard of Earthsea*."

"For the record, I wanted to escape into a fantasy world since the first time I read the *Dragonlance Chronicles*," Eriko corrected. "I upgraded my reading level to Le Guin a few years later."

"Are you in a rush to wake up, or stop hallucinating, or come out of whatever coma has put us here?" Tobias said.

Eriko wrinkled her nose.

"I'd rather be a thief in sword-and-sorcery-land than a barista back home," she said.

"I'll remind you of that the first time we have to slay a cursed latte here," Tobias said. "Speaking of, do they have coffee in these fantasy settings, or is that something that isn't historically accurate?"

"You're an elf," Eriko said. "I'm betting we can find coffee."

She felt a tickle along the back of her neck and slowed her pace for a moment, partially turning her head to look behind her. Just as carefully, she turned her face to look ahead again.

"So, I think we're being followed," she said.

"What? Where?" Tobias said, spinning around.

"Welp, there goes our element of surprise, Elvis," she said.

Surrendering to whatever was about to happen next, she turned around completely, watching as the figure that caught her attention—bedraggled, covered in a brown hooded cloak—disappeared down an alleyway.

"Crap," she said.

"Hey, he's not following us anymore," Tobias said. "I win. I am awesome at this game."

"You're really not," she said, ducking into a passing shop. Tobias followed her in. They were instantly hit with the powerful smell of brewing beverages—different teas, fragrant and flowery, and the dusky scent of coffee boiling.

"What can I get for you," an older woman said behind the counter. Eriko guessed she was a half-orc by the greenish skin and hint of tusks jutting up from her lower jaw. Her hair was iron gray, and her modest blue dress contrasted interestingly with a series of intricate tattoos running up her right arm, reappearing out of the top of the dress to crawl up her neck.

"Is that coffee I smell?" Eriko asked.

"That it is," the orcish woman said. "Two?"

"Thank you," Eriko said. "My friend is paying."

"I—what?" Tobias said.

"You made bank playing at the tavern last night," she said. "You can afford it."

The proprietor set down two small, delicate china cups, shallow and perfectly round. Eriko took a sip. It had the deep, heady strength of a fine Turkish coffee back home.

"Oh, I love this world," Eriko said.

"I'm just going to go out on a limb and say that it's probably considered rude to put milk in mine," Tobias said. The orc woman glared at him. "No milk. Gotcha."

The shop was mostly empty, save for one other pair, an off-duty guard talking with a younger woman. They had the awkward cuteness of a couple just getting to know each other.

"Another one went missing?" the girl asked. Eriko leaned back slightly, listening.

"Third one," the guard said. His voice was incredibly young. Eriko stole a glance at his face and saw he barely had even the hint of stubble on his chin.

"How is no one panicking about this?" the girl asked.

"The chief wants to keep it quiet til we know more," he said. "That's why I need you to not tell anyone either."

"Why tell me at all if I can't talk about it, you ridiculous man," the girl said. Her tone was playful, but Eriko could hear real fear in her voice.

"So as you know to lock your windows at night, and make sure your mother does the same with your little brother's room," the guard said. "Three little ones. Stolen in the night. This last one was right here in town, too. The others were out in the farmlands, so the panic's been slow to build, but once word gets out…"

Eriko leaned her elbows on the counter and bumped Tobias with her shoulder.

"I don't think this coffee will come out of these clothes if you make me spill it," he said. "Please don't ruin my glam rock outfit, Eriko. I'm serious. You know I'm not a vain man, but I love these clothes."

"Coffee stains add character," she said. "And I think that couple behind us are quest-givers."

"You're really going to play the game," Tobias said. "Go on quests, kill ogres and dragons, that sort of thing."

"What are you going to do?"

"Well, if I don't wake up back in my own bed in a few hours, I'm going to make the most of it by getting rich singing a whole bunch of pop songs none of these yokels have heard before," he said. "Think about it. I could be the Beatles of this place! You can be my Ringo if you want. I'm not selfish."

"So, you're not going to help me find the others," Eriko said.

"Oh, I want to find the others! You think I'm not going to look for my sister? I just don't want to engage in daring acts of heroism. I don't want to die."

"Maybe dying is the only way we get home," Eriko said.

"Or maybe if we die here we die back home," Tobias said. "I wouldn't rule out the worst-case scenario."

"I thought you were the optimist in your family," Eriko said.

"I come from a family of optimists," Tobias said. "But none of them have been trapped in a virtual reality medieval death trap. I'm working within different parameters."

Eriko heard a soft clatter of plates and stealthily watched as the guard cleaned up and prepared to go.

"Gotta head to the gates. There's a caravan due in," the guard said. "I'm on inspection duty."

"I'll see you later on?" the girl said.

The guard beamed at her.

"Of course," he said.

After the young couple exited, Tobias and Eriko exchanged a pair of half-hearted looks.

"I guess we could go see who's coming into town," Eriko said.

"Beats sitting around being a creep listening to people," Tobias said.

"Oh, I'm going to be a creep and listen to people there," Eriko said. "I just want a wider variety of options."

Chapter 6: This is what magic feels like

Tamsin could feel mystical words creeping around in her skull like poetry.

It was more than a little upsetting.

Morgan had returned to the front of the wagon to talk more with Bobrick, leaving Tamsin inside. I swear, she thought, if this is real, it's some kind of world inside Jack's mind, that's exactly the sort of stupid name he'd give a throwaway character in a story. They'd propped the tarp open so she could sit right behind them and join in on the conversation, but mostly the driver rambled on about the chief exports of Moderate Expectations, like rhubarb and radishes, and how some weird new culinary trend had picked up steam among humans that they'd heard was popular with the elves where they'd refuse to eat animal flesh, which was the stupidest thing Bobrick had ever heard of, begging your pardon, young lady, didn't mean to insult elves in general, he said, but he didn't know how life was worth living without bacon.

Eventually the conversation made Tamsin's mind drift. She started tugging at those poetic magical words in her mind, turning them over and over like found art.

This must be what magic feels like, she thought. But maybe not, Tamsin wondered. Maybe the way this world works is, just like the game they'd been about to play, the way the players made it work. Maybe magic works this way because, after years of reading fantasy and adventure books, after hours upon hours spent with Harry Potter and Harry Dresden and Harry D'Amour—there's a lot of magicians named Harry, apparently, she thought—that what she was experiencing now was her own mind making sense of magic, applying rules that were logical to her.

Or maybe she was overthinking things, Tamsin thought. I still haven't even cast a single spell yet.

The conversation on the front of the wagon came to an abrupt halt, disrupting Tamsin's reverie.

"Gods dammit," Bobrick said.

"Tam," Morgan whispered. "Trouble."

Tamsin peered carefully out from behind the tarp acting as a door to the wagon. She could see a man standing in the middle of the road. He looked worse for wear, dirty and tired, but he smiled, casually brandishing a sword in one hand.

"Welcome to the Shallow Woods," the man said. "You may not be aware of this, but there's a small tax to use this road. "I'm here to collect."

"Get a job," Bobrick said. There was a sharp whistle, followed by Bobrick grunting in pain. The old man started cursing bloody murder.

"You didn't have to shoot him with an arrow," Morgan said, his voice deep and suddenly filled with authority. Was he getting into character too, Tamsin thought? Or was this covering for his own anxiousness?

"Careful now, friar," the man in the road said. "We prefer not to draw blood from a man of the cloth, but you wouldn't be the first."

"Bloody bandits," Bobrick said, his voice thick with pain. "We ain't got anything! We're just a traveling caravan!"

"Might want to shut your friend up unless you want to be driving that cart yourself," the man in the road said. "We'll just have a look through your things, take a modest token fee, and you can be on your way."

The hell with that, Tamsin thought. She slipped out the back of the wagon, eyes peeled for the archer who shot Bobrick. More magic words crawled through her brain, and she took a chance, whispering them softly. The air around her shimmered with an almost invisible glow. She looked at her hands, and saw that all around her, there seemed to be a sort of shield... a force field? Surrounding her.

Magic shield, she thought. Let's see what else I've got.

She saw movement up on the high ground to the right of the wagon. Without thinking, she grabbed onto another set of words in her mind, these ones glowing with the light of burning embers. Automatically, she threw her hand toward the movement, pointing.

A ball of flame erupted from her fingertip, moving with ridiculous speed toward the hidden person. It struck, exploding, setting fire to leaves and brush and, apparently, to an archer who had just aimed an arrow at Tamsin. The archer screamed and ran down the hill, body on fire like an outtake from a stunt scene in a movie.

"Great," she heard Morgan say, followed by a stream of curses as something squealed like nails on a chalkboard. She looked up to see an arrow, bent at the haft, careening into the air, apparently blocked by Morgan's heavy armor. He yelled to Tamsin. "Next time a little head's up! Initiative order matters!"

"Sorry!" she said. She closed her eyes, trying to grab onto more magic words, but the screaming of her target and the aggression in the man's voice as he barked orders at unseen lackeys made concentration difficult. Finally she caught hold of a few words, glowing like moonlight, and spoke them aloud. A dart of energy the size of a sparrow flew out of her hand, spun through the air, then splashed against the robber's shoulder, knocking him backward.

"Forget it! Kill them! Make them an example of..." the man in the road said, and then his voice faded into silence. Tamsin stole a glance and saw that he now looked down at his chest where an arrow protruded just below the sternum. As the robber reached town to examine the arrow piercing his gut with his fingers, another projectile hit him higher in the chest, piercing a lung. He staggered, falling to one knee, then fell to the ground.

"Oh," Tamsin said, all the mystical symbols in her head jumbled as worry overtook her.

"They killed him!" Someone yelled behind her. Tamsin spun just in time to see another robber running at her, a blade in one hand, aimed down, ready to stab at her. Tamsin's hands reached for her belt, looking for anything, a knife or something, to block the oncoming attack with, but came up short.

I don't want to die in this game, she thought.

And then robber was blown from his feet by a spinning battle axe.

The enormous weapon flew out of nowhere, brutally pinning the would-be attacker against the wagon. Tamsin heard strangely familiar laughing.

"I had no idea if that would work," Cordelia said, emerging from the forest looking, bigger, stronger, and definitely greener than Tamsin had ever seen her.

"What happened to you?" Tamsin said.

"We can talk later," Cordelia said, viciously yanking her axe from the side of the wagon while shoving the dead robber off with one foot. "First, duck."

Cordelia gripped her axe in both hands as if to swing a baseball bat. Tamsin did as she was told, dropping down as she heard heavy footsteps running up behind her. Then, before Cordelia could attack, she heard a creepy, wet thump.

Looking up over her shoulder, she saw Morgan, war hammer in hand, hopping down from the wagon. The crumpled body of a robber lay at his feet.

"Considering I can't hammer a nail without crushing my thumb, this is alarmingly natural," he said, hefting his hammer.

"That's all of them," another familiar voice said. Tamsin jumped to her feet and ran out from behind the wagon. Jack, dressed in greens and browns with a bow in his hand, stepped out of the foliage and into plain sight.

"That was you firing those arrows?" Morgan said. "You don't even have the eye/hand coordination to play a first-person shooter game."

"I think we all… know what our characters know," Jack said. He pulled his hood back and smirked at Tamsin. "I promise this is not what our games are usually like."

"Morgan's been filling me in," she said. She grimaced. "My brother?"

"Haven't found him yet," Jack said.

"Or Eriko," Cordelia added.

Tamsin felt her stomach twist.

"We'll find them," Morgan said.

Above them, they heard Bobrick moan pitifully.

"If you weirdos are done talking nonsense, I could use a bandage," he said.

Morgan and Jack exchanged a knowing look.

"You think?" Morgan said.

"I don't know," Jack said.

"Well, I'll give it a shot," Morgan said.

"To do what?" Tamsin said.

"Well, if you're our wizard and just threw a fireball out of your hand without, y'know, knowing actual magic, I'm wondering if the healing spells my character is supposed to have work as well," Morgan said.

Bobrick moaned again.

"You've got a good test subject at least," Tamsin said.

Cordelia hopped up onto the wagon and easily lowered the slender old man down to Morgan, who placed him on the ground. Morgan concentrated for a moment, hand over the arrow wound in Bobrick's shoulder. Light pulsed from Morgan's palm, then spilled down into the wound. The arrow fell out easily. Tamsin watched in a combination of horror and amazement as the bloody wound sealed shut.

"I hate bandits," Bobrick said.

"Not a fan myself, old-timer," Morgan said. "You okay if I drive the cart if we put you in the back to recover?"

"You say that like you think I like driving a wagon," Bobrick said. "You tell me to take a nap, I ain't sayin' no."

Chapter 7: Reunited

"We are one hundred and ten percent being followed," Eriko said. Tobias almost yelped when she dug her fingers into his upper arm.

"Why does being followed mean you have to pinch me?" he said.

"I don't think you're taking this seriously enough," Eriko said.

Along the edge of the village they'd found that Moderate Expectations was surrounded by a wooden wall, ranging in height from ten to fifteen feet in places—probably as a defense in the event of raiders, Eriko hypothesized. Asking around, they learned that farmlands stretched for miles in every direction, but the walled structure was a safe place to trade and to hide when the various bad things—bandits, mostly—made trouble. They had been skirting the edge of that wall, along which various stalls selling vegetables and tools, were lined up like a state fair. Ahead, the main gate to the town, guarded by a motley crew of constables or soldiers, remained open, with light foot traffic moving in and out.

"Not taking this seriously enough," Tobias said. "What is there to take seriously? We're absolutely, definitely hallucinating, Eriko. None of this is real."

She pinched him again.

"Ow."

"That feel like a hallucination?"

"I don't know," he said. "Please stop pinching me."

"He's at six o'clock. Look at him."

Tobias leaned past Eriko's should, trying to spot their alleged tail.

"I don't see him."

"Your six, not my six."

"You didn't specify."

"Why are we friends?"

"Because I make you look smart and you make me look pretty," Tobias said. "Or is it the other way around?"

"Just look behind you."

"Are you sure that's six o'clock?"

"I don't know. Just look," Eriko said. "But try not to be obvious about it."

Tobias turned around dramatically and stared at the passersby behind him.

"Wow," Eriko said. "Why don't you just yell out and ask what his name is?"

"I think that's a great plan," Tobias said. "Who am I looking for?"

"Older guy, faded brown cloak, beard… you know what? He's gone," Eriko said. "He disappeared. Probably because you looked at him."

"How did I look at him when I didn't even see him?" Tobias said, spinning back around to Eriko.

"Never mind," she said.

Past Eriko, Tobias saw a wagon looking worse for wear trundle in through the town gates. He was fairly certain one side of the wagon was covered in drying blood. And sitting on the wagon was, finally, a familiar face.

"Oh!" Tobias said.

"What?" Eriko said.

"Look!"

"Where?"

"There!"

"Why?"

"Morgan!" Tobias said, leaving Eriko standing in the street. She trotted to catch up with him.

"Morgan looks like he walked off the set of *Kingdom of Heaven*," she said.

Their friend, who eyed the town's streets from above his perch with tired anxiety, was dressed entirely in heavy armor save his head. He wore a gold and red surcoat covering much of his torso, emblazoned with a sort of archaic, abstract sun.

Again, Tobias took off without waiting, leaving Eriko to catch up. He held his arms out at his sides.

"Morgan, you big beautiful bastard," Tobias said.

Morgan looked at him with confusion, then fear, then with a growing grin across his face. He hopped down from the wagon as best he could in his armor. The men through their arms around each other.

"About time you showed up," Morgan said. "You're okay!"

"More than okay."

"Hey, big guy," Eriko said, punching Morgan in the chest lightly so his breastplate made a soft clanking noise.

"Just hanging out in town, playing some music, making friends," Tobias said.

"Y'know, just getting our RP on," Eriko said.

"Meanwhile we're fighting off bandits in the forest," Morgan said.

"Tobias!" Tamsin yelled, hopping out of the back of the wagon and running into her brother's arms.

Morgan looked up at the wagon.

"Best get this out of the way, old timer," he said.

"Look at you lot, with friends greeting you at the town gate. Must be lucky to be loved," the old man said.

Morgan tossed him a pouch from his belt that clinked when the old driver caught it.

"Thanks for the lift, Bobrick," he said.

"Thanks for the healing magic," Bobrick said. "I'd tell you this coin purse is too much, but a man needs to make a living."

"Keep it. You've earned it," Morgan said.

The old man tipped an imaginary cap then ushered his horses onward. As the wagon moved slowly away, Tamsin ran her fingers over Tobias's face.

"You've got the ears too," she said.

"Twins even on the other side of the looking glass," he said. He took in her appearance—traveling robes, a belt dotted with pouches filled with spell components, her hair brushed simply away from her eyes.

"You're a wizard, Tamsin," he said.

"Not how I'd hoped it would happen, but I guess I'll take it," she said. "Hey, I can cast fireball, want to see?"

Everyone from the party other than Tobias sad a firm 'no' and backed away slowly.

"Have you see Jack and Cordie?" Tobias said, the smile fading from his face.

"Actually," Tamsin said, looking over her shoulder as two cloaked figured entered the gate. One pulled back his hood, revealing the familiar face of Jack, a bow slung over his shoulder. Beside him, an unfamiliar figure moved with unexpected power.

"Oh," Tobias said.

"Yup," Cordelia as she and Jack joined the group. She wore her hood up to obscure her face.

"Well, green really is your color, Cordie," Tobias said.

"I think you'll be okay here looking like that," Eriko said. "We bought coffee from a half–orc this morning."

"You had coffee," Cordelia said. "I beheaded two men today, and you've had coffee."

"You put it that way, I almost feel guilty," Tobias said.

"Almost," Cordelia said.

"Yeah, but not really," Tobias said. "Glad you were the one doing the beheading and not the other way around though."

"Thanks," Cordelia said. "So. Now that we can assume we're not in some sort of too-much-caffeine-before-bed nightmare and we're really here... what do we do next?"

"Well," Tobias said, fighting back a laugh. "I do know a tavern we could go to."

Chapter 8: Really specific character descriptions

"We can, if nothing else, determine that we are not having a pizza-induced nightmare we're all going to wake up from in a few hours," Morgan said.

They'd commandeered a table in the corner of the tavern, still a bit early in the day for the place to have grown overly crowded, but full enough they kept their voices hushed as they talked. Eriko scanned the room for anyone who might be eavesdropping. Aside from the bartender and barmaid, whom they'd learned from Tobias were named Darv and Ena—both of whom seemed to love having the bard in their establishment—no one paid them much mind.

Cordelia had been worried her half-orc looks would draw attention, but if anything, the religious vestments Morgan wore drew more looks. Eriko caught Ena's arm as she brought their first round and asked about it.

"We don't see too many battle clerics in these parts," the barmaid explained. "They're more common in places that see more conflict. We're pretty far from contested lands."

"I'm making people nervous," Morgan said.

"Maybe a bit," Ena said.

"If anyone asks, you can tell them I'm just passing through. I came to see some old friends before going off to the front,"

Morgan said, giving Ena one of his ten gigawatt smiles. The barmaid nodded and hurried off.

"Playing the role of a priest has brought out the liar in you," Eriko said. "I like it."

"I don't know if these people are real or not, but if I can lie and make them feel less weird around us, I'll take it," he said.

"So, I guess what we need to now is figure out how we... get home," Jack said. "Whatever that means. I mean we're here. We're physically here."

"We can feel pain," Tobias said.

"All I did was pinch you," Eriko said.

"Pain is pain, Eriko," Tobias said, then winked at her.

"You're ridiculous."

"And proud of it," Tobias said.

"Would it be so bad if we were stuck here?" Tamsin said. She had her slender hands wrapped around a mug of mulled wine she hadn't sipped. "I mean... This is a lot more interesting than what any of us had going on in real life, right?"

Jack opened his mouth to protest, then scrunched his brow.

"Trying to figure out what you have to go home to that would be better than being a ranger with a magical wolf sidekick, aren't you," Tamsin said.

"I... huh," Jack said. "No, no, we need to get back. Or out. Or whatever. We can't stay here. Cordelia..."

"I'm not going to lie, guys, I don't hate being a half-orc," Cordelia said.

"You are a remarkably good-looking half-orc," Tamsin said.

"I can't tell if you're screwing with my mind or not," Cordelia said.

"You're like a combination of Gamora from *Guardians of the Galaxy* mixed with Imperator Furiosa and one of the background Amazons from Wonder Woman," Tobias said.

Everyone turned to look at him.

"That is insanely specific," Jack said.

"I've literally been sitting here figuring out how to describe what she looks like for like twenty-five minutes," Tobias said.

"I swear, Tobias, if you put that brain toward doing anything useful you could cure cancer," Tamsin said.

"Okay," Cordelia said, taking a swig from her mug. "So we've established I'm not Swamp Thing. Can we talk about where we are and what we do next?"

Jack turned to Eriko.

"You said there's a wall around the town," he said.

"More like a glorified wooden fence, but yeah."

"And outside, we have bandits, a trade road…" he closed his eyes for a moment. "I didn't have a ton of time to look it over, but I'm pretty sure that's what the starting area for the game we were playing looked like."

"Was it really called Moderate Expectations?" Eriko said.

"No, it was sort of left open-ended," he said. "It's a sandbox game."

"You're gonna have to explain that one to me," Tamsin said.

"You get to explore at will. It's not on a straight track," Morgan said. "Instead of a set beginning and end, the players can move around and discover their own path."

"And we just appeared out of thin air into that sandbox," Eriko said. "That's wonderful."

Eriko felt an eerie sense of dread washing over her. No, not really dread, per se—more like foreboding. Her nose itched. She tuned out the conversation with her friends. Slowly, she leaned forward in her chair and stood up.

"Where you going, Eriko?" Tamsin said.

Eriko held up a hand as if to shush her friend. She stepped away from the table and made a slow, casual circle of the tavern. Finally, she saw what she was looking for. Deftly, she crept up behind the man in the same brown, hooded cloak she'd seen following her and Tobias earlier. She drew a knife from her belt and stepped up behind him, placing the point just above his kidney.

"Care you explain why you've been following us, friend?" Eriko whispered. "Don't make a scene. This is a nice establishment."

The man's body tensed, then relaxed, sensing how close the knife was to digging into his flesh.

"I'm a Red Sox fan," the man said.

"What?" Eriko said.

"I owned a Jeep with two hundred thousand miles on it. I collected *Batman* comics," he continued. "I'm not from here. And neither are you."

"What are you talking about? Why are you following us?"

"I'm the last one left alive from my campaign," the man said, his voice tightening with fought-back tears. "And I want to help make sure you don't turn out the same way."

Chapter 9: The watcher

Morgan found himself staring across the table at the stranger Eriko had dragged across the tavern at knifepoint. Her tactics were going to have to be a conversation for another time, but for now, they had a bigger situation on their hands.

He was much older than Morgan and his friends, with a gray-flecked beard, weathered eyes—weathered eye, really, since one disappeared behind an eyepatch—a body that was lean and hard from years on the run. He looked every bit like an adventurer who had fallen on hard times.

And he claimed to be from the real world, just like them.

"What's your name," Jack asked. Jack stood, hood up so that a shadow fell across his eyes. It was funny, Morgan noted, how much they had all begun to automatically take on characteristics of the characters they played. Tobias lounged with a casual languidness he didn't have back in the real world. Eriko never stopped watching the room. Cordelia absently sharpened her axe with a grindstone at every quiet moment.

"I'm... Oh, I can tell you my real name," he said, as if the opportunity was a Christmas gift. "I'm Bennett. My character here, this character, I'm called Anders, but back home I'm Bennett. There's been nobody who has known me by that name in so long."

"How long… how long have you been here?" Tamsin asked, leaning in.

Bennett took a long sip from a mug of ale Tobias had set in front of him.

"Time moves weird here," he said. "By my count… I've seen no fewer than fifteen winters. How much time that is in the real world I have no idea."

"Fifteen years," Jack said. "Shit."

"How did you get here?" Cordelia asked.

"Same as you I'm guessing. Were you playing that stupid game?" Bennett said. "Looks like a fancy knockoff of HeroQuest or some such?"

"Yeah," Jack said softly.

"That's what gets you," Bennett said. His hands shook, Morgan noted. Nerves, exhaustion, drink, he couldn't tell. "That's what gets everyone."

"Everyone," Morgan said. "So, we're not the first… people from back home you've found?"

Bennett shook his head.

"Two other groups," Bennett said. "Once early on, my friends and I met a group in our travels. We traded a few stories, but everyone was just having fun at the time. They were headed to a dungeon in the mountains to the south. Never saw them again."

"And the others?" Eriko asked.

"A few years back. I tried to warn them," Bennett said. "They wouldn't listen. But I tried to warn them."

"Warn them about what?" Eriko said.

Bennett reached for her hand. Morgan watched as Eriko almost recoiled. Bennett was missing his pinky on that hand, bandaged over to hide the maimed digit.

"That what happens here is real," Bennett said. "It doesn't feel real, and the game… the game wants you to take risks. It rewards you for taking risks. But what happens here…"

"I take it you showed up here with two eyes," Tobias said.

"Tobias," Tamsin said harshly.

"No, no, it's a valid question. Yes, I lost my eye here," Bennett said. "And my finger, and I've got more than my share of scars. But the game rewards risk takers. It doesn't steal people from the real world to be farmers or peasants. It wants you to be heroes."

"And that's how you knew we didn't belong here," Eriko said. "Because we look like adventurers."

"Well, that and your bard kept dropping anachronisms," Bennett said. "I overheard him call himself the elven David Bowie or something and I knew you were like me. Not that the anachronisms matter. The locals will ignore you if you talk about television or cell phones, or just act mildly confused. It's easier if you stay in character to talk with them, but they won't punish you for slips."

"Why are you alone?" Tamsin said. She took a long sip from a tall glass of wine she'd asked the barmaid for. Morgan could see color in Tamsin's cheeks. She was on the verge of a panic attack. We need to keep an eye on her, he thought. This must twice as weird for her as it is for the rest of us. "You said you met other groups, and you had friends."

"My friends and I... we thought, if we beat the game somehow we'd go home. Right? So we played along. But..."

"What happens here is real," Jack said.

"Slings and arrows of outrageous fortune, in the literal sense," Bennett said. "My best friend was the first to go, and it wasn't even through combat. He thought if he died in the game he'd... I don't know, he'd respawn back home. He'd somehow be free and could clean up the game and bring us all back. He jumped off a parapet."

"And that didn't work," Tamsin said.

"For all I know, he's home," Bennett said. "Maybe they all went home. I don't know. But the pain we endure here is real. I... I have to believe death is too."

"How'd you survive so long on your own?" Cordelia asked.

Bennett took a long swig from his mug again.

"I'm a rogue, like this one here," he said, pointing to Eriko. "The game might want to kill you, but it doesn't want you to starve. Petty theft and pickpocketing, small jobs here and there. It'll sustain you, even as it calls you to greater adventure."

"But those adventures don't lead home," Morgan said.

"I don't know," Bennett said. "I don't honestly think we were wrong. I think we pursued the wrong stories."

"Pursued the wrong stories?" Morgan said. Then he winced. "We're in a sandbox."

"Yeah," Bennett said. "And there's no way of finding the right... quest or story arc that will lead you out."

"Whoever created this game is a jackass," Tobias said.

"Bennett," Cordelia said. "You said the right stories. How will we know if the right story finds us?"

The older man was about to speak when someone stormed into the tavern, kicking the doors open violently. The newcomer was drenched—they'd been so engrossed in Bennett's tales, they hadn't noticed the weather pick up outside.

The stranger staggered around, ripping a cap from his head.

"She's gone," the man said. He was red of face and beard, burly but ordinary in most respects.

"Calm down, now, Hink," Ena, the barmaid, said. "What's happening. Tell us, now."

"My little girl, someone's took her," the newcomer Ena called Hink said. "Broke in through her window and she's gone..."

A murmur rose up around the tavern. Glasses clinked as men rose from their seats and leather creaked as sword-belts and armor was adjusted.

"Ain't the first one neither," Hink said.

"Oh, no," Eriko said under her breath.

"What," Morgan said. Eriko waved him off.

"Guards were talkin'. They knew someone was stealin' children in the night. Weeks now. Nothin', not a word to us. Help me," Hink said. "I need to find my girl."

Morgan grabbed Eriko's wrist. She made a face at him—I don't know? She seemed to ask—but it was Jack who spoke up instead.

"I'm a ranger," Jack said. Morgan almost laughed in spite of the terror of the situation at how in-character Jack became in that moment. There was a languidness to his speech patterns, a folksy quiet. "I can track. My friends can fight if it comes to it. We'll go."

"He's going to get us all killed," Tobias said. "I kind of love it."

"Thank you, sir," Hink said, rushing over to Jack's side. "I'll take you to my home. Maybe you can find tracks before the rain washes them away."

"Jack," Morgan said. He gestured with his eyes toward the twins.

Jack shrugged.

"Do we all go?" Eriko said.

"I'm in," Cordelia said, rising to her full height and tossing her axe onto her shoulder. She looked to Morgan. "Might need a man of the cloth if the kid's hurt. Or if we get hurt ourselves."

Morgan rose as well.

"You two should stay here," Morgan said to Tamsin. "This isn't your fault. The rest of us can at least pretend we've done this before."

"I'm coming," Tamsin said.

Tobias glared at her.

"I can't tell if these people are fiction or not, but they feel real," she said. "And I'm not going to let some little girl die in the rain."

Tobias stood up begrudgingly too.

"I'm going to get my fancy bard vest wet," he said. "I was just starting to get used to it."

"Bennett?" Morgan said.

"I'll be here when you get back," he said. He gestured with his maimed hand. "I'm not much use out in the field these days."

Tobias tossed a gold coin to Darv behind the bar.

"Can you feed our friend while we're gone, Darv? We're going hunting," the bard said.

"I'll see what I can do, elf," Darv said. "Stay safe out there."

"I don't think there's anything quite so ominous as someone telling you to stay safe," Tobias said. "But thanks."

Chapter 10: Into the rain

"So the fun part is over," Tobias said, hiding beneath an embroidered cloak, water cascading from the tip of his fancy hat.

"At least you had a fun part," Cordelia said. She'd drawn her axe and held it casually at her side, her grip high on the haft to keep better control of the blade. This new body was taking some getting used to, she thought. The strength was amazing, a vitality she'd never felt in the real world, but she felt vaguely dangerous at all times, as if she might break someone's neck reaching across the table for the salt shaker.

The constitution that went along with her new orcish body seemed to be less troubled by the weather, at least. She felt the cool rain seeping through her clothes and armor, but it felt more like a passing chill thought than actual discomfort. Leaving Tobias to whine toward the back, she stomped up closer to the front of the train, where Jack was following close behind Hink, whispering with Eriko.

"So—you can really do this then?" Cordelia asked.

Jack nodded at her.

"I think it's a matter of just believing we know how to do these things," he said. "You'd never swung a two-handed battle axe before this morning, right? And you're a right killing machine with it."

"My perception is through the roof," Eriko said. "I thought I was paranoid before, but I notice everything. It's almost superhuman."

"And both Tamsin and Morgan cast spells," Cordelia said. "I suppose if we can do all this, you should be able to track footprints in the mud."

"I know I can," Jack said. "I didn't pay it much mind when we were headed here, but like Eriko, I see things I wouldn't have before. Broken branches, flattened grass. It's like in this world I'm attuned to look for signs like that."

"You don't seem the least bit freaked out by this," Cordelia said. "Where's your wolf, by the way?"

Jack gave her a halfhearted smile, barely visible beneath his green hood.

"Oh, I'm at level eleven of freaking out," Jack said. "But what other choice do we have? And…"

Jack whistled sharply. Something moved in the underbrush. Hink, startled, moved into a fighting position, but Jack put a hand on the bigger man's shoulder. Out of the rainy forest, the black and gray shadow of Jack's animal companion bounded up to them.

"We have backup if my tracking, um, skills prove insufficient," Jack said.

Hink shook his head, then gestured up ahead.

"There's my house," he said, pointing toward a modest wooden structure on the edge of town. "My little girl, Madsin, her room is around back."

"How do we handle this?" Cordelia asked.

Jack turned to Morgan.

"You're usually party leader, Father," Jack said, putting a touch of humor in the title. "What say you?"

Morgan winced as if Jack had said something offensive. Shaking his head, he started pointing around the group.

"You and Cordie go look for tracks out back, through the window. Eriko, why don't you go examine her room, if that's okay with you, Mr. Hink," Morgan said.

"Hinkley, but Hink is fine, Father," the big man said.

"Tam and I will wait out front in case something goes wrong. We'll keep an eye on the street," Morgan said.

"What about me?" Tobias said. Catching a glare from Morgan, he shrugged. "I'll go with Eriko then. Inside sounds better than out here."

Eriko darted off, disappearing in through the front door. Tobias followed awkwardly after. Jack and his wolf skirted the edge of the home. Cordelia trotted after them.

"He got a name?" Cordelia said.

"Huh?"

"Your dog."

"Oh," Jack said, scratching the wolf behind the ear absently. "I don't know. Got a name, boy?"

The wolf looked up at him expectantly.

"Not much of a talker, huh?" Jack said. "Why don't we call you Silence for now, then, huh?"

The wolf seemed indifferent at best, trotting off in search of tracks.

They reached the back of the house, just below Madsin's window, and Cordelia let out a long sigh.

"I don't need hunter's intuition to know that's a bad sign," she said. The wooden outer wall below the window had been abraded with deep scratches in the stone. She touched the scratch marks with her fingertips. "Something climbed in through that window."

"Something with claws," Jack said. He knelt in the mud. "Look."

Cordelia saw what he gestured toward—a deep impression in the mud, foot-shaped, broad with sharp nails. Cordelia let her axe slide down in her hand, ready to swing.

"That is so alarming," she said.

"Signs of a struggle," Eriko said, leaning out the bedroom window above them. "Hink, do you have a dog or any animal your little would spend time around?"

"We have some cows," he said. "Why?"

"Just a hunch," Eriko said. She dropped out the window, splashing in the mud. Inside, footsteps echoed as Tobias left the way they came in.

The wolf growled in the darkness. Jack and Eriko exchanged glances and both drew their weapons. Behind them, Hink raised a makeshift club. Creeping toward a copse of trees along the edge of the property, they found the wolf already there, staring into the dense shadows.

"Together," Jack said. They walked in a triangle formation toward the thicket.

And then a child's voice cried and a massive shadow lashed out, sending Jack sprawling on the ground. Everything seemed to slow then; Cordelia saw blood fly from Jack's face, purple in the rainy moonlight. She charged at the shadow, her axe above her head, but as she swung downward, she hit nothing but earth, toppling forward. Two of Eriko's knives whiffed by with a distinctive snap-hiss as they spun, striking nothing.

Cordelia pursued, aware of Eriko close on her heels. They reached the fence on the edge of town just in time to see the dark figure vault the wall, climbing one-armed, the other stuffed with the squirming figure of a child under its arm. But in seconds, it was up, over, and gone.

And then it was over. Hink felt to his knees bellowing into the air. The others, Morgan, Tamsin, and Tobias, came running, only to see their friends scattered and defeated. Morgan quickly looked to Jack's face, who pulled himself away, rushing to the wall.

"What happened?" Morgan barked, war hammer in hand.

"Dammit," Jack said, hands pressed against the wall, looking up.

"We need to get around," Eriko said. "How do we get over the wall?"

Hink remained on his knees, fists clenched with rage. Morgan knelt down in front of him.

"Hink. Look at me," Morgan said. "Look at me. How do we get

outside the wall?"

"The south gate's the closest," Hink said softly. "It's too late, it'll take you a half hour to get around the town line from there…"

And then the air lit up like morning. Cordelia recoiled from the light, feeling a wave of heat wash over her, blinded by the sudden flash. Eriko swore in an overlapping combination of English and Japanese, the combination somehow making the cursing seem even more vulgar.

"We'll fix it later," Tamsin said.

Cordelia blinked until her vision returned to normal. When she could see clearly again, she watched as Tamsin, her hands steaming in the rain like hot pavement, walked through a scorching hole in the town's barrier, the gap just a little taller than Tamsin's full height.

"Come on," Tamsin said, looking back. "I made the door. One of you needs to lead the way. I don't know where we're going."

Tobias trotted past the group, putting a hand on Morgan's shoulder as he did.

"Aren't you glad my sister picked the wizard?" he said.

Morgan's jaw hung open at the scorched hole in the wall. Shaking his head, he looked to Hink.

"Stay here," he said. "I'm sure the blast will bring the guards. Explain to them what happened, and we'll leave signs for you and the guards to follow. Okay?"

The man nodded, dragging himself to his feet.

"We'll be back soon," Morgan said reassuringly.

Cordelia stepped through the damaged wall and into the damp forest beyond. She looked over her shoulder at the mourning father watching them as they left. And she had a sense, in her heart, that Morgan's reassurances would soon be proven hollow.

Chapter 11: Pursuit

Tamsin couldn't believe the rage she felt inside herself.

This isn't real, she thought, stomping through the wet brush and mud, cursing when her wizard robes got caught on branches and brambles. None of this is real. Why am I so angry that something stole this child? It's all hallucinatory.

But we don't know that for sure, she corrected. She felt the heat from her fireball on her face. The rain in her hair was cold, raising goosebumps on her skin. And that child's cry had sounded as real as could be. This might not be our reality, but it's real enough, she thought.

And so she powered on.

Jack and Eriko ranged ahead, almost out of sight, staying just close enough that the rest of the group could keep them visible. Jack turned to look back at them, and he seemed little more than an abstract painting, a green-cloaked figure in watercolor.

"Great game night, huh?" Tobias said, catching up beside her. He'd wrapped his own cloak all around him like a poncho. "Next time Morgan and Cordelia invite us along, let's say no."

"Little late for that, Tobias," she said.

He laughed, hopping nimbly over a branch. Her brother moved with an easy grace here, she noticed. He wasn't what you'd call oafish at home, but neither was he anything like this.

"You almost look like you're having fun," she said, circumventing a large tree.

"Oh, absolutely," Tobias said. "Catching pneumonia while chasing a monster was exactly how I wanted to spend my Friday night."

Something cried out in the darkness, sharp and inhuman. The whole group came to a halt.

"What was that," Tobias said.

Cordelia brushed past them, axe ready.

"I think we'll find out soon enough," Cordie said.

Morgan unslung his hammer and held it with both hands.

"Do either of you have any light spells?" Jack yelled back to them.

Morgan and Tamsin exchanged hesitant looks.

"Do I?" she asked.

"Maybe?" Morgan said. He closed his eyes and held a hand over the head of his hammer. The weapon began to glow faintly with a warm, golden glow. He opened his eyes and held the weapon aloft like a torch.

Tamsin concentrated, looking for the words to the right spell in her mind. Arcane sigils materialized behind her eyes, and she spoke them aloud in a language she didn't understand. A small globe of light materialized next to her.

Morgan headed for Jack's position, and Tamsin, unsure what else to do, followed. Her light had a flashlight-like quality to it, unlike the warm fireside feel of Morgan's.

Tamsin discovered she could direct her globe of light with her mind, and so she caused it to drift around the edge of the group, illuminating the forest floor.

"What are we looking for?" she asked.

"Anything," Jack said, wandering out of the light and once again becoming a blurry shadow. "The trail stops here."

In the darkness, Tamsin heard Jack slowly draw a sword. She heard the same noise again, closer, and saw her brother had done the same. Weirdly, with the rain-matted cloak and now-messy bard's clothes, Tobias looked less like a performer and more like a dandy from a Shakespearean play, the sort of bravo who wore finery but knew his way around a blade. He held it out in front of him like a fencer.

"Well you're full of surprises," she said.

"I have no idea what I'm doing," he said. "It's all about the presentation."

Cordelia made a silent gesture for them to stop talking. She cocked her head to one side, listening.

Then Eriko yelled.

"There!" Eriko said, pointing.

For just a split second, Tamsin could make out a grotesque face, fleshy and pink, with yellow teeth and red eyes, huddled in a branch ten feet above. It screamed at them with an inhuman wail and darted off, a silent bundle under one arm.

Eriko broke into a run without hesitation.

"Wait!" Morgan yelled, but Eriko's dark red cloak disappeared into the darkness. And, inexplicably, Tamsin found herself running as well.

"Tam, stop!" she heard Tobias hell, but she held tight in her mind the bundle in that creature's arm, because it breathed. She saw the rise and fall beneath the fabric that held it tight. The stolen girl still lived.

Trees and leaves rushed by in a blur of black, brown, and green. The rain spattered against her face as debris from the forest stuck to her robes and skin. She saw Eriko ahead of her, the bouncing of the cloak as her friend ran full speed, dodging stumps and stones sticking up out of the ground. Tamsin used Eriko's movements to her own benefit, letting her friend's sharper vision spot obstacles for them both to avoid.

Too late, she realized she could barely hear the sound of the others behind them. There as a distant clanging she knew had to be Morgan's armor, and Tobias called out her name, but the darkness seemed to swallow his voice.

"Eriko, the others," Tamsin started to say.

Then Eriko disappeared.

One second Eriko was running, and the next her cloak flipped up, the dark-haired woman seemingly dropping out of existence. She wasn't completely gone, Tamsin knew, because she heard her swear every curse word ever created, in between grunts of frustration and pain.

"Eriko?" Tamsin said.

And then the earth gave out beneath her and she found herself falling, falling, rocks digging into her arms and legs, root tugging at her wizard robes. Her head banged against something that must've been a tree root. Dirt kicked up and into her mouth, nose, eyes. She heard Eriko again, a solid bark of air being forced from her body, and then a few seconds later, Tamsin made a similar noise as she slammed into the ground.

Tamsin rolled over onto her back and looked up. Above her, a dark tunnel led up to the night sky, just a pinhole of midnight blue far above.

"I think we made a mistake," she said, before darkness overtook her.

Chapter 12: The den

Well, now I know we're really in a game, Eriko thought as she pushed herself up onto her knees at the bottom of the cave she'd fallen into. In real life I'd have two broken legs and internal bleeding. I must've succeeded my saving throw on the fall.

She took in her surroundings slowly, listening as rocks and earth fell from above. She was underground, she could tell that much; and it wasn't so much a cave as it was a tunnel, clearly dug out of dirt rather than stone, with roots from trees visible in the walls. The ground, aside from where it had been torn up by her fall, was densely packed as if often traversed. The smell was staggering, somewhere between a men's restroom and a cat's litter box. It made her eyes water. She could see, which confused her at first, until she realized the light came from Tamsin's glowing orb, which had followed them down the hole.

Tamsin. Ugh, Eriko thought. Not my first choice to have stuck down here with me. Better to have someone who could at least pretend they'd been in a situation like this before. Cordelia was notorious for rushing in to bail Eriko's character out when she split the party. They had tactics together. Just please don't panic, Tamsin, she thought.

Eriko crawled over to her friend and brushed the dirt out of her face.

"Tam," she said.

"I hate this stupid game," Tamsin said.

"Yeah, me too," Eriko said. "You okay?"

"I feel like I felt down a laundry chute," Tamsin said. "What is that smell?"

Eriko looked around and saw a single tunnel leading out of the open space where they'd landed.

"I'm just going to make a wild guess," Eriko said. "That's what a predator might smell like."

"Like the movie monster, or just like, a carnivore?" Tamsin said.

"The latter," Eriko said. She stood up and then helped Tamsin back to her feet as well. "Why'd you follow me?"

"I thought you knew where you were going," Tamsin said.

"Okay, if we survive this, here's a good rule to live by," Eriko said. "I am Captain Bad Decisions in these games. It's sort of my thing."

"So you're saying don't follow you," Tamsin said.

"Stick with Morgan. He's the planner."

"I really wish you'd told me that back at the dining room table."

"Yeah, me too," Eriko said. Slowly, she started toward the tunnel.

"Where are you going?"

"Might as well see where we are," Eriko said. She spat on the floor to get the grit off her tongue. Tamsin followed close by, her light at her side.

The tunnel curved to the left, a rough pathway with a well-worn floor and crumbling walls. They came across a pile of blankets and furs, almost a bed, and a collection of odds and ends from the surface. Children's toys, a dagger, a pie tin.

"Eriko," Tamsin said.

Eriko looked to where Tamsin pointed. Hanging from the wall was a set of blades, all serrated and cruel, filthy with rust and dried blood. Some looked like torture devices; others, food preparatory instruments.

"Stay close to me," Eriko said, pulling a pair of daggers from her belt.

The women explored deeper into the tunnel, making their way around another curved path. Eriko saw a block of stone that might have been used as a table, a fire pit, currently cold, and a...

"Tamsin, don't look," Eriko said.

"What?" Tamsin said.

"Don't come in here."

"Why," Tamsin said, ignoring Eriko's warning and striding into the room. She gasped, and Eriko slapped her palm across Tamsin's mouth to stop her from screaming as she stared at the pile of bones in the corner.

Small bones. Delicate. Human. Scored with a knife's edge.

"It eats..." Tamsin whispered.

"Stop," Eriko said. She grabbed her friend by the shoulders and shook her. "Look at me, Ravenclaw. Are you listening? You're a badass magician who throws fire from her hands and I'm a stabbity stabby stab killer rogue. You got that? Whatever this thing is, we can take it. Nothing steals children unless it's afraid of badasses like us."

"Like us," Tamsin said.

"Right?"

"Yeah," Tamsin said. She looked at the pile of bones again and sneered. "I want to kill the shit out of this monster."

"Then let's be ready. You ready?"

"I hope so."

"Okay then," Eriko said. "The first thing I need you to do is figure out how to shut that light off."

"And then?"

"Make sure you know how to throw another fireball," Eriko said.

Chapter 13: Not the game I was expecting

Morgan ran through the brush like a bull, his armored frame smashing through branches and knocking down small trees. So much for a dungeon crawl he thought. This has turned into some sort of survival horror situation. Not the game I was expecting, that's for sure.

Tobias was easy to spot ahead of him in his bright cloak, yelling for his sister. He'd lost sight of Jack entirely, but he could hear Cordelia parallel to him, running in the same direction.

"Where'd they go?" he heard her day. "Tobias, wait!"

"Where is she?" Tobias said, turning back to look at both of them, throwing his arms up in frustration. "They weren't that far ahead of us."

"I heard Eriko swearing again," Morgan said, stopping to catch his breath. The armor wasn't as heavy as it should be—he couldn't run in real life mail armor, not like this, so the fictional facets of the world included a little bit of suspension of disbelief with things like armor, he guessed. He raised his hammer—also not as heavy as something twice the size of his head made of solid metal should be—and used the mystical light shining from it to look around.

The forest was too dense, he thought. They'd lost sight of Modest Expectations, and the trees above them were so thick they wouldn't have been able to see the moon even if they hadn't run out in a downpour.

"Where the fuck is Jack," Cordelia said. "Did we lose him too?"

"You don't think that thing is… picking us off one by one," Tobias said. He'd lowered his sword to the ground, his hair plastered to his face, eyes wide with worry. "I mean, is that what's happening?"

"It steals kids, Tobias," Morgan said. "Something that hunts babies isn't going to want to tangle with us."

"Right," Tobias said. "Morgan, none of us has even been in a bar brawl in the real world. We're not scary."

"Listen to me," Morgan said. "Here, we're what we have to be. Are you listening? I don't know how we got here or why it happened, but right now, we're not Morgan the student teacher or Tobias the guy who didn't get the gig for the car commercial at his audition the other day. Got me? If we're going to survive in this reality, we have to be what we need to be."

"I'm a minstrel," Tobias said, his head bobbing in resignation.

"After we find your sister, I'm going to tell you about some of the stuff I've seen bards do in games like this," Cordelia said. "You're so much more capable than you know."

"Shit," Tobias said, a nervous, wry smile crossing his face. "And to think I picked the bard because I wanted to hang back and sing songs while you guys did all the hard stuff."

Morgan barked out a quick laugh, and was relieved to see Cordelia smiling as well.

"Now let's go find our friends," Morgan said. But as he looked back at Tobias, he saw two glowing red eyes in the dark behind him. "Tobias! Duck!"

Tobias spun around. Everything seemed to transition to slow motion. The bard recoiled as the creature, an arm covered in whitish fur, ending in a dark gray, clawed hand, lashed out. Then a blur of green launched into view, knocking Tobias aside. Blood flew through the air, staining the rain. The monster cried out in pain. Tobias' body landed on the forest floor with a thump.

Cordelia ran forward, yelling out a war cry.

Jack's body rolled until it landed at Morgan's feet. Time returned to normal.

"Jack!" Morgan yelled, dropping down to his prone friend. Jack's hand grabbed hold of Morgan's calf.

"I think I got him," Jack said. He dropped his short sword, edge stained red with blood, and pulled back his hood.

Tobias swore. Cordelia gasped.

"Holy shit," she said.

"How bad is it?" Jack said, gesturing to his face. Three ragged slashes ran upward from chin to cheekbone, somehow missing mouth, nose, and eye. Bright blood poured down his face, pooling in his collar.

"Let me try to heal you," Morgan said, grabbing his friend by the shoulders.

"No, save it," Jack said. "Time for that later. We gotta follow him. He's still got that kid."

"You're an idiot," Cordelia said. She helped Tobias to his feet.

"What were you doing?" Tobias said.

"He was stalking you," Jack said. "I was trying to get a shot at him with my bow when he moved in. He's so fast. He would've gutted you."

"So instead you saved my guts with your face."

"I was actually hoping to block him with my sword, but I missed," Jack said.

From the darkness, a wolf howled.

"That your dog?" Cordelia said.

"Yeah. I… I don't know how I know this, but he's telling me he's found something."

"Better than hearing him cry out like he's being eaten," Tobias said.

"Let's go," Jack said, leading them away.

As they moved, Cordelia yanked something from a tree branch. A scrap of blue cloth.

"Tamsin," she said.

"He got her?" Tobias said.

"I don't think so," Morgan said. "Looks like there's just some trampled branches."

The wolf, Silence, trotted like a shadow out of the brush, eyes shining in the dark. He made eye contact with Morgan—well that's unsettling, he thought—and then turned and walked away.

The group followed. Maybe thirty feet away, the wolf stood over a hole in the ground, deliberately dug out and well camouflaged.

"A nest," Cordelia said. "I'll go first."

Morgan started to protest, but Cordelia held up a hand.

"Orc. Axe. Natural ability to see in the dark," she said. "Fight me, big guy, I'm the best option."

"Okay," Morgan said. He watched as Cordelia, with grace incongruous to her orcish frame, slipped into the tunnel and quickly made her way down.

"I'm next," Tobias said. Without waiting for permission, the bard disappeared into the den as well.

Jack turned to his wolf.

"We'll be back," he said. "Keep an eye out for us. Howl if anything approaches."

The wolf, of course, didn't respond, but casually walked away, taking up sentry duty in a copse nearby.

Jack and Morgan looked at each other.

"This is all my fault, Morgan," Jack said. "I did this."

"Did you know the game was going to teleport us to some alternate reality?" Morgan said.

"No," Jack said.

"Did you want it to teleport us to some alternate reality?"

"No."

"Then the only thing you did wrong was buy a board game from Lonnie, who probably overcharged you for it because he thought it was vintage, like he always does," Morgan said. "If you start a pity party I will smack the living hell out of you and I will not heal your face when this is over."

"No pity party," Jack said.

"Good," Morgan said. "Now you go in the hole first. You know I hate this stuff and I don't want you to be able to see my claustrophobia face when we're climbing down."

Chapter 14: Now it's a proper dungeon crawl

Cordelia's boots hit the ground with more noise than she was hoping for as she dropped from the gap in the cavern ceiling. Her eyes adjusted quickly to the darkness, an ability she was suddenly glad the orcish body she was trapped in possessed. The air was rank, thick with rot and ammonia. It was enough to make her eyes water.

This, though, felt familiar. She and her friends had been playing games like this their whole lives, and this world they'd ended up in seemed to very much want to play by the rules of those games. No more running through the sandbox setting of a forest, she thought. Now it's a proper dungeon crawl.

Tobias struggled to escape the tunnel in the ceiling, feet dangling with a complete lack of dignity above her. She reached up and pulled on his leg, freeing him from a root that had caught his tunic, and with one arm all but caught him like a football, setting him down on the floor.

"That could've been smoother," he said.

Jack came next, dropping down with far more practiced ease. Morgan brought up the rear, making an uncomfortable amount of noise.

"Sorry," he said. "Stupid armor."

"Always the cleric ruining stealth," Jack said.

"So, what is this thing?" Tobias said. "Like a troll or something?"

"Stealing little kids from their beds at night," Cordelia said. "It's a bogeyman. Or whatever they call things like that in this world."

"We're chasing the boogey man," Tobias said.

"Bogeyman," Cordelia corrected. "There's lots of names for them in myths. Every culture has them, so they end up in games like this a lot. It's something everyone's afraid of."

"What are we going to do?" Tobias said.

"We're going to kill it," Cordelia said.

"I mean what are we going to do to get to that part."

"Well, normally I'd send our rogue ahead to check for traps, but since as usual our rogue has split the party, as she always does..." Morgan said.

"I'll go," Jack said, heading off before anyone could stop him.

Cordelia gave Morgan an unpleasant look.

"There something in Jack's character sheet about having a death wish?"

"He thinks this is all his fault," Morgan said.

"Well, he did buy the game," she said.

"Can we... not... do that right now?" Morgan said. "Let's find everyone first and we can play the blame game after."

"Every party needs a pooper," Cordelia said before heading off after Jack.

She didn't get far before running into Jack's outstretched hand, telling her to wait. Wordlessly, she questioned him with a glance. He pointed to the ground. Cordelia shrugged, irritated. Jack pointed again. She knelt to check out what had him spooked and saw multiple sets of footprints on the ground. Some were monstrous, scratched up by exposed claws; but alongside those were two sets of footprints, both booted, slender enough to hint they might be female.

Eriko and Tamsin were here, she thought.

Tobias sidled up beside her and immediately recognized the

prints, which, Cordelia had to admit, surprised her. She hadn't thought he'd be that perceptive.

"My sister is here," he said.

"Shh," Cordelia said, giving him a dirty look.

"Why are we going into the dark to find him?" Tobias said.

"Keep talking so loud and he's going to find us," Morgan said.

"There's four of us. One of him. Let's draw him out. Back at the entrance," Tobias said. "Why are we walking into his trap?"

"Guys," Jack said. "That almost makes sense."

"Of course it makes sense," Tobias said. "You want someone to think outside the box? Bring the guy who has never played the game before."

"Okay. Okay, we'll try it," Morgan said. "The corridors are too tight anyway. We risk getting bottlenecked."

"What are we doing to do, ask him to come out and play?" Cordelia said.

"Guys," Tobias said, holding out his arms dramatically. "You brought a bard. Use him the way the gods intended. To make a stupid amount of noise."

Chapter 15: The kitchen

The cave, it turned out, was more pockmarked and complex than Eriko had first noticed. The kitchen—that's what this is, she knew, her stomach a roiling pit of disgust—had dips and corners, something that might have been a pantry, and another tunnel leading down into a sort of makeshift storeroom. The storeroom itself seemed barren and unused. She hustled Tamsin into that tunnel, out of sight from the cooking fire and butcher's table.

"I'm going to set that bastard on fire," Tamsin said. Eriko locked eyes with her.

"The kid," she said. "He might still have the little girl. Wait until you know you won't hit her."

"I must know some other spells," Tamsin said.

"Then start concentrating and trying to remember," Eriko said.

She reached for Tamsin's belt and pulled open a distinctly square-shaped pouch, revealing the top of a book.

"Spell book," Eriko said.

"I have one of those?"

Eriko pulled it from the pouch and handed it to Tamsin.

"Try reading it," she said. "Just… read, like, quietly."

Tamsin nodded, carefully turning the pages, squinting in the dark.

"I can't see shit," she said.

"You're an elf. You should have like, dark vision or something."

"I read the character sheet. Low light seems to indicate there has to be some light…"

"Read quieter," Eriko said.

"I…" Tamsin said, then cut herself short.

The sound of ragged breathing and heavy footsteps echoed faintly from within the cavern ahead.

I'm a rogue, Eriko thought. I'm stabby. I'm sneaky. I should be able to sneak up and stab him before he does anything to that kid, or to us, or…

Her heart raced. It was one thing to play rogue on the streets of the town, without risk. But this was life or death. If her confidence faltered—is it confidence? Are our real bodies back home, rolling dice, unaware that rolling a one meant maybe dying? Or are we just here, truly here, body and soul, relying on skills and abilities we have no idea how to use?

Doesn't matter, she told herself. You're Rouge the Rogue, the party-splitter, always the thief, always the assassin. You've been playing this character your whole life in one game or another. You're a badass, Eriko. Get your shit together and do this.

Then the monster staggered into the kitchen and dropped the unconscious child on the table like a slab of pork and Eriko's limbs went numb.

The girl groaned, which Eriko knew had to be a good sign—he hadn't killed her already, though she was too quiet to be fully conscious. She should be screaming in fear and panic. The monster stepped away, casually examining a wall of carving instruments, lifting one, then another, serrated or straight-edged, all filthy and rusted. He grunted to himself and strode over to the fire, striking metal against stone until the sloppy pile of firewood began to crackle.

He picked up a blackened pot from the floor and hung it over the fire, then retrieved a jug of water and filled the pot.

He's making little kid stew, Eriko thought. Her grip on her daggers went white-knuckle. Do it, Eriko, do it while his back is turned, get him... but that back was massive, rippling with animalistic muscle, the back of his head predatory and monstrous. He sounded like a caged tiger at the zoo.

The child whimpered in the dark. Eriko felt Tamsin's hand on her shoulder. The women exchanged a look. Now or never.

And then: someone started singing a Queen song in the distance. They lyrics to "Bicycle Race" were singularly incongruous to everything in this cavern; light, funny, unexpected, almost comforting.

Tamsin's eyes went wide. She mouthed her brother's name.

"Tobias?"

The monster stood up violently, throwing a wooden spoon it had been stirring the pot with aside. It grabbed two rusted carving knifes from the wall and stomped furiously out of the kitchen toward the singing.

"Come on," Eriko said.

She leapt from their hiding place to the table, finding the little girl still wrapped in a rough wool sack. Eriko yanked the bag open. The little girl—wide-eyed, hair in disarray, a brutal bruise growing across her face—yelped in surprise, but then opened her mouth when she saw Eriko's face.

"Come on, Madsin. We're here to get you out of this place," Eriko said.

"Are you going to save me from the monster?" the child said.

"We sure hope so," Tamsin said.

Eriko pulled Madsin from the sack and Tamsin scooped her up, the little girl wrapping her arms and legs around her torso tightly. Eriko drew two daggers from her belt, and she was shocked at how natural it felt.

"Who's singing?" Madsin asked.

"My idiot brother," Tamsin said. "I think we're going to have to save him too."

Chapter 16: Every party member has a job to do

So I'm the bait, Tobias thought, wailing about how he wants to ride his bicycle in his best Freddie Mercury impression. He had considered diving into some David Bowie instead, but for some reason the lyrics left his mind. Never had any problems calling up the words to a Queen epic, though, so he let loose, immediately regretting not choosing "We are the Champions" instead.

Cordelia, positioned just to the left of the gap in the wall the creature would emerge from, gave him a comically quizzical look.

"Seriously?" she mouthed.

Still, it was effective. He very soon saw the monster's shadow appear in the hallway ahead. He nodded at Morgan, who had taken up position opposite Cordelia, both of them with their two-handed weapons at the ready. Somewhere in the darkness to Tobias' left he knew Jack waited with his bow already drawn.

And I'm the bait, Tobias thought. This is awesome. I always wanted to be the bait. Every party member has a job to do, I guess. I guess if I were in charge I'd make the bard the bait too.

The creature, the bogeyman as Cordelia had called him, appeared at the end of the corridor. He's big, Tobias thought. Bigger than he looked out in the forest, as if he'd compressed himself to hide his bulk. But here in his home he was built like a wall of fur and muscle, pushing seven feet tall, shoulders wider than any human he'd ever seen, with massive black claws gleaming at the tips of his fingers and toes.

The bogeyman smiled. His teeth were like blackened razors.

Tobias stopped singing.

"Hi, gorgeous," he said. "With a face like that, you should be on the *Bachelor.*"

The bogeyman broke into a run, his footfalls heavy enough that Tobias could feel them through the soles of his boots.

"Not a reality TV fan, I guess," Tobias said. "No problem."

The monster reached out for Tobias with an impossibly long, apelike arm.

Tobias didn't even hear Jack's bow release. The arrow silently sunk into the palm of the bogeyman's hand, bursting out the other side, deflecting the blow aimed at Tobias' throat. In the same instance, Cordelia swung her axe, an upward arc that landed dead-center in the monster's guts, driving him backward with a wet, grinding noise. The horrible violence didn't stop there though, as Morgan—the big man dwarfed by the creature's size—took a home run swing at the back of the bogeyman's head, landing with a grotesque smack of steel on bone.

It should've killed him, Tobias thought. He should've been decapitated and bisected in a split second. But the creature lashed out, backhanding Morgan and sending the cleric slamming into the stone wall behind him, his armor clanging on impact. The monster reached down and yanked Cordelia's axe from his guts with his own hands, blood pouring forth, pulling the weapon so hard that Cordelia was torn from her feet, refusing to let go.

Jack leaped in front of Tobias again. I need to do something, Tobias thought, I have a sword, I'm not useless, watching as Jack carved two wicked cuts across the bogeyman's chest then ducked out of the way of a clawed swing. Tobias felt something slam into his gut and realized Jack himself had kicked him, pushing him out of range of the bogeyman's reach.

"Over here, you baby-killing bastard," Morgan said as his

hammer lit up with a gold-white glow. He swung again in a brutal arc and the bogeyman tried to catch the hammer in one huge paw. And catch it he did, Tobias witnessed, his jaw hanging open in amazement. He caught the goddamned hammer, Tobias thought, his breath catching in his throat. But then the air filled with the smell of burning flesh and the monster released his grip, roaring in pain as the hammer itself seared its palm.

"Man, I love playing a war priest!" Morgan said, readying for another attack.

The bogeyman swung wildly, knocking an unprepared Jack off his feet with the back of his arm, howling as he found himself confronted by both Morgan and Cordelia.

Then he turned his eyes on Tobias.

"Oh shit," Tobias said, and the bogeyman ran at him, ignoring both of the more capable fighters for the bard, still sitting on the ground like a fool.

But before he reached him, the bogeyman arched his back in pain, screaming a high-pitched wail. He spun and shook as if trying to reach the worst itch he'd ever needed to scratch. As he turned, long arms reaching over his shoulders, Tobias saw the red-cloaked figure of Eriko hanging there, a dagger driven deep into the thick muscles of his trapezius on either side of his neck. She had her feet planted on his lower back, using the daggers for leverage to stay put. It didn't last though—one massive hand caught hold of her cloak and sent Eriko flying across the room like a doll.

And then Tobias saw his sister framed in the corridor entrance, looking ragged and muddy but strong and angry and brave. She had the little girl in her arms, whom she set down gently on her feet.

"I only seem to know one stupid spell," Tamsin said, her hands beginning to glow with flame. "But if I've ever met someone who deserves to burn, it's you."

She unleashed her fireball once more, striking the bogeyman with perfect aim in the center of his chest. The monster opened its mouth to scream, but it was as if the cry was swallowed up by the heat of the spell. He coughed, and smoke drifted out of his mouth instead of sound. The room filled with the stench of burning fur, and meat, and leather. Then the bogeyman collapsed, his body languid and lifeless, fur turning from white to black as the flames consumed him.

"My sister," Tobias said. "Team Ravenclaw."

Tamsin gave Tobias a weak smile, then knelt beside the little girl and put her arms around her. Morgan grunted as he hauled Jack to his feet.

"You're going to let me cast a goddamned healing spell on your face now, ass," Morgan said.

Jack, winded from the bogeyman's backhanded strike, just nodded. Morgan's hand lit up with the same golden light his hammer had possessed during the fight, and the cleric placed his palm against Jack's cheek.

"Huh," Morgan said. He grabbed Jack's face roughly and turned it to one side. "Looks like it scarred anyway."

"At least I still have both eyes," Jack said.

"I bet if you'd let me fix this an hour ago…"

"Don't go healer-guilting me, Morgan," Jack said. "It's fine."

"Got a spell for healing a busted ass?" Eriko said, dragging herself off the floor and gingerly withdrawing her daggers from the bogeyman's back. "I feel like I was just shot-putted."

"You two okay otherwise?" Cordelia asked.

"Yeah," Eriko said, eyeing Tamsin. "As okay as we can be given what we found."

"I'm afraid to ask," Cordelia said.

"The other kidnapped children… won't be going home," Tamsin said. Then, to the little girl: "Your daddy's waiting for you, Madsin. We're going to bring you home. Okay?"

Madsin nodded silently and put her head on Tamsin's shoulder.

"Well," Tobias said. "That leaves us one obstacle."

"Another bogeyman?" Eriko said. "Tell me there isn't a second bogeyman."

"I hope not," Tobias said. "I was thinking about this."

He pointed at the tunnel leading up to the surface, which

opened almost eight feet above their heads.

"Are you kidding me," Morgan said.

"Anyone know how to roll a strength check for climbing?" Cordelia said.

Morgan looked at her, despondent.

"Not funny."

Cordelia shrugged.

"I wasn't really kidding."

Chapter 17: Little victories

It was nearly dawn when they arrived back in town via the hole Tamsin had blasted in the wall.

The climb from the bogeyman's warren had been an undignified and ridiculous process, involving gracelessly shoving nimbler members of the party up through the ceiling to attach rope to help the others who remained below upward, and then a slow, messy ascent using roots like ladder rungs. Madsin rode up clinging to Cordelia's neck before returning to Tamsin's care on the surface, where Silence the wolf still waited patiently.

Jack led the way back, unable to explain how he instinctively knew which way to go despite the forest looking the same in all directions. Tamsin soon tired of carrying Madsin, who transferred to a piggyback ride on Morgan's back for a while, where she fell into a quiet, silent slumber.

"Survived our first dungeon crawl, huh?" Eriko said, whacking Jack on the arm as they crested a small hill and finally spotted the town.

"Small cave, one monster... I think we just completed the tutorial," he said.

"I guess things get worse from here, huh," Eriko said.

Jack shrugged.

"I don't think we're going to poof back to our reality just by completing this one quest. Not after what Bennett told us."

They found Hink waiting at the damaged wall, with several town guards who had taken up sentry duty. A few others were there as well, including a tall, iron-haired woman they hadn't met before.

"Wake up, Madsin," Morgan said softly.

The girl's eyes opened, and then she squirmed off Morgan's back and ran for her father's open arms. Hink scooped her up and spun her around, wrapping her up in the sort of hug only possible when you thought you'd never see someone again.

"Monster's dead," Cordelia told the gathered group. "Bogeyman. Had a nest a few miles out in the woods."

"The other kids… won't be coming back," Eriko said. "I know there are families looking for them, but we don't bring good news there."

The iron-haired woman watched Hink with is daughter for a moment, then nodded to herself.

"You did more than we could have asked of you. I suspect there was no homecoming for those children before you even arrived in Modest Expectations," she said. "I'm Miriam. I'm the closest thing we have to a mayor here, I suppose. And I'm overdue in welcoming you."

"You welcome every newcomer to town?" Eriko asked.

"Just ones who step in and help us when no one else can," she said. "Whether it was dumb luck that brought you to us or the will of the gods, I don't particularly care. I'm just grateful."

"Um," Tamsin said. "Sorry about your fence."

Miriam smirked.

"Fences can be fixed. It's a small price to pay for…" She looked to Hink and his daughter once more. "For that. You did him an even greater kindness than you know. Hink's wife and son died of sickness two winters ago. Madsin is all he has left in this world."

"Then we're even gladder to have helped," Morgan said. He looked to the others. "I'm, um, Father Bastion. These are my companions, Raven, Rouge, Oberon, Nimue, and…"

Cordelia smiled widely.

"Orchid."

"Well then," Miriam said. "Welcome to Modest Expectations. Are you staying long?"

Again, Morgan looked to his companions. Eriko shrugged and wasn't even the least bit subtle about it.

"We're not sure. We planned to meet here and head out, but we didn't have any specific plans," Morgan said.

"Well, I hope you'll stay. We're a bit of a frontier town and can always use strong fighters," Miriam said. "If not though, at least let us put you up for a few days and make sure you're fed. You're staying at Darv's inn I expect?"

"It does have the best tavern in town," Tobias said, grinning.

"Not that it has much competition," Miriam said. "Consider your rooms paid for. A thank you for the good thing you've done today. And let me know if you plan on staying. You seem like the adventuring types, and we may have some work for you if you're up for it."

"We may very well need the work," Jack said. Miriam raised an eyebrow at him. "You know how idle hands and adventurers go together, I assume."

"You're not my first band of adventurers I've seen in our little town," Miriam said. "I should see to Hink and Madsin. Please, though—come find me if you'd like to talk more."

The mayor turned away politely and walked over to the father and daughter, putting a comforting hand on Hink's shoulder.

"Well, I'm glad they're not mad about the fence," Tamsin said.

"What do you think?" Morgan said. "Do you think the game wants us to stay here? Do we move on?"

"And go where?" Cordelia said. "I think maybe the game works like… like a video game. You start in one zone, learning how to play, and then you keep exploring further and further out. I think we're in the starting area."

"The tutorial," Jack said.

"Looking at your face, Jack, it seems like the tutorial won in your case," Eriko said.

"I think it adds character," Cordelia said. "Did getting your face ripped off hurt?"

"I can't believe I'm going to be the one to say this, but can we not pick on him? His face saved me from getting killed," Tobias said. "Thanks for that, by the way."

Jack shrugged. Tamsin looked at him with a worried expression.

"You saved my idiot brother's life?" she said.

"He would've done the same for me," Jack said.

"I'm like, a hundred and ten percent certain I wouldn't have known how to do the same for you," Tobias said. "Seriously. I owe you. I'll write a song in your honor."

"How about you don't write a song in my honor and we'll call it even," Jack said.

"Sounds fair," Tobias said. "Well, since our meals are free... breakfast at Darv's?"

"I'm starving," Cordelia said.

"Sounds good," Morgan said, herding the group away from Hink's and toward the center of town. "I want to hear more from Bennett, in any case."

Chapter 18: I wanted a dungeon crawl, not a mystery

"I want bacon and pancakes," Eriko said as they walked up to the front of Darv's tavern and inn, which, Morgan was somewhat irritated to realize, they still didn't know the name of.

"Does this place even have a name?"

"Oh!" Tobias said. "It's… it's a thing. It's the… Um."

"The sign says the Hungry Lion," Tamsin said, looking up at a sign over the door with a lion proudly sitting in front of a cartoonish hunk of meat.

"Well that's not subtle at all," Tobias said. "Also, I don't think they've got pancakes in Middle Earth or wherever we are."

"We're not in Middle Earth," Morgan said.

"I don't care where we are as long as they have breakfast," Cordelia said, pushing past everyone and through the front doors. Before anyone else could enter, though, she stopped dead in her tracks. "Shit."

"Please, no," Jack said. "We've been up all night, please don't throw us another quest already…"

Morgan charged in after Cordelia, the rest of the party following close on his heels. Inside, the tavern was a mess. Tables and chairs were overturned and broken; a few patrons lay on the floor, not dead but clearly beaten up. Puddles of ale and wine pooled on the floor as well, alongside shattered glass and earthenware.

Tobias ran across the bar, vaulting the counter.

"Darv? Darv, old buddy, are you okay?" Tobias said. Morgan raced to join them, finding Tobias helping the bartender into a sitting position, a bloody cut across his forehead.

"Oberon? Oberon, it's you. You're a welcome sight," Darv said.

"Who?" Tobias said.

"Oberon. You. Your name is... Am I seeing things?"

"Oh! No, no, you're right, I'm Oberon, I'm sorry," Tobias said. "It's been a long day. I... um, forgot my name. What happened, Darv?"

The bartender grabbed Tobias' shoulder roughly.

"Where's Ena?" Darv said. "Ena!"

"We've got her," Eriko said. "She's okay. Looks like someone gave her a good knock on the head, but she's in one piece."

"Should've seen the number I did on his face with my tray," Ena said. "Ach, my head feels like a boiled egg..."

"Were you robbed?" Tobias said. "C'mon, Darv. Focus here. Tell me what happened."

Darv rubbed his head, his hand coming away bloody from his wound.

"They took your friend," he said. "The old fella."

"Bennett," Morgan said, throwing his head back in frustration. "Does anyone see Bennett?"

Jack and Cordelia bolted outside as if to pursue, but Morgan shook his head, knowing it was too late.

"How long ago did this happen, Darv?" Morgan said.

"Late," the bartender said. "They came in after we were trying to close up for the night, ushering people out and the like. They moved so fast we didn't even have a chance to shout at 'em to get out."

"Did they take anyone else?" Morgan asked.

Darv shook his head. He crawled over to the counter and opened a metal drawer.

"They didn't even take any of our coin," he said. "Nothin'. Just your friend."

Cordelia strode back inside, looking disappointed and disgusted.

"Nobody's seen anything, of course," she said. She picked up a fallen chair and righted it absently. "So much for getting any more answers about how to get home."

Eriko sat down in the hair Cordelia had picked up. Cordelia gave her a dirty look. Eriko ignored her, crossing her legs casually.

"I guess we better settle in for the long term then," Eriko said. "Good thing we have work lined up."

Tobias popped open a bottle of whiskey behind the bar, poured a shot for Darv and handed it to him, then poured a shot for himself.

"If we're sticking around, we need a name," Tobias said.

"No, we absolutely don't need a name," Morgan said.

"The Dungeon Crawlers," Eriko said.

"That's super original, Eriko," Cordelia said.

"Anyone else using it?" Eriko said. "No? I like it better than some pseudo-Ren Faire title."

"I happen to like Ren Faire, you snob," Morgan said. "But the Dungeon Crawlers works for me."

Jack walked back in, his wolf at his heels. He looked quickly at Tobias holding a shot of whiskey aloft, shrugged, then picked up a chair for himself and plopped down wordlessly.

"To the Dungeon Crawlers, then," Tobias said, throwing back his shot. "May we not die horribly, crawling through a dungeon, without ever finding our way home."

"I'll drink to that," Morgan said. "Too bad finding our way home won't be as easy as picking a name."

Epilogue: There is always someone watching

The old wizard felt it the moment the new group arrived.

It had been a long time since anyone had found their way into his world. The trap was no longer being manufactured in those other realities, he knew—something he'd like to change somehow, if he could find a way to travel there—but copies of the trap, or the "game," as it was so cleverly disguised, still circulated. And it still lured new souls into its web sometimes.

He rose from his bed and pulled on a robe over his patchwork pajamas, pulled a floppy cap onto his head. He pulled out a classic scrying sphere, a crystal ball in the most classic sense, and looked within.

Six strangers, lost in his world. New souls to become heroes or victims or both. They all end up both in the end, he knew. He'd watched them all, over the years. Some arrived full of fearless abandon; others with trepidation and fear. All eventually decided they needed to take action. He'd seen them die in dragon fire or acid pits; he'd seen them slay gods and necromancers; wipe out undead armies, or become vampires or liches themselves. In many ways, the game was a social experiment. What do ordinary men and women do when they have a chance to be something extraordinary? Sometimes they do become heroes. Others become... what was that turn of phrase one such travel once called his merry band of misfits? "Murder hobos," he said. "We've become murder hobos, wandering the countryside killing and looting."

They all had their entertainment value, the old wizard thought. Watching them was better than not. This world was very much alive with or without the strangers, but it certainly was more entertaining with them in it.

He watched as the new group slaughtered one of those vile, baby-eating bogeymen. The wizard found himself chuckling at the almost cartoonish level of violence they heaped upon the monster. Well, they're violent, but their heart is in the right place.

Let's see how long that lasts.

He placed the crystal ball in a structure shaped like a three-clawed hand, designed to hold the sphere in place. He waved his hand and a small fire started beneath a cold kettle. Tea while I watch, he thought. I've missed the entertainment of strangers.

Don't disappoint me, he thought. It's so much more fun when they put up a fight.

Book 2:

The Dungeoneer's Bestiary

Chapter 1: Why does everything we fight eat people?

Her entire gaming life, Eriko had loved playing stealthy characters. Thieves, rogues, assassins, games like this had no shortage of backstabbers. Give her some sort of sneak attack and a pair of daggers and she was a happy player.

The thing about playing rogue-types, Eriko thought, was that you usually could hang back and watch your meat shield take the hits so you could dive in and do a bit of backstabbing. Let the other guy take it on the chin so you can get the devious work done.

And this, Eriko thought to herself as she stared up at a stinking, hulking ogre poised to bash her brains in standing in the middle of the creature's makeshift camp, is why I don't play warriors.

The ogre, a grotesque mockery of the human form, a ten-foot tall slab of meat and muscle covered under a wobbly layer of flab, brought his club down in a ponderous arc. Eriko dove out of the way with an almost superhuman grace she did not possess in the real world and which she was growing more and more thankful for every day. The ogre's weapon, more the leftovers of a tree trunk than an actual crafted club, splintered as it hit the ground, kicking up mud and dirt.

"Little help here? Rogue in trouble!" Eriko yelled.

"I'm kind of busy over here!" Cordelia said. Eriko stole a glance to her left to see Cordelia, still an alien sight in the half-orc form she'd taken in this game world, swinging her massive battle axe wildly, opening a wound across the sloping belly of another ogre. This only seemed to anger her opponent, who roared and returned the blow with one of its own.

"I got you, sneak thief," Tamsin said. Before Eriko could figure out where their rookie-player-turned-elven-mage was, a fireball lit up the battlefield, striking the first ogre with the sound of a gas grill lighting up. The air filled with the stench of what Eriko immediately identified as burnt bacon. The stink almost caused Eriko to gag.

"We have got to teach you some new spells," Eriko said.

"You're welcome," Tamsin said, but before either woman could gloat, Eriko watched as the now half-cooked ogre stood up to his full height, ready to continue the fight.

"Oh, come on," Eriko said.

And that was when Tobias started singing. In an almost pitch-perfect imitation of Joe Cocker, Tobias broke into "You Are So Beautiful," immediately drawing the ire of the ogre, almost as if the otherwise non-verbal creature knew he was being mocked. They'd recently discovered that Tobias had some sort of bardic music-based magic that could manipulate minds in subtle ways, but Eriko wasn't entirely convinced his music was magical this time. More likely, the barbecued ogre was as irritated with Tobias as almost everyone was at some point or another. The creature turned away from Eriko to charge the bard, who threw back his bright purple cloak and thrust forward his cutlass-style sword. With a fencer's grace, Tobias ran the giant creature through, the blade piercing the ogre's heart.

"Stop enjoying this so much," Eriko shouted.

Tobias yanked the sword free of the ogre's body just as the massive frame collapsed on the ground.

"I am having the time of my life," Tobias said. "I don't know why you're all so…"

Before he could finish the thought, Tobias was batted into the air by a swaying, apelike arm. A third ogre roared at him, but whether in grief over his dead compatriot or just at Tobias' general annoying behavior it was unclear.

"As… you… wish…" Tobias called out in his best Cary Elwes impression before landing with a pathetic thump in the brush fifteen feet away.

"Fireball! Tamsin, fireball now!" Eriko said.

"I… I think it's recharging, hang on," Tamsin said, muttering and fumbling the arcane words of the spell.

"You're making the cleric hit things," Morgan said, emerging from a nearby copse of trees, maul in hand, his armor creaking and clanking. "The cleric is not supposed to have to hit things."

"You like hitting things," Eriko said.

Morgan shot his million-dollar smile at her.

"Oh, I do love hitting things," he said. Morgan uttered a few mystical words himself and the head of his maul began to glow with warm golden light. He swung it ferociously into the gut of the ogre like a baseball bat, then reared back to swing again. But before he could, a stream of blood began pouring down from the ogre's greasy hairline, and with a horrible, wet noise, the creature fell forward, revealing a gore-covered Cordelia behind him.

"Thanks for your help with the other one, guys," Cordelia said.

"You looked like you had the situation under control," Morgan said.

Still hidden away in the vegetation, Tobias called out in a muffled, exaggeratedly weak voice.

"Hey cleric," he said. "Can you come put your bard back together again?"

"You hurt?" Morgan yelled.

"My pride needs stitches. Also, I think I broke my ass," Tobias said.

Morgan shrugged and walked calmly over to where Tobias had disappeared. Tamsin trotted down from an incline in the earth where she'd been casting like a sniper.

"Where's my brother?" she asked.

"Morgan's patching him up," Eriko said.

Tamsin looked over her shoulder to where the two men were talking and shrugged.

"He sounds okay," she said.

Eriko felt a swell of pride for her friend. When they'd first arrived a month ago, trapped in a very real version of the cursed fantasy board game they'd decided to play together, Tamsin had been a Level 20 worrier, about everything in general, but her twin brother's safety especially. They'd spent the past four weeks doing odd, and usually violent, jobs, protecting the town of Moderate Expectations. The newly minted heroes took down bandits and chased off monsters, and through all of this, Tamsin seemed to have come to trust her brother's competence during a fight. Or if not competence, at least his pure dumb luck, which Eriko had begun to suspect was some sort of class feat associated with his being a bard.

"So, it's just the three of them then," Tamsin said.

"That's what the writ from Miriam said, and that's the number we killed," Cordelia said, hefting one of the ogre's weapons, an axe that the monster wielded one-handed but required two for Cordelia to lift. She turned it from side to side admiringly.

Cordelia had adjusted almost hilariously well to her role in the game, Eriko thought. Rather than being freaked out at living in a powerful half-orc body, bigger and stronger than she'd ever been in the real world—not to mention greener, and toothier—Cordelia appeared to revel in the physicality of it. She loved to fight in this world, relished in taking as many hits as she gave out, battling with an exaggerated barbarian rage that felt to Eriko more than a little bit like a therapeutic endeavor. Back home, Cordelia had been, maybe not quite a wallflower, but certainly unassuming. Here, she walked the line of being pure id.

"I think I just found my new weapon," Cordelia said.

Eriko took a long, hard look at the axe. The blade looked like it was carved with the general idea of what an edge looked like, adorned with poorly treated animal parts, and topped with the yellowing tooth of a very large mammal.

"That is vile," Tobias said, hobbling out of the woods to join them.

"Stop limping," Morgan said. "I healed you fine. You're being dramatic."

"You just told the bard to not be dramatic," Tobias said. "Which I think is an oxymoron. Are those teeth?"

"Teeth?" Tamsin repeated.

Cordelia turned the weapon side to side again.

"Oh, yeah," she said. "I see it now."

"Those are human teeth embedded in the hilt," Eriko said. Her mouth went dry and her stomach twisted.

"The ogres literally jammed a person's teeth into the handle as a decoration," Tobias said. "That looks like a someone turned a gum infection into a melee weapon."

"I'm literally going to be sick," Morgan said.

"You don't like teeth?" Tobias said.

"Toby," Tamsin warned.

"I need to walk away for a minute. I can't look at that thing," Morgan said.

"Oh look," Cordelia said. "They're not all from the same person. See? They're different sizes!"

"I'm walking away too," Eriko said. "I didn't survive fighting three ogres so you can make me toss up my breakfast."

Eriko left the rest of the group to admire or gag at the ogre war art, heading over to where the creatures had built what might have been called a camp. Ogres weren't known for their civility, at least not in this game world, but they had built a fire, and left piles of the spoils they'd collected terrorizing Moderate Expectation about, organized into what Eriko surmised were "weapons," "food," and "shiny things."

She saw something in the food pile that immediately completed the stomach-churning process begun by Cordelia's tooth-studded axe.

"I told you we could do this without Jack, didn't? Oh—Oh!" Morgan said, walking up behind Eriko. "You okay?"

"I think I found Old Man Hobbins," Eriko said, wiping her mouth. Eriko righted herself and felt a wave of sympathy as she watched Morgan turn a shade of sickly gray.

"That's Old Man Hobbins," he said.

"At least they hadn't... started preparing him for dinner," Eriko said. Steering clear of the "food" pile, Eriko began prodding at the "shiny things" pile, finding several gemstones that might have some value, a cracked mirror, a horseshoe with most of the horse's lower leg still attached—she wondered briefly how the ogres decided if the leg should end up in the "shiny" pile or the "food" pile—a few sacks of coins she tucked into her belt automatically, and at the bottom of the pile, a leather-bound book.

Curious, she opened it up. The pages crawled with spidery symbols and letters she couldn't understand, but she immediately recognized.

"Hey Tamsin," Eriko said. "I got something for you."

Tamsin meandered into the camp as well. Behind her, Eriko could see Tobias and Cordelia having a ridiculously intense conversation about the tooth-axe, which Eriko silently vowed to burn the minute Cordelia wasn't looking.

"What's up?" Tamsin said, her fingers absent-mindedly touching the tip of one pointed ear. It was a funny habit she'd picked up since they arrived here, as if even a month later the magician still couldn't believe she had become an elf. "I—oh shit, is that Old Man Hobbins?"

"That's Old Man Hobbins," Morgan said, his voice tight with disgust.

"They were going to eat Old Man Hobbins?" Tamsin said, her voice rising.

"Looks like it," Eriko said.

"Why does everything we fight here eat people?" Tamsin said, her voice swelling with what in any less violent a circumstance have been a humorous amount of empathy and annoyance.

"Not everything," Morgan said.

"The bogeyman," Tamsin said.

"Well, yeah," Morgan said.

"The rat-thing in the graveyard."

"Technically, those were corpses it ate," Morgan corrected.

"That dire bear," Tamsin said.

"To be fair, that bear ate everything it laid eyes on," Eriko said.

"Including two villagers!" Tamsin said. "This world is horrible. It's horrible and it's full of people-eaters!"

"Here," Eriko said, handing Tamsin the tome. "This'll take your mind off it."

"Why are you handing me your diary," Tamsin said.

"It's a spell book," Eriko said. "Take it. Maybe you can learn something other than fireball and that lantern spell you use at night."

"I do know that mystical shield spell too, you know," Tamsin said.

"You say you know that spell, but we've never seen proof of it," Tobias said as he and Cordelia joined them. "For all we know you just pretend to cast a magical protective shield on yourself."

"The same could be said about your 'magic' songs," Tamsin said.

Tobias shrugged insolently.

"True," he said. "Find anything else inter—oh shit, is that Old Man Hobbins?"

"Yes," Morgan said, his tone exhausted. "Yes, it is Old Man Hobbins."

"I guess we should carry him back to Moderate Expectations," Cordelia said. "Maybe Jack'll be back by the time we return."

"Considering we have no idea where he is, I wouldn't bet on it," Eriko said.

"On the bright said, he doesn't get a cut of the ogre bounty," Tobias said. "More money for us, right?"

The rest of the group stared at him in silence.

"I'm remembering this the next time I ask to stay behind to play a gig while you're out fighting bandits," Tobias said.

Chapter 2: Tracking the past

Whatever this world is, Jack thought, however real it feels, it definitely has glitches.

He'd left his friends behind to deal with the latest quest the mayor of Moderate Expectations asked of them so he could continue what the group had begun calling Jack's side job: searching the surrounding areas for signs of whoever had taken Bennett. Bennett, another person from the "real" world, disappeared their first night here, stolen away by strangers in a violent assault before he could tell them anything more about this alternate reality.

They'd asked around town, put Eriko's snooping skills and Tobias' charm to work, and come up with nothing. And so, they sent Jack out ranging, as rangers are supposed to, to track the kidnappers. Whether he found a living Bennett or a body, they wanted an answer.

But you don't always get what you wish for, Jack thought, crouching to scratch the wolf at his side behind the ear. The black and gray canine—wolf by name, but exaggerated, almost a caricature, like a wolf you'd dream up in a storybook rather than in nature—was his silent shadow, always at his side or near enough to come running if Jack needed him. He'd taken to calling the animal

Silence for obvious, literal, if uncreative reasons.

As his friends gelled into a cohesive fighting team, Jack found they didn't need him as much. He certainly didn't benefit from them stomping loudly behind him as he went on his hunting patrols, so they started split up. At first it spiked Jack's anxiety levels, but they'd all found that if they trusted themselves, the skills that belonged to their character classes—Morgan's healing magic, Cordelia's combat prowess, Jack's woodland knowledge—all flowed naturally, like they'd "downloaded" the skills from the Matrix or something.

Jack had a hard time with this. He was a city boy through and through, and had never spent much time with outdoorsman activities. Suddenly being able to spot barely visible animal tracks or knowing instinctually what plants were safe or poisonous was strange. Feeling safer and more competent out under an open sky was even stranger.

But, he thought, the glitches make it more bearable. Like bugs. Part of his aversion to the outdoors back in the real world: bugs. He was a mosquito magnet. He'd never met an insect that didn't want to bite him. But out here, it was as though all the wonderful things about nature—the soft wind in the trees, the gentle warmth of golden sunlight, the smell of earth and life—were almost overwhelmingly pleasant, as if this world had forgotten the little inconveniences and discomforts of traversing unspoiled wilderness.

Idealized, Jack thought. That's the world. It's an idealized forest. A fairy tale woods.

These woods were not without their terrors, but those were also storybook-styled. Monsters or traps, dramatic storms or land formations that didn't make sense. Once, on one of his solitary hunts, he came across a tiny house in the forest, no paths leading to or from it, a thin swirl of smoke uncoiling from its perfect little chimney. He knew, in the deepest parts of his guts, that if he knocked on that door an old crone would open it, and nothing but trouble would follow. He gave the house wide berth and moved on.

There was unreal beauty here, too. He woke one night to find himself face-to-face with a pixie, illuminating the dark forest with warm golden light. The doll-sized woman looked at him curiously as he opened his eyes, laughed, and darted off into the night sky, never to return. It felt like a profoundly private moment. Unlike almost everything else he encountered when he went on these walkabouts, he never told his friends about the pixie. It felt too personal.

Several weeks investigating, and he'd still come up with nothing about Bennett's whereabouts. The side benefit to these excursions was that he now had a remarkably clear map in his head of the surrounding area, miles in every direction outside Moderate Expectations: he knew places where goblin villages had taken up residence; a spot where a solitary giant led a lonely, but peaceful, existence with a small herd of enormous cattle; a river that dropped off into a magnificent waterfall, where beautiful, disembodied voices sang to themselves from the water below.

I think I'm falling in love with this world, Jack thought. The feeling made his stomach churn. It went contrary to the feeling of guilt he'd carried since they first arrived. He had been the one to suggest a game night, and he'd bought the cursed game that trapped them here. Sure, no one knew this would happen, but in the end, Jack could find none but himself to blame for their predicament. This was the reason he'd been viciously determined to find Bennett and figure out a way home since the start.

But this world grows on you, he realized. It is scary and violent and confusing, but it is also full of magic and beauty. It's so many things we wish for back home and know can never be real. Here, in this strange world, a place he still didn't know the name of, all their dreams and nightmares were made flesh and blood.

I've got to start bringing at least one of the others with me on these trips, Jack thought. I'm starting to get melancholy and stupid. Too much time alone. Maybe Eriko or Cordelia would want to come along. Morgan could keep the other two out of trouble.

He'd become so lost in thought that he couldn't stop himself from crying out when he turned to his left to see a man sitting on a rock watching him.

"Holy shit!" Jack said.

"Lost in your thoughts?" the man said. He was older, with receding gray hair and a full, if somewhat unkempt, gray beard. Dressed in green robes, he had a long, ornately carved staff resting casually against his shoulder.

"Look, I'm just going to cut to the chase. Are we going to fight?" Jack said.

"Only if you want to," the man said. "I'd rather not."

"Me neither," Jack said.

"Good," the man said. "I've been observing you. I felt the need to step in, because I've begun to feel bad for you and you seem extraordinarily persistent. You're not going to find him out here."

"You know the man I'm looking for?" Jack said.

"I know most everyone who makes their way into this world by accident," the man said. "I'm Malcolm, by the way."

"Jack," Jack said automatically.

"That's your… home name, isn't it? Not your 'here' name," Malcolm said, framing the air-quotes with his fingers.

"Yeah. I've been going by Raven here. Which feels stupid," Jack said. "Does it matter if we use our real names? You're one of us then? Not from here?"

"I've been here so long I've gone native," Malcolm said. "But yes. I'm from Toronto originally."

"Boston," Jack said. "How long is long enough to go native?"

Malcolm shrugged.

"Time moves differently here," he said. "But it feels like a lifetime."

"And you never found a way home," Jack said.

Malcolm stood up and stretched his back. There was a surreal calmness to him. This was his home, Jack realized. He was looking at man who had no intention of ever going back.

"I never tried," Malcolm said. "Jack, can I tell you something I haven't told anyone in a very long time?"

"Sounds vaguely creepy, but okay," Jack said.

"Back home I was very sick. I was dying," Malcolm said. "And I don't know if being here stopped it, or if you leave your sickness back in your real body, or hell, if I went on to live out the rest of my life and die while some other part of me stayed here. I don't know. I don't want to know. All I know is that here, nothing hurts. At least not the way it does back home. Here I wasn't burdened by doctor visits or treatments. All I had to do was live."

"Why are you telling me this?" Jack said.

"Because I've been watching you."

"Again, creepy."

Malcolm laughed.

"I can tell this world is getting to you. And I showed myself to you just now because I think you deserve a warning."

"I love warnings," Jack said.

"Think carefully before you become obsessed with going home. Just make sure home is worth going back to."

Jack's mind flickered to the pending layoffs at work, the mounting bills, the little worries that kept him up at night.

"Why are you just hanging around Moderate Expectations, Malcolm?"

"Because it's where my group started as well," he said. "In a way, it's the closest thing I have to a home on this side of the game."

"Did the rest of your group die like Bennett's?"

Malcolm coughed out another laugh, more a bark than a chuckle.

"No, no. A few decades adventuring together, you need some space. Most of my friends are still alive." A shadow fell across his face. "We lost a few. But it's inevitable in a world like this. You can't escape the violence."

"Did you know Bennett's group?"

Malcolm scowled at the name.

"Not everyone plays the game the same way, Jack. This game wants you to be important. That doesn't mean everyone will be heroic. You can be important and not be the hero."

"He seemed nice enough."

"His friends spent enough time as… what's the delightful term I heard someone use a while back from the real world? Oh, 'murder hobos.' A lot of us who make our way into this world fall into the temptation to let our less appealing instincts take over."

"He didn't mention that," Jack said.

"And his friends were far, far from the worst from our world who have come here. Truthfully, it's been a while since we've seen anyone new. I imagine the game is often rotting away on shelves somewhere."

"I got it at a going-out-of-business sale."

"How unfortunate," Malcolm said. Jack couldn't tell if he meant it was unfortunate they'd found the game, or unfortunate the game seemed to be disappearing entirely from the real world.

"Yeah," Jack said. "So, what happens now? Will you help us?"

Malcolm shook his head.

"I'm home, Jack," the older man said. "I can't be of much help. I offer you a little bit of advice. See the world. It will grow with you. It wants you to explore. Take advantage of that."

"I was just thinking we may outgrow the starter zone soon."

Malcolm nodded.

"And my other piece of advice: this world is far more real than you expect. Don't treat the people you meet like NPCs. They are so much more than that."

He pointed at Silence, who watched him intently.

"Him as well. You may feel like you're in a video game. You're not. You're in a world."

"Thank you for that," Jack said. "Will I ever see you again, or are you going to ghost out of here and just watch us like a creep from now on?"

Malcolm held out his arms like he was welcoming Jack into his home.

"I'm here. Make enough noise, say my name loud enough… I'll hear you. Probably."

Malcolm turned to leave. Jack, resigned, just watched him walk away. After a few steps, Malcolm looked back.

"Oh, and Jack—don't trust anyone who seems too helpful," Malcolm said. "This world has existed a long time. There are malicious spirits here, both literally and figuratively."

"Says the creepy guy who appeared out of nowhere in the middle of the woods to offer me helpful advice," Jack said

"Well, exactly," Malcolm said. "I'm just offering some suggestions. I recommend you find your own way, and your own truth."

Chapter 3: Roll a religion check or something

Morgan collected their payment from Miriam, the mayor of Moderate Expectations, with Cordelia along to help carry both the items, and bodies, they'd recovered. As a general rule, Morgan found himself acting as the leader and spokesman for the team, which he didn't enjoy, but didn't particularly mind, either. His role as battle priest seemed to carry a lot of weight in the community, and an inherent trust that he would do the right thing. It worked in the group's favor, but as the weeks went by, that unearned trust had begun to weigh on him.

Heading back to the Hungry Lion Tavern and Inn they'd taken up residence in, Morgan and Cordelia spotted Tobias emerging from the side door of a local tailor's shop, smiling, as he almost always was, at some inner joke no one else was privy to.

"Go on without me," Morgan told Cordelia. The half-orc raised an eyebrow. "I need to talk to Tobias about something."

"Something I can't hear about?" Cordelia said.

"No," Morgan said. "Something that would bore you. You're welcome to stay if you want to."

"Well, now you know I am morally obligated to stick around and eavesdrop," Cordelia said.

"Fine," Morgan said, sighing. He flagged down Tobias, who

strolled over to meet them.

"Calling me over to give me my part of the spoils early?" he said.

"No," Morgan said. "I mean, do you need me to count it out for you here in the street?"

"Nah," Tobias said. "What's up?"

"I need your help with something," Morgan said. The trio began walking leisurely back to the inn together.

"Anything for you, big guy," Tobias said.

"I need your help with this," Morgan said, pointing to the stylized sun that emblazoned his simple tabard.

"A broken heart? I don't have that spell. Don't you have that spell? You're the healer."

"Tobias," Morgan said.

"Hey, if you're in love, good for you," Tobias said. "I have to admit, I'm finding medieval fantasy dating kind of a slog, but if you've found true love…"

"The symbol, Tobias. I need your help with the symbol," Morgan said.

"I don't have points in the embroidery crafting skill," Tobias said.

"Why are you being obtuse about this?" Morgan said.

"Because you're being obtuse about what you're asking for," Tobias said.

"In the bard's defense, I can't tell what you're asking for either," Cordelia said.

"This religion," Morgan said, exasperated. "I'm the priest of some religion I know nothing about. It's been okay so far, but at some point, someone's going to ask me about this fictional god I represent and I know literally nothing about him."

"First of all, it's a her," Tobias said.

"How do you even know that?" Morgan said.

"Because I'm a bard, and everyone talks my ear off," he said. "Someone said it was really nice that we have a priest of Theana the Wise on our side when we protect the town, praise her name."

"Praise whose name?" Cordelia said.

"Theana the Wise, praise her name," Tobias said. "That's how the person phrased it, and then she made a little gesture with her index finger against her forehead, like y'know, when you finish a prayer sometimes back home. Depending on your religion."

"This is a good start," Morgan said. "Definitely a good start. Did she tell you anything else?"

"Well I mean, we weren't really there to talk about you," Tobias said. "We were there to talk about me."

"Tobias," Morgan said.

"What? I'm living my best life here. You want me to lie about it?"

"Tobias, can you find out more about Theana the Wise? Maybe someone's got a book or something we can borrow?"

"How am I supposed to do that?"

"You talk to everyone," Morgan said. "You've got to be able to ask around."

"Religious texts don't often come up during flirty talk, dude," Tobias said. "Why can't you ask around? Can't you roll a religion check or something?"

"That's not suspicious at all," Morgan said. "Hey, stranger, can you tell me more about the religion I'm allegedly a clergyman of?"

"Fair point," Tobias said. "I'll come up with something."

"Thank you," Morgan said.

"Hey, anything for my favorite fake priest," Tobias said.

Chapter 4: The emotional math

Eriko meandered in to the Hungry Lion to find Tamsin sitting by herself near a window, the light spilling in through her fantastical, metallic elvish hair. Eriko stared at the sight for a moment—the elven grace, the perfect daylight, the glittery hair, the delicately pointed ears—and was overcome by the desire to irritate the living hell out of her friend. She walked up to Tamsin and flicked her pointed ear with one finger.

"Ow," Tamsin said, scowling at Eriko. "What was that for?"

"You know, normally when people play these games, they chose to play an elf because they wish they looked like an elf, and you and your stupid brother are so fucking pretty it's like this game just added pointed ears and said: that'll do."

"I can't tell if that's a compliment or not," Tamsin said.

"Kind of both," Eriko said. "I had no idea the two of you were descended from immortal fey creatures the whole time we knew you growing up."

"If it makes you feel any better, I catch these stupid ears on everything," Tamsin said. "Have you ever closed your ear in a door? I now have, and let me tell you, it feels as wonderful as it sounds."

"Sorry for picking on you. I'm not annoyed. I'm just jealous."

"I've known you most of my life, Eriko. You are definitely not jealous, and absolutely annoyed."

"How do you know the difference?"

"You have a specific annoyed face."

"I need to work on that."

"You should," Tamsin said.

"Anyway. How's the book?" Eriko slid into the booth across from the mage and put her elbows on the table. Ena, the co-owner of the bar, placed a stein of beer in front of Eriko without asking. Eriko smiled at her and nodded.

"I can't read all of it," Tamsin said. "I assume that means the spells are above my level."

"Picking up the lingo," Eriko said. "My heart swells with pride."

"But there's several I can totally use."

"Such as?"

"Invisibility, for starters," Tamsin said.

"Best. Spell. Ever," Eriko said.

"There's a spell that is either super useful or completely useless that lets me manipulate a rope, so if we ever get stuck in the bottom of a bogeyman's cave again, it'll be easier to get out," Tamsin said. "Some little illusions spells for making someone look different, a dispel... spell... spell? A spell that dispels spells."

"Tell me there's something in there you can shoot that isn't fire," Eriko said.

"Oh, definitely," Tamsin said. "A lightning bolt spell. I was saving that for last for shock value."

"You did not just do that," Eriko said.

"I did, I did," Tamsin said. "I'm not proud."

"Yes, you are."

"Yes, I am," Tamsin said, fighting back an enormous smile.

"Well, I'm glad we found it," Eriko said. "Pull your brother aside and see if he can learn any spells too. Sometimes in games like this, bards can pick up some minor spells."

"I shudder to think what my brother would do with an invisibility spell."

"Probably the same nonsense he gets up to without it, only nobody would see him," Eriko said.

As she spoke, Jack walked in. Eriko could tell he was trying not to look dramatic, but the green cloak and back-lighting made for an impressive figure, at least until he caught his cloak in the door and choked himself on the fastener.

"You do that almost every time you walk through a door," Eriko said.

"I forget how long this thing is," Jack said, coughing. "Hi."

"Welcome back," Tamsin said.

"Find anything?" Eriko said.

Jack sidled in beside Eriko. He smelled like the outdoors. Not in a bad way. Like earth and wind and drying leaves.

"New spell book?" he said.

"Yup," Tamsin said.

"The ogres had a spell book?"

"Technically the ogres killed a guy and took his spell book," Eriko said.

"That makes more sense," Jack said.

"So, what did you find?" Tamsin said. "Any sign of Bennett?"

"Nope. I did meet a guy from Toronto, though," Jack said.

"Shut up," Eriko said.

"Yeah."

"This place is *so* not exclusive," Eriko said.

"Nope," Jack said. "And he confirmed our suspicion that Moderate Expectations is basically the starter zone. If we're going to progress in the game and maybe find our way home, we probably need to move on soon."

"I was kind of loving it here," Tamsin said. "I like being a local hero. Do we have to go?"

"I have a feeling that, like most games, if we don't go on our own, the game will somehow force us," Jack said. "Might be better if we do it of our own volition."

"I was starting to get bored anyway," Eriko said. "The quests were starting to feel repetitive."

"He said the game wants us to be important," Jack said. "I don't quite know what that means, but…"

"Killing giant rats is not important enough," Eriko said.

"No," Jack said.

"If this is the starter zone, and he knows so much, why was he here?" Tamsin said. "Shouldn't be out there trying to find his own way home?"

"That's the funny thing—he says he doesn't want to go home," Jack said.

"Okay, I haven't brought this up before, but this feels like a good time to say it: do we want to go home?" Eriko said. "I mean I can't speak for you, Tamsin, but I'm in no rush to go back to slinging fancy coffee beverages and worrying about my student loans, and Jack, I know you were five minutes away from losing your job."

"Morgan's dad needs him," Jack said.

"I'm… Tobias and I have some family stuff I am in no rush to go home to," Tamsin said. "And Toby seems to be having the time of his life here. But I mean… are you suggesting we should just stay in the game forever?"

"Not exactly," Eriko said. "Maybe? I don't know. All I'm saying is I don't have a hell of a lot to go home to."

The trio sat in silence for a moment, awkwardly not making eye contact.

"Well this turned super depressing," Jack said.

"Wow," Tamsin said.

"Sorry," Eriko said.

"No, I just… never did the emotional math there. Everything sucks back home, huh?" Jack said.

"Not everything," Eriko said apologetically.

"Almost everything," Tamsin said.

"But, I mean… we can't just stay here, right?" Jack said.

"If we go home and I can't do magic anymore, I'm going to be super disappointed," Tamsin said.

"If it turns out we all just want to like, stay, this would alleviate the profound amount of guilt you have for buying that game in the first place, right Jack?" Eriko said.

"I never figured you for someone who'd find the one bright spot in a situation like this," Jack said.

"I am full of surprises," Eriko said. "Just try me."

Chapter 5: Religious education

Tamsin stood in the corner of the tavern, completely invisible, and it was the greatest thing that had ever happened to her.

Ever since she'd started reading books about magic, the ability to turn invisible fascinated her. Whether it was Harry Potter's cloak or the One Ring or any other variation of the same mystical theme, the concept of being out of sight, undetectable by anyone, had been something she wished for. People tended to like Tamsin right away when they met her, but she was brutally introverted by nature, so the combination of shyness and involuntary attention had never sat well with her. Oh, to be invisible, she thought, to slip a ring on and disappear.

And now, here in this fictional world they were all stuck in, she could.

Cordelia knew Tamsin was here, but only because Tamsin had told her. The warrior sat near the fire, sharpening her axe—her normal axe, fortunately, as the group had been able to convince her to discard the grotesque weapon she'd taken from the ogres earlier—and staring vaguely at the space where she suspected Tamsin was hiding. At a booth just behind Cordelia, Jack and Eriko were catching Morgan up on Jack's encounter in the forest. Cordelia was clearly listening to their conversation, but she'd become less and less patient with idle chatter since they arrived here, and Tamsin suspected something about the character she played—all fighting, little thinking—had begun to creep into her personality.

Tobias swaggered in through the front door, greeted immediately by cheers from the clientele.

"Gonna play for us tonight, Oberon?" one man yelled from the bar, referring to Tobias by his character's name. Tamsin found it strange that they all simply stuck with those names—Oberon and Nimue, Raven and Bastion, Rouge and Orchid—but, she supposed, it lent them a bit of anonymity. Sort of like having a code name.

Tamsin weaved her way through the room to stand uncomfortably close to her brother, unnoticed, as he checked in with the rest of their friends.

"Good news," Tobias said, sliding into the booth next to Morgan. "I got the information you asked for."

"Awesome," Morgan said. Jack gave them both a quizzical look. "I asked him to learn more about the gods, since I'm a cleric and…"

"And none of us know anything about the gods here," Jack said. "Good call. But you sent him?"

"Why do you say that with such disdain?" Tobias said.

"Because you're… you," Jack said. "You're not who I'd send on a quest for subtle inquiries."

"I really didn't have to be subtle," Tobias said. "I'm me. People just sort of tell me things when I ask. It's one of my bard powers I think."

Jack waved his hand, making a face of vague agreement.

"What did you find out?" Morgan said.

"Okay, so you're a priest of Theana," Tobias said.

"I knew that much."

"Right. I'm starting from the beginning," Tobias said. "She's the goddess of wisdom and 'just' war, which I think is another oxymoron. Her priests believe in peace, but also in raising arms to defend the helpless or to defeat true evil. They don't participate in the wars of men over territory or whatever, but you'll always find priests of Theana when the really terrible stuff bubbles up. Undead, dragons, whatever."

"I think I like this goddess," Morgan said.

"Could be a lot worse," Eriko said. "You could be a like, devil priest or cleric of some asshole war god who just wants to fight everybody."

"Yeah, she's well-liked," Tobias said.

"Where'd you learn all this, anyway?" Morgan asked.

"Did you know there's a temple in town? Or, well, it's more of a chapel," Tobias said. "But it's a thing."

"For Theana?" Morgan said. "That's not good. What if I was supposed to check in or something?"

"No, it's dedicated to the goddess of the harvest," Tobias said. "Totally different goddess."

"The goddess of the harvest got a name?" Cordelia said, suddenly interested in participating in the conversation.

"Glutenia," Tobias said.

"Shut up," Eriko said.

"I'm just kidding. She's Aeterna, the Mother," Tobias said. "I've been kind of dating one of the priestesses there."

"Kind of dating?" Jack said. "Weren't you also kind of dating that guard?"

"Look, there's no dating apps here," Tobias said. "Also, I'm incredibly popular. I have groupies. I'm not that strong-willed. Sidebar: I can't really get too serious with the priestess. They have vows."

"You're… helping a priestess of the Mother goddess break her vows," Morgan said, a growing dread in his voice.

"It's fine, don't worry about it," Tobias said. "Also, in case you're about to freak out, there are no vows for Theana's battle priests, by the way. In case you meet someone."

"I have no intention of dating fictional people in a fictional world," Morgan said. "I had enough trouble dating back home."

"Um," Jack said.

"You, of all people, shall offer no dating advice," Morgan said. "I've met furniture that have a better dating track record than you do."

"No, no, hang on," Jack said. "Malcolm, the guy I met today. He said the people here are... more real than we know? I think that's how he said it."

"You're not making me feel better about whether Tobias should be Moderate Expectations' most eligible bachelor," Morgan said.

"I mean, I think he was saying we should be respectful," Jack said. "That we might see them as NPCs, but they have real feelings."

"Shit," Tobias said.

"What did you do," Eriko said.

"Nothing," Tobias said. "I'm just... I'll avoid ghosting on people. Is it okay to break up by text here? How do I text here? Parchment? Do I slide parchment under their door?"

"I cannot believe we're having this conversation," Morgan said.

"I can absolutely believe we're having this conversation," Eriko said.

"Forget about my dating life," Tobias said. "Where is my sister?"

Tamsin immediately gave her brother a wet willy. Shocked and horrified, Tobias spastically kicked his feet out, slamming one knee into the table from below, knocking over his lute with a horrible, yet musical, clang, nearly spilling Morgan's beer, and letting out a birdlike screech in surprise.

"Hi, Toby," Tamsin said, dropping her invisibility spell.

"I hate you," he said.

"I love you," she said.

"You are going to teach me how to do that spell," he said.

"Only if you behave," Tamsin said.

"Anything else I should know about this goddess I'm allegedly representing?" Morgan said, nudging the conversation back on track as Tamsin sat down at the booth.

"Oh!" Tobias said. "My priestess friend gave me a book."

He pulled a heavy, simple, but sturdy tome from his backpack and handed it over.

"The Thirteen: Religion and Mythology of Revery," Morgan read out loud.

"What's Revery?" Tamsin said.

"Oh! Best part of this whole conversation I had today," Tobias said. "You know how all along we've felt like there was no way to ask what the hell this world we're actually trapped in is called?"

"You didn't," Eriko said.

"I didn't have to! Just came up in casual conversation. We're in Revery."

"So this world is basically named... daydream," Eriko said. "I think I'm in love."

Morgan and Tobias both gave Eriko a long, questioning stare.

"What?" she said. "I can be a romantic sometimes. Don't look at me like that. Anyway. Tell us more, Tobias."

"Well, Moderate Expectations is in the unclaimed country," Tobias continued. "It's not part of any larger empire or kingdom, though there's some concern we'll be annexed by the Ruby Imperium in a few years."

"The Ruby Imperium sounds hot," Eriko said.

"I know, right?" Tobias said.

"You find anything else out we should know about?" Jack said.

"Oh, a bunch. I'll jot it all down and we can decompress," Tobias said. "I also learned that if someone offers you some Basilisk's Breath, you should say no."

"You learned that from a priestess?" Tamsin said. "Wait. No. Don't tell me anything. I don't want to know."

"It's a drug, Tam," Tobias said.

"I said I didn't want to know!"

"I didn't take it! I just learned you shouldn't use it," Tobias said.

"You're turning into a fountain of useful and useless information, Tobias," Jack said. "Thanks for this."

"Hey, what can I say. I'm all ears," Tobias said, wiggling his pointed elven ears.

Tamsin gave him another wet willy.

"What! Why?" he said.

"I'm trying to discourage more bad puns," Tamsin said.

Chapter 6: Smoke on the horizon

Morgan woke up the next morning as he had for the past three weeks, forgetting where he was. The others seemed to be adjusting more readily, or at least faking it. For Morgan, every day began with the startling realization they were still here. He sat up in bed, a bed far too comfortable for a medieval setting, he knew. Which was part of the charm of this fictional world, with its comfortable bedding, good dental hygiene, lack of overwhelming body odor, and other quirks that both broke the immersion but made the environment far more livable.

The group had been renting three rooms at the Hungry Lion, each with two beds, but they kept their adjoining doors open, for the most part. No one said it out loud, but they were all still too disoriented, too homesick, to want a room of their own.

Tamsin and Tobias tended to bunk down in one room, and Eriko and Jack, both chronic insomniacs, would crash in another where they could talk in the infuriating darkness without bothering the others. Morgan's usual roommate was Cordelia, which worked well, both of them heavy sleepers and early risers. Today, though, Cordelia had awoken even earlier, and stood in her patchwork leather armor, staring out the window.

"You okay, Cordie?" Morgan asked, rubbing the sleep from his eyes.

"Something's burning," Cordelia said, not turning away from the window.

Morgan slid from bed, pulling a rough tunic over his head, to join her by the window. Their rooms were several stories up in the inn, high enough to see over the wooden wall surrounding Moderate Expectations. The sky to the east was filled with black smoke.

"What the hell is that," Morgan said. "We should go check it out. Are the others awake yet?"

"I'm up," Jack said from the doorway between the rooms, yawning and looking like he'd lost a fight, as he did every morning. "What's going on?"

Cordelia pointed out the window. Jack swore.

"I'll get my stuff," he said.

As Morgan began to pull his armor on, a knock came at the door. Cordelia opened it. Outside, the striking, iron-haired Mayor Miriam stood flanked by two members of the town's professional, if not particularly intimidating, guard.

"I'm sorry to wake you," the mayor said.

"You didn't," Morgan said, buckling on his chest piece. "I assume you're here about…"

Morgan thumbed at the window behind him.

"We're sending some of our guards out there to investigate, but if it's some sort of attack, we don't want to leave ourselves undefended," Miriam said. "If you could…?"

"We'll go," Morgan said. "We were practically on our way already."

"Thank you," Miriam said. "And don't worry, there will be payment."

Cordelia waved her hand dismissively.

"We can talk about that later," Cordelia said. "I just want to make sure nobody's hurt out there."

Jack, standing alone by the window tying on his green cloak, muttered softly, mostly to himself.

"From what I can see from here, it's less a question of if people are hurt but how many."

***

After rousing the others—Tamsin was up and getting ready the minute Morgan said "fire," though Eriko and Tobias required some aggressive cajoling back to consciousness—the group headed out of town through the east gate on borrowed horses along with a half-dozen of the town's guards.

Outside the town proper to the east, north, and south, Moderate Expectations quickly turned into farmland, part of the town itself but apart from it. They'd traveled past the farms and the families who ran them often in their time here, sometimes stopping to talk or buy food, but mostly to get a feeling for the people they protected as they worked for Miriam and her colleagues. These were the people most at risk from ogres and bogeymen, after all, outside the comfort of the town's walls, away from the watchful eye of the guards.

It didn't take long to find the first burning farmhouse. Livestock had been sloppily slaughtered and left to rot, supplies ransacked, crops slashed and torn down. Morgan lowered his eyes when he saw what was clearly a human body lying in a field. He was certain if they moved closer he'd discover he knew the person.

They passed two more farms, each with survivors sitting shocked and shaken outside. The guard captain leading the expedition silently ordered a pair of his soldiers to split from the group to check on the farmers as the rest of the group continued on. After the fourth burning farm, Jack dismounted and walked toward the smoldering wreckage.

Eriko and Morgan exchanged a look, then Eriko slid from her horse as well, tossing the reins to Morgan, and followed their ranger. Morgan and the others joined them, though remaining on horseback.

They found Jack hunched over, examining the ground.

"Tracks," Jack said. He looked up at his friends, then to the guard captains, then to Morgan specifically. "Three toes. Big. Heavy, whatever it was. I don't recognize the tracks though. I've never seen anything like it."

"Trogs," an unfamiliar voice said. Morgan whipped his head around to find the owner.

Of all the stereotypical fantasy tropes they'd encountered so far, it surprised Morgan that this was the first dwarf they'd seen. The stout man leaned on a shovel, his arms bare and covered in blood and soot, his face and gray beard stained with both as well. Bald on top, he wore what was left of his hair in a braid in the back. A heavy leather apron covered his chest. He looked as though he walked out of a storybook.

"Been on the surface forty years, and I've never seen a trog beneath the open sky until last night," the dwarf said.

"I'm sorry," Morgan said. "I'm, um, Father Bastion. These are my companions. We…"

"I know who you are," the old dwarf said. "Small town, a bunch of fame-seeking adventurers are hard to miss."

"We don't seek fame," Morgan said.

"I do," Tobias said, sliding awkwardly from his horse. "What's a trog?"

"Troglodytes. Y'see them more often back home," the dwarf said. "Word is they once were men, like you folk. But they retreated below the surface and, well, like so many things that hide in the darkness, the darkness had its way with them."

"These creatures attacked you?" Eriko said.

"Yep," the dwarf said. "Too many of 'em to count. Used the darkness to hide their numbers. Clever like animals, they are."

"Is this your farm?" Cordelia said.

The dwarf eyed Cordelia's half-orc face with suspicion, but answered.

"Nah. My forge is on the other side of the field. Was, rather. It's a pile of ash now."

"I didn't catch your name, friend," Jack said.

"I didn't give it," the dwarf said, sizing Jack up. "Ingo. Ingo Hammerhand."

The dwarf sighed, taking in the carnage around them again.

"Bastards," he said. "I'm just glad my wife didn't live to see the day. Trogs under an open sky."

"Do you know where they came from?" Morgan asked.

"Why, you thinking of going after them? You might be crazier than you look," Ingo said. "There was a commotion at the mine last night. Woke me from a sound sleep. I assumed they had another cave in—the owner's been skimping on safety for years. But then…"

Ingo opened his arms as if to present the carnage all around them.

Morgan and his group looked back and forth, silently planning. Cordelia nodded to him.

"Can you point us to the mine?" he said.

The dwarf laughed.

"I'll do you one better. Let me grab my coat and I'll show you there myself."

Chapter 7: One big medieval OSHA violation

The sky rumbled with the threat of a thunderstorm, and Tobias felt his heart sink. They'd been caught in so many storms on their recent adventures he bought a protective carrier for his lute, a sort of waterproof leather case, padded on the inside to keep it from getting jostled too badly. He'd never been a musician in the real world—a singer, sure, but he had not an ounce of talent no matter what instrument he'd tried to learn—but it didn't take long here in the game for him to become protective of the tools of his trade.

Tools, plural, Tobias mused. He learned last week he could also play the fiddle and flute, though he only owned the latter, borrowing the former from a traveling minstrel for a jam session. He also learned that day that "jam session" was not a term the people here in this world understood.

Tobias felt a single drop of rain hit his nose. He was about to start complaining when the group arrived at the mine, and he immediately realized he would prefer to be rained on than go into said mine.

"That place is one big medieval OSHA violation," he said out loud. A few of the town guards accompanying him looked at him askance—the default reaction, he had quickly discovered, to any anachronism he said publicly—and he caught his sister sighing at him out of the corner of his eye.

Ingo marched right up to the entrance of the mine, a beautifully crafted battle axe slung across his back. Cordelia and Morgan followed close behind while Jack hopped off his horse and began scanning the ground. Tobias caught Ingo giving Cordelia serious side-eye.

"Hey," Tobias stage-whispered to Eriko, who leaned lazily on the pommel of her saddle. "Did you catch that? I think the old dwarf is totally racist toward Cordelia."

"Well, we're in a classic fantasy setting," Eriko said. "Dwarves and orcs, man."

"Still. Sort of a dick move," Tobias said.

"I'm not defending it," Eriko said. "I'm just saying I'm not surprised."

"They definitely came back this way," Jack said, interrupting. "Tracks everywhere."

"Did they walk single file to hide their numbers?" Tobias joked. He was supremely happy to see Jack, who had been Captain Emo for weeks, bark out an involuntary laugh.

"Not funny," Jack said.

"I thought it was funny," Tobias said.

"What happened here?" Cordelia said, picking up a bloody pickaxe from the ground then tossing it aside.

"Folly is what happened here," a new voice said. An older man, clearly a miner by his clothing, hobbled toward them, cradling one arm in the other.

The town guards drew their weapons. Morgan held up a hand as if to calm the soldiers.

"It's just Horace," Ingo said. "Calm yourselves, lads. He's the foreman."

The newcomer, Horace, nodded at the dwarf.

"Glad to see they didn't get you, old-timer."

"You as well," Ingo said.

"What do you mean, folly happened here?" Tamsin said, her voice all business.

Horace sat down on a broken cart, groaning as if his entire

body hurt.

"Been saying for months the mine is tapped out," he said. "Months. But the cheap old bastard wanted us to dig deeper."

"We're kind of new," Eriko said. "Who's the cheap old bastard?"

"Mine's owner, Steban Dyme," Horace said. "Said he could smell ore just beyond our reach. He wasn't wrong, I'll grant him that. But we took down a wall and by the gods, it was as if hell itself passed gas in our general direction. Knew there was evil in there and we just opened the door for it."

"What happened to the miners?" Morgan asked.

"The noise must've brought the creatures. Came bubbling up out of the dark soon after," Horace said. "We work into the night sometimes—day, night, it don't much matter when you're underground. These... things killed a bunch of us. Dragged a few into the darkness. Then came up here, burning, pillaging. Murdering. I've never seen anything like it in my life."

"I have," Ingo said quietly.

"They came back though," Jack said. "I can see the tracks. They went back into the mine."

"Aye," the miner said. "I watched them. They didn't much like the sun. Came running back just before dawn, dragging food, livestock... I didn't see any living people with 'em, but they definitely took some of our dead."

"Everything in this stupid world wants to eat people," Tamsin said.

"How many," Cordelia said.

The miner shrugged.

"Two dozen, maybe," Horace said. "A raiding party."

Morgan and Cordelia exchanged a long look.

"The game wants us to be important," Morgan said.

"You can't possibly be thinking what I think you're thinking," Eriko said.

"This is what we're here for," Morgan said.

"To be heroes," Cordelia said.

"I had no idea you people were suicidal," Tobias chimed in. Tamsin shot him a look. "What? I'm in if you are. I'm just saying. Y'know."

"They're going to come back," Jack said. "We can pursue them and catch them unawares, or we wait for them to come charging back up out of the tunnels tonight. Either way, it's a fight."

"Just throwing it out there—they're subterranean critters. We'd be fighting them on their own turf," Tobias said. Everyone looked at him as if he'd just started reciting rocket science. "Guys, I know I hide my geek, but I've read enough fantasy novels to know a thing or two. I'm not as stupid as I pretend to be."

"He's not wrong," Eriko said. "We don't know their territory."

"But I do," Ingo said. "You go, I'll be your guide. These shits killed friends of mine and burned my home to the ground. I want to take a few of their heads off. And you've got a reputation. I know the lot of you can fight."

Morgan turned to the guard captain, still mounted on his horse.

"You can head back, look for survivors. Maybe round them up and get them behind the town's walls for now in case we fail. They'll be safer there than on their own," Morgan said.

"Good point, Father Bastion," the captain said. "You want some of my men to back you up?"

"No," Morgan said. "If we aren't successful, you'll need all the help you can get."

"I'll come with you as well," Horace said.

"Absolutely not," Cordelia said. "No offense, but you can't fight, and if there's dozens of them…"

"Let me at least take you as far as the place we broke through," Horace said. "The tunnels can get twisted if you don't know the way."

"Fair enough," Eriko said, handing the reins of her borrowed horse to one of the guards.

The others followed suit, knowing if things went badly, the horses wouldn't live long waiting for their riders here outside the mine. Better they take these poor beasts back to town to wait for the worst, Tobias thought, patting his sorrel on the neck before giving his reins to the guard captain.

"I still think this is a stupid idea," Tobias said.

"Stupid ideas is what we do," Eriko said. "Are we going to change that now?"

Chapter 8: This is why we check for traps

Cordelia could feel the old dwarf's eyes burning into the back of her neck as they made their way down the cool, darkened tunnels of the mine. In another life—literally another life, her pre-orc life—she would have ignored it, but ever since they arrived here she found herself less and less willing to tolerate behavior she didn't like.

"Got a problem, Ingo?" she said

"No, no problem," the dwarf said. "Your people live underground though, aye?"

Cordelia rolled her eyes.

"I've never spent a minute of my life living underground. Or, to be blunt, around 'my people,' either. So stuff it, Popeye."

"Never knew orcs to be so sensitive," Ingo said.

"There's a difference between sensitive and impatient with bullshit," Cordelia said.

Horace, the miner, cleared his throat, awkwardly interrupting. He showed them a rough gap in the otherwise deliberately carved caverns, debris from a cave-in scattered on the ground.

"Here's where we broke through," he said. "A few hours later they came bubbling up like a pox."

Cordelia stepped through the break in the wall. Inside, there was a very different feel. It was murkier, for one, with an organic smell to it that felt more like a terrarium than a mine. The walls were smoother, slick, covered in lichen in places. The lichen glowed with a soft, blue-green light, enough to see by.

"This is terrifying," Cordelia said. Ingo followed close behind, and then Eriko.

"This is what, eight, ten feet of earth away from the mine?" Eriko said. "These miners could've been this close to these creatures for years and never known it."

"The world is a honeycomb of tunnels beneath the ground," Ingo said. "There's parts of the world you can walk for weeks without seeing the sun and get to where you're going. It's filled with beasties of all sorts, and surface folk can go their whole lives never knowing it's there."

"This is pure, unadulterated nightmare material," Tobias said. "Hey, I have an idea. Let's cave this in and go back."

"That's a… I was going to say that's a terrible idea, but why aren't we going to do that?" Tamsin said.

"Ingo?" Morgan said, awaiting an answer.

"I see your point and don't disagree," the dwarf said. "But they know there's food above them now. They're like insects. You can bury the opening to an ant hill, but they'll dig their way out in another place."

"They'll really come back up again if we bury the tunnel?" Morgan said

"You see what they took with them?" Ingo said. "They hit the jackpot. They're going to want more. Stuff like that doesn't grow down here in the dark."

Jack put a hand on Horace's shoulder.

"You head back. Maybe see if collapsing the tunnel is a backup plan in case we don't make it back."

"Not what I'd call ideal, but I'll do what I can," Horace said. "Good luck down there."

Jack knelt down to examine the ground for tracks, but the dwarf already started heading into the tunnel.

"This way," Ingo said.

"How do you even know that?" Jack said.

The dwarf pointed at his eyes.

"My eyes are better in the dark than yours. I can see the footprints clear as day."

Eriko pushed her way past the dwarf, who glared at her.

"I'll go first. Scout ahead."

"By yourself," Cordelia said.

"I'm the rogue! I sneak! This is literally my job."

Giving Eriko a head start, the rest of the group followed.

"So, what can we expect from these trogs, Ingo?" Morgan said. "Any advice for fighting them?"

The dwarf nodded.

"They ain't bright. They fight stupid. Their strength is in their numbers and their ferocity. They don't have much sense of self-preservation, unlike the rest of us, and you know not caring if you live or die is a pretty solid advantage in a fight in the right hands."

"That's alarming," Tamsin said.

"Any magic users? Healers? Guys we should watch out for in the battle field?" Cordelia said.

"They may have a shaman or two, but magic don't come naturally to trogs," Ingo said. "They're scavengers, really. Scavengers with a sadistic streak. Comes from being underground with no contact to civilization for too long."

"Got it," Tobias said. "We're going up against semi-intelligent suicidal cavemen who eat people. I hate this game. I hate this game so much."

After some time, they entered an expanse where the cavern widened, the walls rising up high. The faintest bit of sunlight trickled down from a break in the cave far, far above them. Eriko waited for them, hands on her daggers.

"What do you have, Eriko?" Morgan asked.

Eriko pointed. Before her, the cavern floor opened up into a pit deep enough no one could see the bottom. Along one side of the pit, a curving arc of stone acted almost like a ramp into the darkness below.

"And she's buying a stairway to heaven," Tobias sang half-heartedly.

"Wrong direction, unfortunately," Eriko said. "This legitimately looks like a bad idea incarnate."

"It's not too late to go back," Tamsin said.

Jack turned his attention skyward, to the bit of daylight shining in.

"Hey Ingo," Jack said. "These trog things good climbers?"

"Most creatures of the underworld are good climbers," Ingo said. Jack gave him a questioning look. "I'll have you know we dwarves are excellent climbers when we have to be. We live in the bloody mountain. You think we can't climb?"

"We cave in the entrance and they just climb up there and out the top," Cordelia said. "And then we're dealing with the same problem, just from a different source."

"Hey guys," Tamsin said.

"Yeah," Jack said.

"Guys, I have a bad feeling about something," Tamsin said. Jack squinted at her.

"Like a mage's intuition bad feeling, or...?"

"No, I feel it too," Tobias said. "You don't? It's a low..."

Before Tobias could finish his sentence, a single stone rolled down from the wall above, just in front of the opening they'd stepped out of. Ingo grabbed Tamsin, closest to the opening, by the wrist and pulled her back several feet.

"Get back," he said. "All of ya, get back!"

One rock turned into many, and those turned into may more. With a deafening rumble, the unrefined stone in the tunnel gave way, collapsing on itself as if deflating. The fall kicked up dust and filth, covering the adventurers in gray grime. The cavern went very dark for a moment, then began to glow with the pale lichen light, the sky no longer visible.

"Elf ears," the dwarf said. "I'm sorry. I'm so very sorry. I should've noticed it myself."

"No," Jack said, examining the wreckage, one hand calmly scratching behind Silence's ear. Cordelia almost laughed when she saw his wolf sitting calmly beside him—the critter was so quiet and so unassuming she hadn't realized it followed them into the cave. "Look at this."

"Guys, we were supposed to be on the other side of the tunnel when we collapsed it! Who is running this operation!" Tobias said.

"What do you have, Jack," Cordelia asked.

Jack pointed to broken wood and rope.

"I thought you said they were stupid," Morgan said. "That looks like a trap."

"That's… the bastards rigged the tunnel to collapse," Ingo said. "I swear to you, I've never seen this before. Trogs are dumb as rocks. Never seen them engineer anything more than a tarp."

"This is why we check for traps, people!" Eriko said. "Don't touch things until I've had a look at them!"

"You were already in this room!" Tobias yelled. "You check for traps, that's your job!"

"Shit! Okay, fine, I missed the trap," Eriko said. "My bad. That's on me."

"So… we're stuck down here," Tamsin said.

"Aye, lass," Ingo said.

"Well, let's look on the bright side," Morgan said.

"I hate it when you're the optimist in the group," Eriko said. "Whenever you're the optimist I know things are bad."

"We don't have to argue about our plan anymore, right?" Morgan said.

"Fair enough," Eriko said. "Down we go I guess, huh?"

Chapter 9: Don't touch anything

The winding ramp quickly proved to be more natural formation than crafted stairway. It was unevenly shaped, often requiring a bit of deft navigation to get across narrow or broken areas. The twins needed a hand more than once, more for lack of confidence than ability. At one point Morgan slipped enough that Jack felt his heartbeat in his throat for minutes afterward.

After a while, the glow of the lichen grew insufficient, and both Tamsin and Morgan cast their light spells to illuminate the walk. Jack and Eriko traded off taking the lead, Jack's innate ranger skills letting him find the surest footing while Eriko remained doubly paranoid they'd encounter another trap.

Finally, Jack felt the ramp give way to more solid footing as they reached the bottom. The stone ground beneath his feet radiated cold he could feel through his boots. He drew both short swords from his belt and held one out in front of him as if testing the air with the blade.

"What are you doing?" Tamsin asked taking up position behind him.

"Just checking," Jack said.

"Okay, here's the deal," Cordelia said. "Don't touch anything."

Tobias reached the bottom and poked at the ground with the

heel of his boot.

"This reminds me of that scene in the *Empire Strikes Back*, in the asteroid field," he said. "What do you mean, don't touch anything?"

"In these games, traditionally, everything is dangerous in underground areas," Morgan chimed in. "Bugs that eat metal, giant rodents…"

"Lots of stories about characters running ahead of their group and splashing full-speed into roaming piles of living acidic jelly," Jack said. "Eriko?"

"I know, I know, don't split the party," Eriko responded. "Why do you treat me like I have poor impulse control?"

"Because you have terrible impulse control," Jack said.

"Living acidic jelly," Tamsin said. "Are you serious?"

"I can't say this is a top five in my own personal nightmares, but it's pretty high up there," Tobias said.

"Tam," Jack said, softer, not intended for the whole group. "Can you shine your magical light on the ground for me?"

Tamsin nodded to him. Jack crouched down, easily finding the troglodyte tracks.

"That way," Jack said, gesturing to one of the shadowy gaps in the wall around them.

"Okay, Ingo. Now's the time to tell us anything else you think we should know about these trogs," Cordelia said.

The dwarf again had trouble disguising his distaste for her, but answered.

"They used to be ordinary humans, like some of you," he said. "And they're about human height, I guess, give or take. They can be sickly or strong in equal likelihood. They don't have good stock."

"These feet don't look human," Jack said, staring at the heavy, wide footprints with three toes, more pig like in shape than human.

"They don't look much like humans anymore," Ingo said. "Their heads are oversized. Big teeth, beady eyes, malformed sometimes. The dark magic in the underground took its toll on them. Or maybe their misdeeds led to their malformation. Either way, they are a far cry from the humans above. Vicious and strong and sadistic the way only the stupid and cruel can be."

"Do they have kids?" Tamsin asked.

Ingo looked at her as if she'd started speaking in demonic tongues.

"What?"

"The trogs. If we find them, do they have kids? Like, are we going to have to fight families?" Tamsin asked.

"Dammit," Eriko said.

"Now is not the time to develop an overabundance of empathy," Ingo said.

"You're about 19 years too late for that," Tobias said. "Guys, we're in a game world. I don't really see a problem. Chances are we won't see anything but trogs and boss trogs."

"But they must be hunting to provide for something, right? A village or whatever? Hunter/gatherer cultures…" Tamsin said.

"I am now questioning every game I've ever played since I was five years old and whether or not I've regularly been committing genocide," Morgan said.

"Me too," Cordelia said. "You've just given me an existential crisis and I think I hate you a little bit for it."

"What if we come across little trog babies when we find the hunting party?" Tamsin said.

"Then we kill 'em," Ingo said.

"Whoa," Eriko said.

"Little trog babies turn into big trog hunters and big trog hunters kill your family and burn your house to the ground," Ingo said. "Don't ask me to have sympathy for 'em. You haven't been on the receiving end of a trog hunt."

"I can't kill babies," Tamsin said. "Even if they're psychopathic monster babies."

"Fine, don't," Ingo said. "Who recruited the soft touch?"

"That'd be my fault," Tobias said. "She got all the empathy when we were born. I got all the looks."

Ingo glared at Jack and pointed angrily at the entrance to one tunnel.

"This way, lad?" the dwarf said. Jack nodded. Ingo stormed off down the tunnel. Cordelia gave Jack a long look then followed the dwarf, then Morgan and the others joined. Tamsin hung back and put a hand on Jack's arm.

"We're not really going to... kill a whole village of these things, are we?" she asked.

"I'm not," Jack said. "The thing about games like this is there's always an alternative to charging in and killing everything. That's the easy option. It's the lazy option."

"So our job will be to try to convince everyone to choose the harder option," Tamsin said.

"Possibly," Jack said. "The man I met in the forest said that the people here are more real than we'd expect, so I don't think you're wrong to worry about this. But these sort of games also have a way of course correcting. It might be possible these trogs exist solely to force us into action. It may just be a roving pack of cannibalistic monsters and all this moral quandary stuff won't matter."

"But if we find baby trogs?"

"I will not kill baby anything, Tam," Jack said. "I got your back."

"Now who's the soft touch?" Tamsin said.

"You've known me forever," he said. "I'm a closet pacifist at heart."

"And yet here you are, armed to the teeth and hunting monsters."

"Everyone needs an outlet," Jack said.

Tamsin smirked at him and headed off down the tunnel to join the others. Jack looked down to see Silence the wolf staring up at him. Despite being incapable of human expression, Jack sensed a hint of humor in the wolf's eyes.

"What," Jack said.

The wolf made a soft barking noise, more of a huff than a woof, and trotted after Tamsin.

"Great," Jack said. "My fictional wolf makes fun of me."

Chapter 10: The fungus has eyes

The group spread out a little bit, Ingo and Eriko in the lead, Morgan hanging back a bit, Jack and Tamsin bringing up the rear. Tobias, seeing an opportunity, tapped Cordelia on the shoulder.

"So, when this is all over, are you doing to push Ingo into a bottomless pit or anything?" he said in a stage whisper.

"What?" Cordelia said. She looked genuinely baffled.

"He's being a total bigoted jackass to you because you're an orc," Tobias said. "I want to push him off a cliff. Or, I mean, give him a stern talking-to about it."

"Toby, you think I'm not used to that low-level bullshit aggression from old guys like him?" Cordelia said, truly breaking character from her warrior persona for the first time in a long time. "Hell, back home I have people yell at me to go back to Mexico. My parents are from Queens. My grandmother was born an American citizen in Puerto Rico. I've been hearing stupid shit like that my whole life."

"But it doesn't bother you?"

"Of course it bothers me, because it reminds me of what happens in the real world, but... I mean look, I know you have your own issues with bigots, Tobias."

"Not like you," Tobias said. "People just like to tell me I don't exist or I haven't made up my mind yet. I'm not…"

"Hate's hate, kid," Cordelia said. "All I'm saying is there's enough hate back home that I'm not going to let some fictional character's hate for me because I'm a fictional character be the thing that ruins this particular day. Mountain dwarves don't exist. Orcs don't exist. And I'm not really in the market for allegory right now. This shit's hard enough in the real world without acknowledging cheesy, overly symbolic fantasy racism."

"Gotcha," Tobias said.

"Thanks for thinking of me, though," Cordelia said.

"In a ham-handed, insensitive, and uncharacteristically violent way," Tobias said.

"I'm feeling really forgiving today. I'll file it under 'it's the thought that counts,'" Cordelia said. "And you know I'm not minimizing what you have going on back home either."

"Not even a little bit," Tobias said. "You got my back too."

"Forever and always, doofus," Cordelia said.

Their conversation was abruptly interrupted as Tobias walked full-speed into Morgan's broad back. They'd entered a larger cavern, this one better lit by the glowing lichen they'd seen earlier. Huge mushrooms grew here like short, colorful trees.

"This is strange," Ingo said.

"No kidding, this is strange," Tobias said. "These mushrooms are eight feet tall. This is like some nightmare version of Alice in Wonderland."

Ingo drew his axe from its sheath, and Cordelia followed his lead. Eriko, still at the lead of the group, had a hand on each of her daggers.

"If we find a Cheshire Cat, I'm going to just run screaming out of here," Eriko said. "I'm not even going to pretend to have any dignity if that happens."

The dwarf looked around at the entire group with a grimace of exhaustion and vague disgust.

"I mean this is strange because this sort of growth is usually deeper underground," he said. "In the deep caverns, you see fungus oases all the time, but we can't be more than a few hundred feet below the surface."

"Can we focus for a minute on the fact that we're a few hundred feet underground?" Tobias said. "Giant mushrooms or not, that just kicked my anxiety into eleven."

"Guys," Cordelia said.

The dwarf grunted. Cordelia pointed just behind him.

"The fungus has eyes," Cordelia said.

And then one of the giant mushrooms reached out and picked Ingo up off the ground. Colorful tendrils wrapped around the dwarf, lifting him roughly into the air and waving him around like a rag doll.

"No way!" Tobias yelled as the others launched into action. To his left, Morgan lifted his hammer to charge, but his forearms and wrists were entangled in tendrils from another mushroom. Eriko immediately drew her daggers and started cutting Morgan free. The room flared with fiery light, and Tobias whipped his head around to see his sister preparing a fireball spell.

"Do not sauté the mushrooms yet!" Tobias yelled. "Abort, abort!"

And then Tobias felt his feet go out from under him as Cordelia shoved her way quickly past him, knocking him to the ground. He watched, viewing the battle upside-down from his back, as she leapt into the air, two-handed battle axe pulled back, slashing through the tendrils holding Ingo in place. The tentacles had started to choke the dwarf, wrapped around his neck, his eyes bulging as his face turned an alarming shade of red. Three swings from Cordelia's weapon and the dwarf dropped to the ground with a grunt and a thud as the tendrils, eerily bloodless, writhed and then grew still. Not slowing down, Cordelia planted the blade of her axe between the strange yellow eyes of the mushroom creature, seemingly to no effect.

"Little help!" Jack yelled. Tobias crawled to his feed to see Jack, held only by one ankle, but struggling to swing his sword without hitting his own foot, being dragged into the copse of mushrooms behind him. The bard pulled out his sabre and slashed his friend loose, helping the ranger to his feet. Morgan stomped furiously on a tendril, swearing and sweating, and Eriko cursed out her short blades as she fought off a pair of vines herself.

Cordelia stood between the monstrous fungus and Ingo, who dug into the tendrils around his neck with thick fingers, gasping as his airways opened again.

"Burn," he rasped.

"Everyone down!" Tamsin yelled. Tobias belly-flopped onto the ground without hesitation as Jack crouched down in a far more dignified way. Cordelia covered the still-struggling Ingo with her own body, and Morgan put his armored arm and shoulder over Eriko's body, covering his head own with a gauntleted hand.

Tamsin began chanting the incantation and the room burst into flames. The mushroom creatures hissed and crackled as they cooked in Tamsin's magical fire, the room taking on an earthy, greasy stench. A moment later, the flames sputtered and went out.

"All clear, guys," Tamsin said.

Tobias looked up to find the mushrooms hadn't been obliterated so much as cauterized off, leaving rows of fleshy white stumps sticking up from the ground.

"Good job," Tobias said. "We just defeated a pizza topping."

Cordelia helped Ingo back to his feet, the old dwarf avoiding eye contact. Eriko absently fixed her fauxhawk. Jack got back on his feet and walked cautiously between the stalks toward something just out of sight.

"What you got, Jack?" Morgan asked.

"Give me a hand," Jack said. Morgan joined him, and together, the two dragged something heavy out into the light.

A body.

Human, mostly, and big, though it showed signs of decomposition, almost mummified in places. Three toes on each foot, and the creature's hands looked almost human as well, but its fingers seemed to have fused together, pinky with ring finger, index with middle, the thumb on each hand unchanged. Its face was man-like, but exaggeratedly square-jawed, with deep set eyes, bushy eyebrows, yellowed teeth filed to points.

"That, my friends, is a trog," Ingo said.

"Good looking guy," Morgan said, nudging the corpse with his foot. "Looks like a charmer."

"Oh good," Eriko said. "Only have to fight what, two dozen of these?"

"Look on the bright side," Tamsin said. "They're not tougher than evil mushrooms, right?"

Chapter 11: The men who would rule this world

Malcolm sat calmly on a log, basking in the midday sun. He could feel the heat burning the places on his scalp where his hair had thinned. Living here, he'd lost a lot of his vanity, for better or for worse. He listened to the birds, to the wind in the leaves.

Somehow, despite everything, this place had become home to him. And that was why this meeting today, as distasteful as he found it, was necessary.

After a while, he saw the man he waited for appear. Dressed all in black, trudging forward reluctantly, as if he found being out among nature uncomfortable, the newcomer leaned on an ornate staff and his face beneath a heavy black cowl.

He was flanked on either side by an armored human skeleton, one carrying a sword and shield, the other a bow and arrow. Their armor was old, and ornate, like a Roman soldier's in a movie.

The man in black stopped twenty feet away. He drew back his hood, revealing a gaunt face, a well-kept black beard, a tightly shaved scalp covered in tattoos.

"Malcolm," he said.

"Leo," Malcolm said. "You really didn't need to bring an escort."

"They're not for you," Leo said. "There's worse things than an old druid in these woods and you know it."

Malcolm shrugged.

"All these years, and you still look at me like a dog left me on your lawn," Leo said.

"This place changed you," Malcolm said.

"This place changes everyone," Leo said.

"You have to admit, you went all in with your role," Malcolm said.

"We were friends in our home plane," Leo said. "Do you really think if I knew what would happen I would have chosen to play a necromancer?"

Malcolm laughed.

"You always did like the emo roles," he said.

Leo shrugged.

"True enough. But this is what I became, and it's let me do a lot of things none of the rest of us could."

"Why do I have a feeling you have bad news for me," Malcolm said.

"Because I never come find you with good news," Leo said. "I thought I sensed an incursion. Has there finally been a new group to appear here?"

"Yes. I met one them. Observed the others."

"And?"

"They're scared, but excited. Like we were. And unlike that group of weird ones who broke the Loophole a little while back, they seem like they're ordinary people, like us," Malcolm said.

"I wish I'd met the last group," Leo said. "They found their way home faster than anyone we've ever seen."

"They had help from the other side. No one ever has help from the other side."

"But this group is…"

"Exactly what you'd expect. Extraordinarily ordinary," Malcolm said. "But you didn't come here to talk about some gaming group who stumbled into this world."

Leo's eyes darkened.

"I found a Wound, Malcolm," he said.

Malcolm felt the skin across his body tighten. His stomach fluttered.

"So, it's true, then," he said softly.

"The Belief Engines are going cold, Malcolm," Leo said. "When was the last time you saw a dragon in flight?"

"Giant, scaly canaries in the coal mine, aren't they," Malcolm said. "Right, then. The world is sick. We're not the ones who can fix it."

"And to think, we once thought we could rule this world," Leo said. "Now we're just a couple of revenants, trying to stir up enough trouble to keep this place from..."

"I know," Malcolm said. "I'll do what I can."

"I'm going to investigate the Wound more closely. Maybe I can figure out some alternate way to close it," Leo said. "If you never see me again, you know what happened. Try not to be too happy about it."

"That's not funny," Malcolm said. "As much as we disagree on things, you're the last person here who remembers me from the other side."

"Did you tell them our companions are all dead?"

"I lied," Malcolm said. "They don't need to know our friends are all gone."

"Do you ever think about the others?" Leo said.

"All the time," Malcolm said.

Leo looked at his free hand as if it belonged to someone else.

"All this power over life and death and I could never bring them back," he said.

"You're not a god, Leo."

"But I could've been," the necromancer said.

"Maybe in the next campaign," Malcolm said.

Leo huffed out a laugh that sounded like a tomb door closing.

"That's a hell of a way to look at mortality, my old friend."

Chapter 12: Accidental architects of the earth

Cordelia took the lead for a while, her orcish eyes giving her far better sight in the dark than Eriko's. Ingo joined her at the front of their party. The two shared an awkward, uncomfortable silence, broken here and there by questions from Morgan about what they saw ahead in the dark, an occasional snarky comment from Tobias, and a hushed conversation between Tamsin and Jack in the back. Cordelia shook her head at the two of them. It'd been a while, even before all this happened, since those two had acknowledged a long-standing and unspoken thing between them. The last place Cordelia had expected to see it resurface was here, but, she supposed, enough life or death situations and everyone starts rethinking their personal relationships.

She wasn't the only one to notice, either, as Tobias caught her eye and made a gagging motion with his finger. Cordelia smiled and turned away, placing her hand on the wall of the cavern. She stopped, noticing an eye-catching, maybe even pretty pattern in the stone.

"Stoneworms," Ingo said. Cordelia looked over her shoulder at him, surprised to hear him speak.

"What's that?"

"These tunnels," Ingo said, joining her by the wall, running a practiced hand along the grooves that caught her eye. "They were made by stoneworms. Big, ugly things. They chew through stone and earth, moving along with these diamond-sharp spines on their skin. They're a strange thing. They don't hunt, they don't intentionally hurt anyone, though they've been known to collapse tunnels by accident or hurt a traveler underground."

"Have you ever seen one?" Cordelia said.

"Once," Ingo said. "It surfaced in a cavern outside the dwarven city where I was born, like a leviathan rising out of the sea. Couldn't tell how long it was, just an endless wave of spikes and flesh. They're mostly gone now, I think. There were never many of them, but they started dying off, a little at a time, and those that lived burrowed deep into the earth and never came back. But much of the honeycomb of tunnels like this all across the world were made by stoneworms. Accidental architects of the earth."

"Wouldn't have pegged you for the poetic type," Cordelia said.

"Funny thing about we dwarves," Ingo said. "We like to whinge and grump, but there's more poetry in our hearts than we care to admit."

Cordelia smiled at the old dwarf, who cleared his throat.

"Look, I... I owe you an apology," Ingo said. "You saved my life back there, but that's not the reason for it. I let my old prejudices get the better of me, and I should have been better than that."

"Water under the bridge, Ingo," Cordelia said.

"One of the stereotypes my people live up to," Ingo said. "Stubborn and rude and unforgiving. It's no excuse, but... there it is."

He held out a hand. Cordelia took it, and they shook. Cordelia started to speak, but Eriko interrupted her.

"Hate to break up a moment, but..." Eriko said, pointing ahead with a dagger.

Cordelia and Ingo shared a quizzical look and joined the rogue. The corridor once again opened, up, this time revealing a thin stream of dark water. The tunnel had three visible paths—one directly across the water, and in either direction the small river flowed. The tracks they'd been following ended at the river's edge, washed away by the water. All around the new chamber hung drifting drapes of cobwebs, thick as silk cloth.

"Not spiders, not spiders, not spiders," Tobias said. "Literally anything but spiders, please."

"Then I suppose you'll only be half-disappointed," a soft, lyrical voice said.

Tobias immediately drew his sword. The others quickly followed suit.

"There's no need for violence, little adventurers," the silky voice said.

"Sis, tell me you have a fireball spell ready," Tobias said.

"Would you hang on for one minute?" Morgan said. Then, to the voice: "We're not looking for trouble."

"Yes, you are," the voice said. Slowly, methodically, the owner of the voice appeared, crawling down delicately from the ceiling. The lower half of the creature was most certainly a giant spider, though not monstrously large, no more than four feet from head to tail. Where the spider's head would be, a thin, pale torso emerged, dressed haphazardly in a tunic woven from spider silk. Equally spindly arms gently moved webs out of the way as it approached. The being had the face of a small elf or gnome, gaunt, delicate, almost haunting until the fangs became visible. His eyes were ridiculously big, with distinctly red irises. "Look at all of you. You are the definition of trouble."

"We're not here to fight you," Morgan said.

Cordelia tightened her grip on her axe, looking for more creatures tiptoeing out of the darkness.

"Of course not," the spider-thing said. He smiled almost charmingly. "You're looking for the others. The beast men."

"You know where they are?" Cordelia asked. "Which way they went?"

"I do, I do," the spider said.

"And here it comes," Morgan said.

"What do you have to trade?" the spider creature said.

"There it is," Morgan said.

"Aren't you supposed to be our level-headed spokesperson?" Tobias said.

"I hate getting scammed," Morgan said. "Creepy little scam artist spider-creatures is where I draw the line on civility."

"Fine," the creature said. "Find them on your own."

He began to skitter away, but Eriko stopped him.

"Wait," she said. "We don't have much to trade you, is the thing."

The spider-thing walked quickly back to her, looking up eagerly.

"You'll make a deal?" he said, flashing its needle-like teeth at her.

"None of us are for trade," Eriko said.

"Fine, fine, that's fine," he said. "What do you have? I'm hungry."

Eriko looked back at the whole group. Everyone shrugged.

"We really don't have much to offer," Eriko said, her voice tinged with resignation.

The spider-thing held up one long, thin finger, then pointed at her.

"Perhaps it's not what you have, but what you don't take," he said.

"You want to loot the corpses," Cordelia said. Eriko shot her a sidelong glance, then shrugged.

"Now we get somewhere," the creature said, elfin eyes gleaming in the dark. "They brought meat. They brought grain. You leave."

Eriko looked to Cordelia, who shrugged.

"Morgan?" Cordelia said.

Morgan sighed.

"We can't carry everything back to the surface anyway," he said. "Are you okay with this, Ingo? The supplies were taken from your people."

"You're right. We'll never get it back to the surface," the dwarf said.

"He could take whatever we had to leave behind anyway," Jack said. "It's not an unreasonable trade."

"See? Reason. You are reasonable people for adventurers," the creature said. "I help you."

"Help might be too strong a word," Morgan said. "Why don't you just answer two questions for us."

"I will answer three if you wish!" the creature said. "Three is a good number. There's magic in three."

"Do not ask three questions," Tamsin said. "I've read enough books to know if a magical creature wants you to ask a specific number of questions, you're going to have nothing but trouble."

The spider-creature looked wounded.

"Your distrust is hurtful," he said. "I only want to help you, travelers."

"Sure, sure," Morgan said. "Question one: how many did you see?"

The spider-elfling began counting on his fingers, then ran out of fingers and started counting on his spiny spider legs.

"Two more than that many," he said. "Twenty."

"Twenty trogs, seven of us," Cordelia said. "I am in love with these odds."

"Second question," Morgan said. "Which direction did they go?"

The creature pointed down river.

"That way," he said. "They followed the river. This way goes deeper into the dark, you know."

"Go team gravity," Eriko said. Everyone looked at her. "What?"

"Okay," Morgan said. "You'll be able to find their camp after we're done?"

"I know these tunnels very well," the creature said. "I will have no trouble finding my prizes."

"So he's going to be following us," Eriko said. "Like a creep. I love this plan. This is a good plan."

Jack shrugged and started for the river.

"I'll take lead," he said.

"I'll help," Ingo said, walking after the ranger. The others began to follow. Then Tobias piped up.

"What's your name, anyway?" he said.

"Don't answer that!" Morgan said.

"Tobias!" Tamsin said.

"Shit," Eriko said.

The spider-thing rubbed his pale hands together.

"Third question! My name is Orsun," the creature said.

"I made a mistake, didn't I," Tobias said.

"That's a fourth question," Orsun said.

"This is why I'm not in charge of riddles," Tobias said.

Chapter 13: Like us but more violent

Maybe an hour later, Jack emerged from the shadowy tunnel ahead of the rest of the group and held a finger to his mouth, silencing them. Morgan fought the urge to sigh.

Maybe I was just hoping we'd never find them at all, he thought. They'd been in plenty of fights together so far, but the overwhelming odds, and the carnage they'd seen on the surface, had his nerves in the red zone heading into this battle.

Jack raised his hands, outstretching all ten fingers, then again, this time retracting his thumbs. Orsun hadn't lied—eighteen trogs ahead, Morgan thought. Then Jack pantomimed something that took several tries to get across, holding one hand high above his head, then out wide, then again, repeating what eventually became clear was an indication of size. He held up one finger, then mimed placing a crown on his head.

"One big one?" Tobias said. Everyone whipped around to glare at him.

Tobias shrugged.

"We were making enough noise already," he stage-whispered. "If they were going to hear us coming, they heard us coming."

"I give up," Jack said. "Come with me."

He led them down a winding corridor that opened into a larger cave, the group's vantage point several feet above the ground. Jack belly-crawled up to the edge. Morgan did the same, then the others, so that they could all look down at the war band of trogs.

They really do look like us, but more violent, Morgan thought. Human aside from their misshapen hands and feet, and bigger, certainly—ugly as hell too, with filed teeth and heavy brows—but human nonetheless. They wore the ragged skins of unidentifiable animals and carried rusted metal or dirty bone weapons. The spoils of their journey to the surface lay all around—bundles of grain or produce, entire cow or horse carcasses, other kinds of meat that Morgan would rather not know the source of.

In the middle of the group one stood out clearly as the leader. A full head larger than the others, broader of shoulder, this one wore a headdress like a crown, spiked with a variety of teeth and bone. He carried a grotesque two-handed weapon that seemed to be little more than a staff that had been studded with every vile sharp instrument the trog champion had ever found.

"That one's mine," Cordelia whispered.

"I'll help," Ingo said.

"There's got to be a way to thin them out a bit before we fight," Eriko said. "I mean I could sneak down and backstab one, but that's not super helpful."

"I have an idea," Tamsin said. "But I'd need a distraction, and another vantage point. Can we get to that tunnel over there?"

She pointed at a cavern opening below and to the right of them.

"There's a path I found that winds around," Jack said. "I can get you down there."

"And I can come up with a distraction," Tobias said.

"No," Tamsin said.

"Trust the bard, sis," Tobias said. "You said you learned an invisibility spell, yeah?"

"I hate this idea," Tamsin said.

"Just do it," her brother said. Reluctantly, Tamsin softly uttered the words to a spell, touched Tobias on the shoulder, and watched her brother fade away.

"I'll give you a head start," Tobias said, unseen. Morgan sensed the bard walk by him and make his way quietly down into the chamber.

"Okay. Tam, Jack, you head to the other chamber. I can hit them from above with a divine spell from here, but I'll wait for your move," Morgan said.

"I'll stealth down and get stabby when Tobias has them distracted," Eriko said.

"And then we'll charge in and make some noise when the mayhem starts," Cordelia said.

Morgan nodded. Jack and Tamsin slipped away. The cleric took a moment to see if he could find Tobias' invisible footsteps below them, but the spell was doing its job, fortunately.

Okay, Morgan thought. So. Theana. I know you're a fictional goddess in a fictional game, and to be honest, I was raised pretty religious so even thinking like this would put my grandmother in an early grave. But the way I see it is, we're stuck here together, and that means I'm here to do the work you need, and you're here to lend me a hand. I can live with that, whoever you are. But we're about to fight a metric shit ton of cannibal cavemen and now would be a great time to introduce yourself in some fashion. If you don't mind.

"Are you talking to yourself?" Cordelia whispered. "Your mouth was moving."

"Y'know, I'm not sure if I am or not," Morgan said. "Figure now is as good a time as any to find some old-time religion."

And then, a soft voice whispered in his ear.

"I'm as real here as you are, my sentinel," a woman's voice said. It sounded both imperious and warm; understanding and unyielding. "And for as long as you are here in this world, as long as you do good, I will be at your side."

"Holy crap," Morgan said.

"The irony of your expletive is appreciated, my sentinel," the goddess whispered.

"And she has a sense of humor," Morgan muttered. "Well, this could be worse."

Chapter 14: A night at the opera

The closer Tobias got to the encampment, the worse the smell became. It wasn't so much the trogs themselves, though they had some pretty impressive body odor going on. But the goods they'd stolen from the surface had started to spoil already, or hadn't been in particularly good shape to begin with. The whole area had a funk of rot filling it up like a green cloud.

Tobias waited until what he felt was the right moment, hoping he gave his sister and Jack enough time to get to their spot. He took a deep breath and did his best musical theater voice.

"Nighttime sharpens, heightens each sensation," he sang, hoping he could remember enough of the lyrics to *Phantom of the Opera's* signature song to get through this. Why am I worrying about my performance? He thought. We're all going to die anyway. Who cares if you flub the lyrics?

The trogs, all together, stopped what they were doing and looked around the cavern for the disembodied voice.

"Darkness stirs…" he continued, louder this time.

He continued to sing "The Music of the Night" with, in his opinion, perfect pitch, the high notes light and airy, the low notes powerful and full. This cavern has ridiculously good acoustics, Tobias thought. I could sing here all day.

The trogs had drawn their weapons, pointing, shouting in a fierce, guttural language, swinging at empty spaces in the cave. One started smashing a club into the ground out of frustration, and another covered his ears, howling. I've had better audiences, he thought. Any time now, Tamsin...

And then he saw his sister appear at the tunnel entrance. Worried that they'd see her, he ran up to the nearest trog, drawing his own saber as he hit that big, beautiful, glorious high note, and slashed the creature across the chest. The trog's cry of pain and shock harmonized with the note surprisingly well.

Tamsin's location began to glow with bright purple-blue energy. Her voice was audible now. There would be no hiding those magic words. Just as some of the trogs began to turn toward her, she unleashed a massive bolt of lightning from the tips of her finger, steaking toward the nearest trog. The creature lit up from within, a like an x-ray after image from a cartoon. The lightning didn't stop there. It leapt from one trog to another, electrocuting them, the creatures dropping to the ground in sizzling, smoking piles of muscle and bone. The lightning arced all the way around the room—Tobias had to cut his song short to duck out of the way at one point—then back toward Tamsin. It streaked upward, splashing into the stone above where she stood with Jack, who had started firing arrows at the now furious and distracted trog war band. As all this happened, a bright white light illuminated the room, and Tobias could hear Cordelia's war cry as she charged...

But his attention focused on the cracks forming in the stone above Tamsin's head. Cracks that split and grew, rumbling, crumbling...

"Tam! Jack! Look up!" Tobias yelled.

One of the trogs charged at the duo. Seeing this, Jack dropped his bow to draw his swords, nearly gutting the barbaric warrior with one swing of his blades. The ranger heard Tobias' cry and looked up, immediately seeing what was about to happen. With one smooth motion Jack sheathed both swords and dove at Tamsin, hooking her around the waist and carrying her back into the corridor they'd emerged from just as the ceiling above them collapsed in a thunderous cacophony of stone and electric energy.

And then they were gone.

Chapter 15: Fools make plans

Eriko had just started to make her way down the edge of the tunnel when everything went sideways.

She was admiring Tobias' singing—really, a solid performance given the circumstances—when Tamsin's magic carved a path of electric carnage through the trogs. The lightning bounced seemingly at random throughout the room, and to fatal effect. Eriko was close enough to the husk of one of the victims to know the trog wouldn't be getting up again in this lifetime.

Another trog noticed Eriko's decent, but before he could take a swing at her, Morgan unleashed some sort of holy hand grenade of a spell, a bolt of majestic golden light lancing down from above and searing another of the trog warriors. The monster who had begun to threaten Eriko turned to look at the source of the light, and Eriko wasted no time driving a dagger into his neck.

Before she could feel like the battle might be going their way, though, she heard Tobias cry out, and saw Jack diving to push Tamsin out of the way of a cave-in. Eriko, never prone to emotional outbursts, caught herself gasping as she watched two of her friends swallowed by falling stone. But before she could do anything to help, she found herself dodging and ducking away from nasty, unclean trog weapons swung with the intent to take her head off.

This is why only fools make plans, she thought. With a sort of cool serenity she never felt in the real world, Eriko spun and slashed, hamstringing trogs and bloodying her dagger with each strike.

Tobias appeared beside her, his invisibility spell dropping as Tamsin disappeared.

"We have to get to my sister," he said, parrying a blow from a trog with his saber.

"We will. Help me," Eriko said, the two weaving a flashing dance of blades across the cavern.

Not for the first time, Eriko found herself surprised at Tobias' skill with the sword. He spent so much time pretending to be a parody of a medieval musician it was easy to forget his character was no slouch in a fight, as well. But as they carved their way toward the rock pile where Tamsin and Jack had disappeared, Eriko felt a looming presence nearby and looked to her left.

The champion had taken notice of them.

He was even bigger and uglier up close than he had been from a distance. A mountain of muscle and hair, thick scars lacing his skin like armor, he wore a belt strung with human skulls around his waist. Well, at least we know the game has declared him "chaotic evil," since nobody good wears human skulls as flair, Eriko thought. As he turned to confront them, Eriko saw that he'd tied several fresher human heads to his belt as well as if to dry out.

I don't know if we can take him, Eriko thought.

"Hey big guy!" Cordelia yelled. Eriko stole a glance toward her friend, her axe stained with trog blood, standing side by side with Ingo, both spoiling for a fight. "I'm gonna add your head to that belt of yours!"

The champion stopped paying attention to Eriko and Tobias, turning his full focus on the two warriors. He roared at them, curdled spittle flying from his vicious, sharp teeth.

"We're all gonna die," Tobias said.

"Let's get your sister! Go!" Eriko said, shoving him along, and not for one second doubting he was right.

Chapter 16: Not the first date I had in mind

Jack came to with an immediate awareness he was somewhere he shouldn't be. Gasping as he regained consciousness, he realized that the place he wasn't supposed to be was partially on top of Tamsin, as they were both pinned down by dark stone.

The pocket of air around them was illuminated by a tiny globe of conjured light. Tamsin, already conscious, smiled at him as he opened his eyes. A tiny trickle of blood ran down from her scalp toward her eyebrow.

"Oh good. You're not dead," she said.

He faked a weak smile as pain across his entire body began to flair.

"Maybe reassess that statement in a few minutes," Jack said. "Are we stuck?"

"We're stuck."

"And our friends are out there," Jack said.

"This could have gone better," Tamsin said. "Thanks for making sure the cave wall didn't land on my head."

"Feels like it mostly landed on mine," Jack said. He wiggled his fingers and toes to make sure they all worked.

"Did you see how many trogs the spell took out?" Tamsin said. "I'm just hoping we didn't leave everyone with like, just one less creature to fight."

"Pretty sure you hit eight or nine," Jack said. "And I plugged at least two with arrows. We pulled our weight. Not bad for two players who only lasted one round of combat."

"You know, this means you've officially saved both me and my brother since we got trapped here," Tamsin said. "My mother would be so proud of you."

Jack nodded, fighting waves of dizziness. Do concussions exist in this world? He thought.

"So," he said, suddenly self-conscious at the fact the rocks had them pinned awkwardly close together.

"So," Tamsin said. They stared at each other in uncomfortable silence for a moment. "This isn't exactly the first date I had in mind."

"What?" Jack said.

"Oh, shit, I was trying to be funny and now it's twice as awkward, isn't it…"

"…more like four times as awkward."

"This is really weird."

"We better not die down here. I don't want our last conversation to be this uncomfortable."

"Why did the two people with clinical anxiety have to get stuck in the cave in together?" Tamsin said.

"You have—how did you know I had…?"

"Morgan told Tobias and Tobias told me."

"Why did Morgan tell Tobias I have anxiety?"

"So Tobias wouldn't give you a hard time when you wouldn't go out with them to some thing or another."

"I feel simultaneously betrayed and strangely relieved I don't actually have to tell you about my anxiety," Jack said.

"Quick, change the subject," Tamsin said.

"Are you still going out with that cosplayer, the one with the perfect anime hair?" Jack said. "Crap, that's not any less awkward than…"

"We broke up anyway, he cheated on me with an *Attack on Titan* cosplayer he met doing an Eren versus the Female Titan photoshoot," Tamsin said.

"I'm… sorry to hear that?" Jack said.

"It's fine. He was too obsessed with his abs anyway," Tamsin said. "What about you, are you still going out with…"

"Oh, no, that went sideways on account of me being unlikable," Jack said.

"You know what's unlikable? Self-pity," Tamsin said.

"If I'm being honest it was mostly because we kept running out of things to talk about," Jack said.

"I assume you never tried super-awkward banter," Tamsin said.

"If only we'd tried, we could've salvaged the relationship," Jack said. He shot her a weak smile.

"On a scale of one to ten, how much pain are you in?"

"Two," Jack said. Tamsin stared at him. "Seventeen. I'm at a seventeen. You?"

"You took most of the impact. I'm at like a six," Tamsin said. "Also, you can put your head back down if your neck hurts."

"I'm picturing Tobias' reaction when they find our bodies. 'Why was he listening to her stomach growling when they suffocated?'"

"We'll be like those mystery bodies on *Lost*."

"Exactly how I wanted to go out," Jack said. "Hey, Tam?"

"Yeah?"

"This has been a good conversation. If we don't die, we should talk more."

"Maybe we will," she said.

Then they both perked up at the sound of soft scratching against the stone.

"You hear that?" Jack said.

"Yup," Tamsin said. "Shush. It's above us."

They remained still and silent for a few minutes, listening to the clacking of moving rocks and the distant sound of combat. Then one of the rocks above them moved.

"I found you," a familiar, and yet still creepy, voice said. "You owe me even more now."

"Orsun?" Tamsin said.

The spider-creature's gaunt little head poked through the stones. He smiled. It was an incredibly alarming sight, a row of needle teeth trying to look reassuring.

"I watched. I saw the rocks fall. I listened!" he said. "Heard your voices. Knew you weren't dead. You talk a lot."

"I never thought I'd be this happy to see you, you bizarre little man," Jack said. "Help us get out of here, Orsun, and we'll make sure it's worth your while, my friend."

Chapter 17: To the death

Cordelia heard the blood pounding in her ears as uncontrolled rage pumped through her veins. She felt like she was teetering on the edge of losing control, and this both terrified and exhilarated her.

I should be afraid, she thought. But she wasn't. Not even a little.

The great, hulking trog champion swung his makeshift weapon like a maniac, forcing Cordelia and Ingo to duck and weave to stay out of its way. The creature seemed impervious to pain, no matter what they threw at him. Ingo planted his axe in the champion's calf, and Cordelia made vicious contact with the trog's abdomen, leaving him bleeding fiercely. But both warriors were battered as well, covered in their own blood, bruised and wounded.

It was no elegant sword fight. This was a battle between barbarians, fighters with no care for their own safety, driven mad by the smell of their own blood.

She swung, missing the champion but burying her axe in the neck of one of his subordinates. She nearly met the same fate as the trog leader attacked, but Ingo shoulder-checked the bigger creature, knocking him off-balance and saving Cordelia's life. She returned the favor, walloping the trog's elbow with a kick to stop him from slashing at Ingo in retaliation.

But it wasn't a one-sided fight. Not only did they have to contend with the lesser trogs interfering; no amount of damage inflicted on the champion appeared to slow him down. He must be a mountain of hit points, Cordelia thought.

Cordelia felt the bones jutting from the champion's weapon scrape across her back, burning as the skin tore. All around them, carnage reigned; she saw the blade dance of Eriko and Tobias, heard the wet smack of Morgan's war hammer, heard cries of rage and pain. It all felt stupid and pointless and thrilling and terrifying at once, these cave-creatures who had laid waste to Moderate Expectations completely unprepared for prey who fought back. And this champion, the oversized creature adorned in human remains, he laughed as Cordelia cut him again and again with her axe, kicked Ingo away like he was nothing more than a child.

Through the pounding in her ears she heard Morgan calling to her. She saw a flash of divine energy, but then she caught the battle priest out of the corner of her eye as he was knocked from his feet by a pair of trogs. Before she could yell out to him, Eriko was there, slashing away, defending their friend as he found his feet again.

Ingo seemed to sense the futility of the fight and charged in recklessly. He sunk his axe into the champion's lower back as the monster turned to face Cordelia, a cruel and hungry grin turning into a grimace of rage. Cordelia saw an opening as the creature seemed to focus all of his attention on Ingo. She roared at him, weapon raised, an incoherent war cry on her lips that felt as if it were coming from a stranger's mouth instead of her own.

The trog champion swiped at her without even looking, his garish weapon smashing into the haft of her two-handed axe, splitting the handle like a toothpick. Cordelia found herself holding a stick in one hand and the remnants of the axe head in the other. Without thinking, she threw the blade at the trog, which skimmed off his hide, drawing blood but doing little real damage.

The champion had her now, she knew. He turned his

overwhelming bulk to crowd her, limiting her ability to swing her powerful arms, and even if she could, she had nothing more than a broken stick to defend herself with. She dodged a swing of the trog's weapon to her left, to her right, the nasty blade kicking up bits of bone and rock as it smashed against the cave floor.

"Lass, here!" Ingo shouted above the din, and Cordelia saw him skim his axe across the floor, a perfect slide to land near her feet. She reached to scoop it up, ducking under what she thought was a strike from the champion intended to end her.

But it wasn't intended for her.

There was a sickening, wet thump, and the sound of fabric tearing. Cordelia heard Ingo exhale hard, wheezing in a way she'd never heard him breathe before. There was no cry of pain, no cursing, no berserker's roar. She cast her eyes up to see the trog champion's weapon embedded in Ingo's chest, opening him from belly button to collar bone. The dwarf grabbed hold of the spiked club with both hands, eye to eye with the champion, blood pouring from his mouth and staining his gray beard.

"Do it, lass. Do it now!" he cried.

The champion seemed perplexed, unable to comprehend what had happened, or how this little man still had the strength to cling to his weapon. Ingo bear-hugged the club, cursing in the foulest of language at the trog leader.

Cordelia gripped Ingo's axe with both hands and leaped into the air, body extended, arms pulled back like a spring ready to snap.

The weapon was smaller than she was used to, but perfectly balanced; a weapon of war forged with love and care. A flawless instrument of death.

She brought the axe down hard, still in the air, legs trailing behind her like a comet's tail. Every muscle in her upper body burned as she unleashed her rage, becoming as much an instrument of death as the blade she held.

The axe parted the trog champion's head without a sound, bifurcating left and right, not stopping until the raised metal heart of the axe struck the bones of his neck.

Everything seemed to stop moving then. The champion didn't fall at first; it was as though he did not yet realize his life was over. He staggered around, eyes wide but not seeing, mouth open, blood running from his lips and ears. He abandoned his vile club, Ingo still impaled on it, and after what felt like an eternity, the champion collapsed, the ground shaking as his frame struck stone.

"No!" Cordelia yelled, watching in horror as Ingo fell to the ground. One of the few remaining troglodytes tried to stop her. Without thinking, she cut him down with a single swipe of Ingo's blade. Absently, she could hear her friends shouting, but all she could do was stare at this dying man, this fool who had been so unpleasant to her and who had just hours ago seemed capable of redemption and change. The only thing you can hope for from someone with hate in their heart. And that potential for change was bleeding out on the cave floor.

Her throat swelled shut as Ingo pushed the spiked club off his body. Feebly, he pushed himself up against the nearest wall so he could sit upright. His legs didn't seem to want to move, and one arm hung useless at his side, the fingers on his hand twitching.

"We'll fix you," Cordelia said.

Ingo looked down at the shredded wounds on his chest and smiled weakly.

"I know you've got a priest with you, but it'll take more than a little healing magic to put me back together again," Ingo said.

Cordelia called for Morgan anyway, helping Ingo say upright.

"Don't you die on us. I was just starting to think you weren't an irredeemable bastard," Cordelia said.

"Good timing, then," Ingo said, coughing. He pointed at the axe she still clutched in her hand. "You keep that. I made it... I made it for my son. He died fighting in the dark like this too. Never got to give it to him."

"Don't do this, you old fool," Cordelia said.

Ingo patted the ground with his one good hand, looked around the now quiet cave absently.

"Good place to die. Good stone. It's better for a dwarf to die beneath the ground. The sky's too big. You get lost in it."

"Ingo, is there anyone…"

"My wife's gone," he said. "But if you… if you ever find yourself east of Moderate Expectations, there's a city on the edge of the God's Jaws mountain range. My daughter. Clementine Hammerhand. Find her and tell her… I should've been a better father. Tell her I died well though."

"I will, Ingo," Cordelia said.

"I'm sorry I was cruel to you when we met," Ingo said.

"You tried to be better," Cordelia said.

"That's all life is, isn't it," Ingo said. He smiled with blood-stained teeth. "A series of mistakes, and each of us trying to be better than we were the day before."

"I think so," Cordelia said.

"I wish I had fewer apologies to give at the end," he said. "And I wish we had better words for all the wrong we do than I'm sorry."

Ingo rested his head on his chest. Cordelia heard him exhale. He did not draw another breath.

Morgan fell to his knees next to her, gasping for air.

He looked up into the air, shouting to some unseen presence.

"Help him!" Morgan yelled, but Cordelia knew it wasn't directed at her. Morgan was appealing to something else, a higher power. "Help me bring him back! Please!"

Morgan put his hands on the old dwarf's body, but nothing happened.

"Why won't you answer me?" Morgan said, again clearly not addressing anyone in the cavern.

Cordelia reached own and closed Ingo's eyes with her fingertips. She slid the axe—a two-hander for Ingo, but one she could wield single-handed—into a loop on her belt. She put a hand on Morgan's shoulder.

"He was ready," she said. "Maybe your goddess understands that sometimes warriors don't want to come back."

"This was supposed to be a game," Morgan said. He climbed to his feet. All around them, the trog raiders had fallen. It was a terrible sight. Cordelia felt a heat in her belly, shame at the blood they'd shed, even if, in the end, it was to stop more bloodshed down the road.

On the other side of the room, Eriko and Tobias struggled to move the stones where Tamsin and Jack had disappeared.

"Come on," Cordelia said. "Let's go help the people who need still need us."

She stole one last glance back at Ingo's body.

"Clementine," she said, and walked away.

Chapter 18: Are we sure we're the good guys?

Tobias clawed at the stones blocking the tunnel where his sister disappeared, fighting off the urge lose his mind with panic and rage. No matter how hard he worked, he couldn't move the rocks fast enough. Beside him, Eriko did her best to help, and even Silence, Jack's wolf, scratched and pawed, trying to get to his human companion.

"We have to get to them!" Tobias yelled, trying to keep the fear out of his voice.

"We're here," Morgan said, joining him at the rock pile. Cordelia soon appeared as well, and with the two of them helping, they seemed to start making some progress.

"What if they're…" Tobias said. "This place is real, right? If you die here you die for real."

"They're not dead," Morgan said, but Tobias found his tone not even remotely reassuring.

Though Tobias thought he was the one closest to having a fit of anger, it was Cordelia who snapped first. Furious at the way the rocks just seemed to tumble and fall to fill in every inch of space they cleared, she started kicking the stone, an ineffective and almost petulant gesture, roaring in rage.

"Nobody else is dying today!" she said, hurling a football-sized stone across the cavern.

Then Silence stopped digging and walked away.

"Oh, that's great, that's real loyalty, wolf," Tobias said. "Just walk away. Not like you were any help anyway. Stupid dog."

"Yelling at the wolf isn't going to make this rock pile move any faster," Eriko said.

"Maybe I can…" Morgan said, standing up to his full height. He muttered a few words, reaching his hand out toward the stones. The faintest glimmer of light began to form around his fingers.

"Holy hell, look at this place," a voice that was not supposed to be in this chamber said. "It looks like a nightmare. Are we sure we're the good guys?"

Tobias whipped around to see his sister entering from a completely different opening in the cave, arm-in-arm with Jack as they supported each other to stay standing. Silence, clearly having heard them coming long before everyone else, was already walking by Jack's side.

Tobias ran to his sister and threw his arms around her.

"Don't ever knock a cavern wall onto your head again, okay?" he said. "I don't want to do this without you."

Tamsin hugged her brother back. She was covered in dirt and dust, battered and bruised, but alive.

"To be fair," she told him, "Jack caught most of the cave-in on his head."

"It's true," Jack said. "I'm never going to be right again."

Tobias pulled Jack into the hug as well.

"Thanks for saving my sister from herself, Jack," Tobias said.

"Hey!" Tamsin said. "My lightning spell was super effective. It was super effective, right? I didn't see how it panned out on account of dropping a wall on top of us."

"It was pretty effective," Eriko said as she joined them. She punched Jack in the arm. "I think your spell took out almost half of the war band."

"Took out," Tamsin said. "Let's not be delicate about it. I killed half of these creatures. That's… I don't know how I feel about that."

"Where's Ingo?" Jack asked.

Morgan shook his head. Jack nodded.

"We paid in blood, then," Jack said.

"Yeah," Cordelia chimed in. "Yeah, we did."

"Is this what this game is all about?" Tamsin said. "Do we just… murder our way across the world and hope nothing murders us back?"

"I think you've described one way of playing every RPG ever created," Eriko said.

"But it's not the only way," Tamsin said.

"It isn't," Jack said. "You just have to decide you're not going to be a roving band of killing machines."

"Can we not do that?" Tamsin said.

"Talking your way out of things is always the harder option," Cordelia said.

Eriko walked away and began poking through the items the trogs had stolen. Despite her usual glee at looting, her efforts seemed half-hearted this time.

"I just… I want to make sure we're the heroes of this story," Tamsin said. "I don't want this to be our thing. Wiping out entire… whatevers."

"I can get behind that plan," Morgan said.

Cordelia nodded to Jack.

"Hey, can I get your help with something? You too, Morgan," she said.

Both men followed her over to where Ingo's body sat, brutalized but strangely at peace.

"I guess we won," Tobias said. "I mean, our path to the surface is buried in rubble and our dwarven guide is dead so we're all going to die down here unless we can find our way to the surface on our own…"

"I can help with that," Orsun said.

Tobias felt the hair on the back of his neck stand up. He looked around frantically or the creepy little spider-thing, and spotted him in the tunnel Jack and Tamsin had emerged from, hanging from the ceiling. Like a spider. A creepy spider.

"How long have you been there!" Tobias said. "Why are you stalking us!"

"Tobias, Orsun saved us," Tamsin said.

"In order to eat you later?" Tobias said.

"I have no desire to eat you. You are profitable adventurers and bring prosperity to my caves," Orsun said.

"He gets creepier every time he talks," Tobias said.

Orsun looked almost upset, his eyes falling. Which was even weirder, Tobias noticed, because, upside down and sticking to the ceiling, looking "down" meant looking "up," and the entire scenario made Tobias' stomach churn.

"You can help us get back to the surface?" Tamsin said.

"Yes, yes, I can show you the way," Orsun said.

"What do you want in return?" Tobias said.

Orsun shrugged. It was so human, so mundanely casual, Tobias didn't know if he wanted to cry or scream.

"What if my brother writes you a song?" Tamsin said.

"I'm not writing a song for Spider-Gollum," Tobias said.

"I would love a song!" Orsun said. "Teach it to me. I will sing your song about me throughout the caverns. They have such great acoustics."

Tobias just shook his head.

"I got nothing. I have no way of disputing that," Tobias said. "He's right. The sound in these caves is amazing."

Chapter 19: So much below the surface

Tamsin watched her friends build a cairn for Ingo and realized she was proud of them.

Tobias had muttered something upon seeing them construct a tomb from the fallen stones about how Ingo hadn't been their friend, that he'd been unkind to Cordelia. But Tamsin knew her brother better than that, and knew his defensive tells. He was feeling what they all were feeling. Until now they hadn't lost anyone who felt "real."

They'd fought, yes, and killed, but those had been obstacles, wordless monsters presenting a clear threat. They hadn't lost an ally, not someone who had spoken to them as people do, and a fictional character or not, a nice man or not. Ingo's passing felt real, and for some of them, it felt partially their fault. It's easy to feel immortal until you've lost someone, Tamsin knew. Until a voice in your life was silenced forever.

Cordelia seemed angry and disappointed. Morgan was quiet and kept looking up, as if awaiting an answer that never came. Eriko stayed away from everyone, watching the makeshift funeral, absently moving a handful of coins she'd taken from the corpses of the trogs back and forth between her hands. Jack seemed far more concerned about the welfare of the living than the dead, eyes darting from one friend to another to observe them as he scratched Silence behind the ear. He caught her watching them and smiled. Tamsin smiled back.

"Okay, Orsun," she said, beckoning the spider-creature to her side. "What's your price for guiding us to the surface again?"

The little monster waved a hand.

"One song is enough. One song and the promise of a future favor. One favor, if you ever come back to my caves," he said. "Is that fair?"

"One song, one favor. I think so," Tamsin said. "Lead on."

It was no short journey Orsun took them on. They had to go deeper into the caves to get around the cave-in, down into a vast opening where a river of red magma drifted by, hot and silent. They passed cave drawings sketched in phosphorescent ink, found the corpses of a team of explorers who had died without a visible sign of a struggle, and Tamsin wondered if perhaps they had just wandered too deep and never found their way home.

They passed the bones of an impossibly large dragon so big the remains formed the structure of an entire cavern, ribs like stalactites, a massive skull that seemed to look at them as they came close.

Orsun stopped their progress at one point, then guided them forward, silently. He pointed. Up ahead, the path opened into a larger space, where tiny lights played and swam through the air. The lights made noise as they flittered about, like a song that never ended. Tamsin realized that Orsun had wanted them to see these lights, to share with them something no other living creature had seen with him.

He must be very lonely down here in the dark, Tamsin thought. There is so much below the surface he sees every day, and there's not a soul he can talk about it with.

They crossed through a chamber where diamonds were scattered like snowflakes. The space looked like a blanket of stars that went on far beyond where her eyes could see.

Orsun silenced them again, later, placing the palm of his hand against the cave floor. Seeing Tamsin watching him, he took her hand and placed it next to his. She felt vibrations in the stone, something writhing below them. Orsun gestured for the group to crouch down, and they complied. A moment later they saw a serpentine creature burrow up through the soil and crest like a whale surfacing from the ocean before disappearing into the darkness again.

Hours passed, but then Tamsin sensed it—fresh air, cool and light, invading the stuffy denseness of the caves. They moved faster now, the tantalizing closeness of the sky begging them to rush. The ascent was so sharp Tamsin felt her ears pop, like on an airplane. But then she could see it, blue sky, the literal light at the end of the tunnel.

"I cannot go any further," Orsun said. "The light, it hurts."

Tamsin knelt beside him and took his hands in hers.

"You will always have a friend in me, Orsun," she said. Tamsin heard her brother exhale disapprovingly, but she ignored him. "I see kindness in you. And I think you know more about the world than you let on."

The spider-creature blushed and looked down at his segmented legs bashfully.

"Be safe, lady wizard," Orsun said. "Come back to my caves someday. I have so much to show you all."

"We will, Orsun. You be safe," Tamsin said.

The adventurers started for the surface, Cordelia leading the way. Tamsin looked back over her shoulder to see Orsun standing alone in the dark, watching them disappear. She held a hand up and he returned the gesture. And then he was gone.

"You okay?" Jack asked, keeping pace beside her.

"I feel bad leaving him here," she said. "I think that just broke my heart. What was he?"

"I don't know," Jack said. "I've never seen anything like it in any game. I guess he's a bit like a drider—a spider-centaur—but that size, all alone, that benign… I don't know what to tell you. Maybe he's one of a kind."

"I don't know that I'd ever want to be the only one of me in the universe," Tamsin said.

"Spoken like a true twin," Jack said. "But I think we're all alone, in our own way. Orsun's place in the world is just lonely in a more profoundly literal way."

Finally, they reached the end of the cavern and stepped into broad daylight. The sun burned Tamsin's eyes. *How long were we below the surface?* She thought to herself. *A day? A week? A few hours?*

They arrived in a landscape they didn't recognize, along the side of a mountain—not treacherously high up, but heavily wooded, and without any hint how far away they'd ranged from Moderate Expectations.

"It's like the end if *the Descent*, but less depressing," Tobias said.

"Where the hell are we?" Morgan said.

"I guess it's a good thing we have a ranger?" Eriko said.

"I only play a ranger on TV," Jack said. "I really have no idea where we are."

"Well, we can't stay here," Cordelia said. "I'm not camping out unless we figure out where we are."

Jack looked around at the group.

"Any suggestions where we go from here?" Jack said.

"East," Cordelia said.

The group looked at her questioningly.

"We owe a terrible old man one last favor," she said. "If we're not going back to Moderate Expectations, we should go east."

"Fair enough," Morgan said. "East it is. You can figure out which way east is, right Jack?"

"I could do that even back in the real world, city boy or not," Jack said. "Follow me."

And so, bloody, battered, but victorious, the adventurers left the underworld behind, with no way of knowing what the next day would have in store.

Chapter 20: To the ends of the world

Leo the necromancer. He hated thinking of himself that way. When he arrived in this world with his friends, he'd been called Mordecai the Unholy, and he'd enjoyed playing that character. He reveled in it. Leo would dress all in black, adorning himself with bones and red stones reminiscent of blood. He would stare at people until they could no longer make eye contact, and speak in a whisper that forced the listener to stand uncomfortably close. His friends were heroic figures. Leo, as Mordecai, was their shadow, the monster they brought along to do the things they could not.

But now most of his friends were dead, and Leo found himself forced to be a hero. Someone had to do it. That was the story of Mordecai the Unholy, after all. Where good men failed, the monster would rise to save the world using whatever means necessary.

I should've played a monk, Leo thought. I might be dead by now, but I wouldn't be dealing with this shit.

"This shit," in this case, was the looming darkness on the edge of the mapped lands of this world. Like a cancer, this darkness seemed to drain whatever it touched of life, leaving nothing but ash and shadow behind.

Leo had been a necromancer for decades now. He had no issue

with death or darkness. But even evil men need a world in which to be evil, and this darkness, this cancer, it felt as though it might consume the entire fictional world. There is no darkness without light, Leo thought, quoting an annoying old priest his group had run into in their younger days. A priest of the Sun God, as good a man as you would ever find, and he looked on Leo, on Mordecai, not as an abomination, but as a counterpoint to a conversation the world had been having since the dawn of time. Leo had found him sanctimonious and obnoxious, and over the years, Leo realized he would never have a better friend.

The priest died in a way Leo and his friends almost never saw in this world: of old age. Natural causes. No one died of natural causes here. The world was too violent.

"I wish you were here, old friend," Leo thought. Malcolm was a good sounding board, but Malcolm's magic was tied to nature, and whatever this was, it was not natural. Leo had his theories and suspicions. And those theories were beginning to prove… if not correct, at least not unfounded, as he found a small bubble of land re-growing some of the life that had been drained of it.

Just a small circle, but it was green, and flowering, and it had been dead as the dust in the bottom of a coffin days ago.

Leo cursed Malcolm for playing so coy with the new players to this game. We need them, Leo thought. Though, as he pondered the situation, he was not sure exactly how much they should know, or how aware they needed to be of how precarious the health of this game world truly was.

Faith in the players. Faith in the game to make them into the heroes they needed to be. Faith in the few remaining player characters still trapped here to maintain their own faith in this magical construct.

Leo studied the grim landscape at the edge of the world.

I've long wanted to live out the rest of my life here, the necromancer thought. But I never really thought about how I don't want to die here.

Epilogue: This town is a graveyard

They worked their way east from the mountains for almost a full day before they saw anything remotely resembling civilization. Tobias had already started complaining—"a bard needs an audience! What am I going to do, busk for bears and chipmunks?"—but after their adventure underground, Jack, leading the way with Silence, was happy for the reprieve from violence.

"I wonder what kind of reward we would have been given by Moderate Expectations if we made it back there," Eriko wondered out loud.

"Considering their farmlands and livestock were devastated by the raid, I'd have trouble accepting much by way of payment," Morgan said.

"And that's why you're the cleric, and I'm the rogue," Eriko said.

Eventually Jack sensed, in that strange sixth-sense way his ranger abilities worked here, that the landscape had begun to change; the plants grew less feral, the ground itself seemed tamer. He followed that sense until he led them to a small village, less than half the size of Moderate Expectations.

"Hey, it's Very Low Expectations," Tobias said.

Jack cocked his head and listened. Tobias kept rambling,

amusing himself with alternative names for the town, but Jack waved his hand at him.

"Guys… I don't think there's anyone here," he said.

Eriko gave him a quizzical look, then darted ahead.

"Hey, please don't…" Morgan said. "Split the party. She always splits the party."

Wordlessly, Cordelia shouldered her way past everyone else and walked slowly after Eriko, letting the rogue take a healthy lead.

Because of the quiet, Jack expected to find ruin—burned-out buildings, bodies in the street, the remnants of some sort of attack. But there was nothing. The town was pristine, if perhaps a little run down, but there were simply no signs of life. Not even a stray dog or cat wandering the main thoroughfare.

"We really shouldn't stay here," Tamsin said.

"What do you think?" Morgan said. "Plague? Did they just move on and abandon the town?"

"Um, guys?" Eriko said from somewhere just out of sight. Her friends rushed to catch up to her and found the rogue standing in front of the town's central building. The windows had been boarded up, the doors chained from the outside.

"So, in game terminology, I think this offers us a choice," Eriko said. "We can open this door."

"Or we could absolutely, definitely, in no way, shape or form, open this door," Cordelia said.

"I think we should open the door," Eriko said.

"You would," Cordelia said.

"Okay, everyone in favor of opening the 'Do Not Open, Dead Inside' style barricaded door, raise their hand," Tobias said.

Only Eriko raised her hand.

"Seriously, guys, you are no fun. You need to step outside your comfort zone once in a while," she said.

"All in favor of getting out of this creepy-ass town as soon as possible?" Tobias asked.

Everyone raised their hands except Eriko, who eventually, and reluctantly, raised hers as well.

"Fine. Ignore the opportunity to delve into a medieval ghost town," Eriko said. "Man, you guys are so boring."

"C'mon, Rouge," Jack said. "I'm sure if we walk long enough we'll find you something to stab and loot."

He turned, giving wide berth to the boarded-up building, and lead his people from the village. They passed by abandoned carts, windows covered up by dust, and a well, long unused.

Leaving no trace, they left the unnamed ghost town, undisturbed.

But had any of them looked back, they might have seen a single, gray-skinned hand reach up out of the well, clawing to escape.

Book 3:

The Ghoul Slayer's Guidebook

Chapter 1: Far from home

It might have been a beautiful hike under other circumstances. Tall evergreen trees launched into the sky like green daggers all around the party. The road they journeyed upon was worn by time, but sturdy and even. The air had a hint of a chill to it but was pleasant and cool, and the sun, just on the verge of setting, had been with them all day, casting an elegant golden light on the wandering adventurers.

Unfortunately, the wandering adventurers had ended up untold miles from their home town, bumbling up out of a dungeon filled with horrors and wonder into a foreign landscape. Being lost and battle-battered sort of took the joy out of a leisurely stroll.

"We have... not even a slight clue how far we are from Moderate Expectations, do we?" Morgan said. The cleric looked miserable, clanking in his heavy armor, his massive war hammer clearly growing heavier with each passing mile.

"Nope," Cordelia said. She honestly felt bad for him. He was, after all, the only party member wearing heavy armor, and while the physics in this fictional world they were trapped in often skewed in their favor, making them stronger, more durable, and more skilled than they were back in the real world, metal armor was metal armor. Stuff got heavy after a while, game-gifted athletic endurance or no.

"I can scout things out, see if I can get an idea of where we are," Jack said. The ranger had his hood up, as usual, partially hiding his scarred face, while his wolf companion, Silence, shadowed him as soundlessly as his name implied. They'd been trapped in the game for weeks and Cordelia still found it hysterical that Jack, a city boy born and raised whom she knew had always been squeamish about things like camping, had chosen to play a ranger that first night and was now their best and most skilled woodsman. The only thing about the character Jack played here that was reminiscent of him in the real world was his soft spot for dogs.

"No, you don't have to do that," Morgan said. "Probably best we all stay together anyway."

"Because of the eerie, abandoned town we left behind back there?" Eriko said. Eriko was still mad at them for not exploring the town further, but they'd just escaped an arduous underground journey and nobody, other than Eriko, was much in the mood for opening boarded windows to find out why the town was no longer occupied.

"Eriko, we'll let you open the next creepy house we find, okay?" Tobias said as he adjusted the strap his lute hung from. Not for the first time on this journey, the bard muttered something under his breath about learning to play a less unwieldy instrument next so he wouldn't have to carry this one all the time.

"Who knows how long it'll be before we see another creepy house?" Eriko said. "It could be months. Years."

"How about a creepy campsite instead," Tamsin, their mage, said.

"A creepy campsite is a poor substitution for a creepy building," Eriko said.

"Well, we have a creepy campsite right now. You want to check it out?" Tamsin said, pointing in the distance.

The group came to a halt, exchanging nervous glances. Jack unslung his bow and nocked an arrow. He looked at Cordelia, who unhooked her dwarven battle axe from her belt. The axe felt strange in her hand. She'd lost her trusty two-hander underground and had a dying, bigoted dwarf gift this one to her. She still wasn't sure how she felt about that whole incident, but a fine weapon was a fine weapon. She adjusted her grip on the haft and readied herself.

"That's a creepy abandoned campsite," Morgan said. He sounded simultaneously alarmed and too exhausted to really care.

"I'll go," Jack started to say, but Eriko took off past him.

"I got this, I got this," Eriko said. "I'm bored out of my skull. I've got this."

"But…" Jack said.

"Let her go," Cordelia said, trying hard to not sound as tired as Morgan. She'd taken a beating in the fight underground, facing off against the chieftain of a band of marauding troglodytes, and she had been struggling all day to hide how much her body hurt. "This is what rogues do."

"This is what Eriko does," Morgan said, not taking his eyes off Eriko as she darted toward the campsite.

"What do you mean, this is what Eriko does?" Tamsin said. She was the least experienced gamer of the party—a group of friends who sat down one night to play a knockoff tabletop RPG and found themselves trapped in a very real, very lethal incarnation of that game, living the lives of the characters they'd chosen to play. Tamsin hadn't been around for all the years Morgan, Jack, Eriko, and Cordelia had thrown away countless nights playing different role playing games.

"Eriko always splits the party," Jack said.

"You guys have been saying that for weeks like it's a joke I'm supposed to get," Tamsin said.

"It means she runs off on her own a lot," Morgan said, hefting his hammer, ready to run to Eriko's aid if she found anything.

"And that's bad because the party is supposed to be a cohesive unit that works well together," Tobias said. He hadn't been part of the others' regular gaming sessions, but the longer they spent in this fictional world, the more Tobias had proven himself to be a deep-dive closet geek.

"I'm not saying Eriko caused every party wipe we ever had when we were gaming, but..." Jack said.

"Most," Morgan said.

"No, all," Cordelia said. "Except for that time when we all rolled so badly against that green dragon."

"Please don't bring up the green dragon," Jack said.

"Too soon, too soon," Morgan said.

In the distance, Eriko rummaged through the small camp. It was made up of a few small, disheveled tents, a few abandoned crates, a long-cold campfire. She waved them over.

"I got nothing!" Eriko said. "There's nothing here."

As the others joined her, Jack sent Silence ahead. The wolf sniffed around the camp curiously, weaving in and out of the tents.

"No blood, no signs of foul play?" Jack said.

"Nothing. No traps, nothing," Eriko said. "It's like they just got up and left."

"Great," Tobias said. "Ghost camp."

Morgan sat down on a nearby tree stump with a groan.

"Oh, that was a mistake," he said.

"Don't sit down! If you sit down you'll never get back up again," Eriko said.

"I'm done," Morgan said. "We've been walking for ten hours, guys. I'm done. I'm out."

"Well," Tobias said, setting down his lute. "We do have a camp."

"No," Jack said.

"Absolutely not," Cordelia said.

"What?" Tobias said.

"Best case scenario, these people were killed. Worst case, this is a honeypot and we're going to get ambushed while we sleep," Cordelia said.

"Let them try!" Tobias said. "Look at us. We've got Oliver Queen over there, and you're Conan the Barbarianette, Tamsin's like Hermione, and Eriko's like, Ezio Auditore or something. We're amazing. Nothing will ambush us."

"What about me?" Morgan said.

"I'm still trying to figure out what you do," Tobias said. He knelt beside the fire and tried to get it lit again, badly, almost cutting his own finger striking his dagger against flint from his pack.

"Said the bard to the cleric," Morgan said. "We'll see how many jokes you have when you need a healing spell."

"It's almost dark," Jack said. "We should find a safe place to camp anyway. We can just set a rotating watch."

Suddenly, there was a flash of light and camp lit up with the warm orange glow of flames. Tobias jumped back as the campfire sprang to life.

Everyone looked at Tamsin, whose hand still glimmered faintly with fire magic.

"What?" she said. "I was tired of watching my brother try to start a fire the old-fashioned way. I like my way better."

Cordelia sighed and sat down next to the growing fire.

"Can't argue with that," she said.

Chapter 2: The eternal hunter

The hunter did not spend much time with his kin.

Kin. Funny word, that. Particularly funny in this context, because his kindred were not his blood family. Not anymore. Not for centuries. Family is what you make it, he thought bitterly, as he often did, and the family he was born with died centuries ago. All he'd had since then...

Was his kindred.

Unliving and undying. Always hungry. Always. The hunter's kin haunted the graveyards of the world, sustained by the meat of the deceased. They called it sacrament, but the hunter knew what it was. It was gluttony.

And for some, it was penance.

And so, the hunter, more often than his kin liked, would do in this unlife he'd found what he had done as a living man. He'd hunt. He would stalk silently in dark forests, his undead eyes unhindered by the darkness. He no longer felt things like a mortal man did, not really, not in the same way. But the bow in his hand, that felt real. That felt mortal and true.

He didn't need to hunt. The curse on his body meant he was always hungry, but also that this hunger would never kill him. But it felt good to do what mortals did, taking down a deer with a longbow, treating the body with a pious respect as it gave its life for others.

He used to leave his kills for the living, like gifts, like offerings. Apologies, really, for the things his kin did to their dead. But then his brothers and sisters started using the hunter's kills like bait, and he had to stop.

No good deed goes unpunished. One of the outsiders said that to him once, the travelers who were not of this world. No good deed. Well, if I can do no good deed and go unpunished, the hunter thought, the least I can do is find solitude.

And so, he hunted. Some nights he'd draw his bow and never fire. Simply knowing he could have a kill was enough. Proving he still had the talent in his hands that he once had as a living man. To know there was something left of himself, the man he once was and could be no longer.

The sounds of his kindred sickened him. The moaning, the gnashing of teeth, the constant rumble of their ever-hungry bellies. The way their conversations always turned to eating.

The hunter knew his transformation was different. He knew he was like them, but not fully one of them, the same way the champion was, the same way their leader was. We are all vile creatures, the hunter thought, but some of us remember. Some of us cannot forget who we were before.

And that is a vicious cruelty, he knew. He envied the stupid among his kin. The ones who could not remember themselves. Oblivion was a comfort when you became a monster. To be a vile creature and remember who you were before… that, that is cruelty. That's what a curse looks like.

The hunter found tracks in the forest tonight, fresh tracks. He stalked them briefly, not to hunt, but because he could sense something different about them. They smelled like the other world.

The travelers are nothing but trouble, the hunter knew. But he knew their flesh would attract his kindred like flies to sugar. The travelers were a hard delicacy to find for his kind.

The hunter grimaced and moved on, following their trail, not sure if he was simply curious, or if some part of him wanted to help.

He'd been like them once upon a time, after all. Something more than what he was now, and most certainly something less as well.

Chapter 3: A history of trouble

Eriko was born to play a rogue.

From the moment she could walk, she always went where she shouldn't. Trespassing, sometimes; other times, just going places others were too afraid to go. She was the child who took the dare to go into the haunted house, or hop over a fence to retrieve a lost baseball. It was never malicious. She was once caught in the back room of a store and accused of shoplifting, but she had nothing on her. She told the manager who caught her she just wanted to know what was through the door.

Compulsive curiosity, she called it. And it was one of the bigger reasons why she had few friends.

I need to know what was in that house, she thought. The boarded-up town hall they'd found earlier that day. You don't board up a building from the outside. It made no sense. Why wouldn't they let her look inside? She found herself irritated she'd let her companions talk her out of scouting the place out.

She found herself doing the math. Two, maybe three miles back? And on a well-worn path. She could go back to the town in the dark. Not a problem. And by the time she'd be heading back it would be daylight. Perfect. I'm gone.

Eriko lay awake in the campsite, listening to the others

breathing. They were taking turns on watch, smartly knowing they couldn't trust the world around them while they slept, and she knew exactly whose watch she was going to sneak away during.

Jack took first watch, then Cordelia. No sneaking past either of them. They knew her too well. Third up was Eriko's mark: Tamsin. I love you Tam, Eriko thought, but you are definitely the weakest link in this group when it comes to reading peoples' intentions.

While settling in for the night, Eriko had specifically chosen the tent furthest from the fire, and made sure it wasn't particularly well constructed so she could slip out from the back. Just a matter of rolling a successful stealth check, metaphorically speaking, Eriko thought. And I'm pretty sure Tamsin's perception skill isn't very high in this game.

Sure enough, after Cordelia retired, settling in loudly in another tent, the quiet started to get to Tamsin. Eriko smiled as the magician started talking to herself softly, muttering almost incoherently, before giving in to singing quietly. Eriko almost laughed out loud when Tamsin, clearly bored and trying to stay awake, snapped her fingers to create a small flame in the palm of her hand and juggled it back and forth playfully.

Seeing her friend fully invested in her spells, Tamsin slowly, carefully, crept back deeper into her tent, and then slithered underneath it, escaping into the cooler air outside. She checked her belt for her knives and thieves' tools, ran a hand through her fauxhawk, and nodded to herself.

Two miles. Back by dawn. Not a problem.

I have got to find out what's in that building.

Eriko stuck mainly to the road, eyes darting over her shoulders to see if her friends had decided to pursue her as often as she looked forward for signs of oncoming travelers. She made good time, though she almost turned her ankle on a stone. Finally, the shadow of the town appeared before her, an absence of light along the road, the cloudless, star-filled sky blocked out by the black shadows of larger buildings.

She saw no signs of life in the town as she entered, but played it safe, sticking to shadows and alleyways until she found the central building in the square. Resisting the temptation to go in through the front door, Eriko did a quiet circuit around the exterior, quietly testing the small number of boarded-up windows on the ground level.

Chewing her lip, she looked up, then nimbly scrambled up to the second floor. The action made her smile. In the real world, she wasn't exactly clumsy or un-athletic, but scaling the side of a building like a squirrel certainly wasn't something she was able to do easily. Here in Revery, though, she was able to pop up along the siding like she'd done it her entire life.

The second-floor windows were blocked as well, though not as securely. Eriko crept around the edge of the building until she found a window with slats big enough she could peer through. The interior was near perfect darkness, the combination of sealed windows and no daylight leaving… well, everything to the imagination, Eriko thought.

Well, nothing ventured, as the saying goes, she thought. Eriko looked down to pull a dagger from her belt so she could pry the wooden slats off the window and take a look inside. I'm probably going through all this and the place is going to be empty, she thought. Or it was a plague and I'm going to get sick and die. This is awesome. Good call. Glad I gave up a night's rest for this. I have a problem, she thought. I have got to stop doing this to myself…

She looked back up, dagger ready to get to work on the window.

And looked directly into the eyes of a pair of eyes staring out at her through the break in the boards.

"Shit!" was all Eriko managed to get out before tumbling backward, sideways, and over the edge of the ledge, falling to the street below.

Chapter 4: Night haunt

Tamsin watched the slow, undignified process of her brother dragging himself out of his tent to take his turn on watch. Whether in the real world or a fantasy one, Tobias was hard to rouse, so much so she was honestly a little bit proud he got up on his own to relieve her.

Tobias stumbled over to the fire and sat down near her.

"My turn," he said, eyes half-closed, body swaying with sleep.

"Maybe I'll wait up a bit longer," Tamsin said.

"No, s'alright," Tobias said.

Laughing, Tamsin snatched up a lock of her brother's hair and whispered the words to a spell. Instantly, her fingertips danced with flames, and so did the hair she had grasped between them.

Tobias let loose an undignified gasp, leaping backward, slapping the flames, and his own face and neck, until they were out.

"You awake now?" she asked.

"You set me on fire!" Tobias said.

"Just a little bit."

Tobias pushed himself back up into a proper sitting position, fixing his singed hair.

"Well, it worked, I'll give you that," he said. "When are you going to teach me some spells?"

"When we're not almost dying," Tamsin said. "Eriko and I were talking about that the other day. That in most games like this, bards can cast spells, so you should be able to, hypothetically, learn some of mine."

"But then you won't be special."

"I'll just have to learn more spells," Tamsin said.

"That's my sister," Tobias said. "Unbridled ambition."

Tamsin shrugged and leaned back, enjoying the cool night air. Tobias caught her smiling.

"What. What cosmic joke are you laughing at," he said.

"Just that... I mean for most of us, we're better here, aren't we?" she said. "I'm a wizard, dude."

"People pay me to sing, which is better than community theater was doing for me," Tobias said. "Eriko certainly seems happier pilfering for a living than slinging cappuccinos."

"Jack almost feels like he's over the guilt of buying the game in the first place," Tamsin said. "And... I don't know. The three of them, Jack and Cordelia and Morgan, they just seem like this is where they belong, not back home."

"I don't know," Tobias said. "Morgan seems lonely sometimes."

"Well, he has family back home who need him," Tamsin said. "I mean I know we have family, but the only person I'd want to get home to is sitting beside me right now. If you weren't here I'd be fighting like hell to get back, but..."

"Twinsies," Tobias said.

"I hate when you do that," Tamsin said.

"I know."

"Sometimes," Tamsin said, brushing a strand of supernaturally silver hair out of her face, tucking it behind one exaggerated elvish ear. "I worry that we'll have to go home."

"That's dark," Tobias said.

"I know," Tamsin said.

"Also, I have the same worry," Tobias admitted. "I love it here. Selfishly, I just... I love this world."

"And this world loves you back," a stranger's voice said.

Tamsin felt her stomach turn to acid. Her brother staggered to his feet, drawing his saber clumsily.

Across from them, sitting calmly by the fire, was a man-shaped thing. It has stark white skin tinged with blue and gray, like a corpse. Its ears were unnaturally long and pointed, its mouth just a little too wide, its eyes red, glowing pinpricks in the darkness. It had a long spear resting casually against one shoulder and wore simple clothes in browns and grays.

"What the hell are you?" Tobias said.

Tamsin readied a spell, her hand sparking with electrical energy. The creature waved her off dismissively.

"You have the sweet smell of another world on you, the whole group of you," the creature said. He made no move to leave or even stand, confidently ignoring Tobias' threatening body language. "I came to investigate. We like creatures from other worlds here. They taste better. They give us strength."

"Why does everything in this entire world eat people," Tamsin said.

"Still worried about never going home?" Tobias said. He pointed his sword at the creature. "What do you want, Nosferatu?"

The creature laughed. It sounded like a crypt opening in the darkness.

"Oh, I'm no vampire, minstrel," the creature said. "And I wouldn't want to be. No, my tribe's a little different."

Before the creature could say another word, Morgan's booming voice rang out in the darkness.

"Begone!" Morgan said, his voice seemingly coming from all directions at once. The campsite was suddenly doused in a glow as bright as daylight. The creature hissed and fled, its face taking on a feral, predatory look before it ran. Morgan strode into the center of the camp, his hammer held above his head, glowing like the sun, shredding every shadow.

Cordelia and Jack emerged seconds later, weapons in hand, shielding their eyes from Morgan's light.

"The hell is going on out here?" Jack said.

"Undead," Morgan said, lowering his hammer. The glow began to fade.

"So I guess we can verify that clerics have powers against the undead in this game, then," Cordelia said.

"It's funny," Morgan said. He looked at Tamsin and Tobias with concern, but Tamsin shook her head. "I was dead asleep and I heard a voice—her voice, Theana's—urging me to wake up, that we were in danger."

"Divine intervention," Jack said.

Morgan shrugged.

"Or a coincidence," Morgan said. "But that spell was almost instinctual—I don't know if it's the game guiding my hand or this goddess, but I didn't even have to think about what to cast when I saw that thing."

"Vampire," Tobias said.

"Something," Morgan said. He glanced around. "Where's Eriko?"

"Oh, don't tell me," Cordelia said. She ripped open Eriko's tent. "Gone."

"He took her?" Tamsin said.

"No," Cordelia said. "She want to look at that goddamned building, didn't she."

"Split the party," Jack said. "She always splits the party."

He looked at Morgan, who nodded.

"You scout ahead. We'll catch up," Morgan said.

Jack took off at a sprint, whistling and calling Silence to his side. The wolf bounded along, clearly excited at the prospect of a hunt.

"We know where we're going?" Tobias said.

"Back," Cordelia said. "Eriko has always been the proverbial curious cat."

Chapter 5: What we never were

Jack raced through the pre-dawn darkness, bow in hand, hood thrown back so that the night air rippled against his scalp. He marveled, not for the first time, at how sure-footed he was here. Back in the real world he wasn't out of shape or clumsy, but he still couldn't get over how much nimbler he was now, never misplacing a step, his endurance better than ever, his movements almost graceful, in a rough and tumble sort of way.

Here we are all what we never were, he thought. Tamsin got her magic. Tobias got his stardom. Cordelia was strong enough that no one ever bothered her. And Morgan could touch someone and save their life with divine magic.

And, as Jack ran so expertly he could keep pace with the wolf at his side, Eriko had the skills to perpetually get into trouble.

Silence pulled ahead of him, huffing quietly as he ran. The wolf turned to look back at Jack, as if to tell him something, and together they stopped. Jack scratched behind the wolf's ears and pulled an arrow from his quiver.

He looked up at the night sky and then at the trees around them, and those strange, innate ranger abilities he didn't have in the real world told him they were very close to the abandoned town. He stepped off the worn path and into the woods for cover, his gut telling him not to brazenly approach, just to be safe.

If all the others were what they never were back home but wanted to be, what am I? Jack thought. Unafraid, he guessed. The wilderness didn't scare him here. He saw the beauty in feral things. A purely urban child growing up, the biggest critter he'd seen in person before college was a raccoon that had grown obese living off human garbage. Here, he could wander for days, not just unafraid but at peace, comforted, surrounded by wild beauty.

He looked once more to Silence, checking to see if the wolf's hackles were up, but he calmly scanned the woods at Jack's side, seemingly unfazed. Above them, the sky slowly shifted from black to deep purple as the sun struggled to begin the day.

Even right now, Jack though. There's peace in this, searching for my irresponsible friend, alone except for magical oversized dog, when I should be terrified, sick to my stomach, being eaten alive by mosquitos. But this is my place now. This is what I am.

Well, maybe not entirely at peace, Jack thought. My best friend is doing her best to get herself killed, as usual. That's not peaceful.

His meandering thoughts were interrupted by Silence, who let out an almost imperceptible growl. Jack turned his gaze to the place in the darkness the wolf's bright eyes stared.

What's out there, buddy, Jack thought, and Silence stopped growling. The two shared an awkward look, and, once again, Jack wondered if Silence could hear his inner monologue. Well, answer me back if you can hear me, Jack thought, but the wolf went back to staring into the darkness and growling. Nocking an arrow, Jack scanned the shadows, seeing nothing.

This is why you don't split the party, Eriko, Jack thought. If I put an arrow through your lung I'm going to feel terrible about it, but it's your fault I'm out here in the woods. You're my best friend, but this is getting old.

And then Jack saw the glimmer of two red eyes in the dark.

Biting back an involuntary gasp, he let his arrow loose, breaking the silence with the whistling snap of his bowstring. The eyes blinked once and darted off, inhumanly fast, gone long before his arrow struck. Fully expecting an attack, he instinctually slung his bow over his shoulder and drew his two short swords, ready for an incoming monstrosity.

But nothing came.

"Well, shit," Jack said out loud. The wolf looked up at him judgmentally. "I'm not going after him. Do you want to go after him?"

Not really expecting an answer, Jack shrugged at Silence, who began ignoring him to look in another direction, back toward the town.

Great, Jack thought. It's Jurassic Park and that was the clever girl. Going to get eaten by a sneak attack from behind...

He heard what Silence had noticed before, the soft fall of footsteps through the brush, moving fast, running. But not the sound of something charging at him—those were the footsteps of something fleeing, afraid...

Before Jack could call out, a small, familiar shape slammed into him, knocking the breath from his lungs.

"Jack!" Eriko said. She was covered in dirt and debris, her undercut fauxhawk completely askew. She bounced back to her feet faster than he did, helping him up with one hand and handing him one of his fallen swords with the other. "Jack, we gotta go."

"What did you do?" Jack said, scooping up his other sword and fixing his hood.

"Um, funny story about that," Eriko said. "You won't believe what's in that building we didn't open."

Chapter 6: Funny story about that

Eriko woke up on the ground in the alley beside the boarded-up building, covered in debris and garbage.

She lay very still for a moment, feeling her fingers and toes, making sure everything still moved. The back of her head felt wet—I hope that's not blood, she thought, grossed out by the idea of an open wound in this filthy alley—and her whole frame felt heavy and bruised, but everything seemed to work as intended otherwise.

Before she could pick herself up, though, she saw something dart across the mouth of the alleyway. Man-sized, but skinny, almost emaciated, with exaggerated ears and a hunched gate. She barely got a look at it, but she could tell it wore rags. And it was fast. Very fast.

Maybe I won't move yet, she thought. She waited for the creature to return, but when it didn't, she rolled over gingerly, forcing herself to one knee.

The eyes, she remembered. The face looking out at her. It wasn't a monster, she realized, despite being startled by it. No, it was the face of a child, a very scared child, dark-haired, and clearly amazed to see a human being standing outside the window looking in.

There's a kid in there, Eriko thought. Not just a kid, as she closed her eyes to try to call to mind what she saw inside the window. There were others behind the first child, too, bodies she couldn't quite make out, maybe other children, maybe adults. Huddled together in the darkness. Trapped inside a building locked from the outside.

What is going on here?

She took stock of the alley, looking for cover. A handful of crates lined one wall. The alley itself terminated in a dead end, or close enough to it, with a solid wooden fence tall enough she'd need rope or proficiency in parkour to scale. Guess I'm going out the other side, she thought.

She caught the sound of nails on stone and ducked behind the crates as the creature she'd spotted earlier darted past the alley's entrance going the other direction. Awesome, she thought. I'm in a stealth level.

Then the creature returned and looked down the alley.

Eriko pressed her back against the wall behind her, willing herself to be invisible. Come on, she thought. I'm a rogue. I'm stealthy. Don't see me, don't see me, don't see me...

The creature walked tentatively into the alley, sniffing the air like a hound.

Oh, great, he tracks by smell, she thought. This is the best day ever. I'm so happy I decided to do this.

Carefully, she slid both daggers from her belt, readying herself to strike. This could go one of two ways, she thought. He's going to come around those boxes, look right at me, call for help, and attempt to eat my face, or...

The creature walked right past her, deeper into the alleyway.

I am the best rogue, Eriko thought. With almost supernatural speed, she drove one dagger straight through the monster's neck, the point of the blade piercing the opposite side, bisecting his throat from the spinal cord forward. The other she drove between two vertebrae near his shoulders, amazed at the way this fictional world granted her the grotesque knowledge of anatomy to know exactly how to do that. The creature let out one quick, sputtering hiss, arms and legs twitching like a spider's, and she yanked the dagger in his throat sideways, very nearly removing his head in the process.

And to think, back home I'm a pacifist, she thought. Using the leverage from her other dagger, she lowered the body to the ground, watching as the glow of its red eyes dimmed and then went out.

Okay, the creepy thing can be killed by non-magical weapons. Good to know, she thought. Moving back behind the crates in case another of these monsters wandered by the mouth of the alley, she poked at the corpse a bit. Deathly white skin tinged with blue and gray, a mouth full of needle-like teeth, nearly hairless, fingers with nails like claws. It definitely looked like something they'd killed before, she thought, but she wasn't willing to jump to any assumptions.

Predatory monsters in a town where children were locked up in a building, Eriko thought. Yup, this is one of those fairy tales that hasn't been edited for kids. I've got to get back to my friends.

She edged her way to the alley entrance and peered into the street. It looked empty, but as a stealthy person herself, she didn't have a lot of faith in that. Still, it was this or nothing, she thought. Eriko took a deep breath and darted out of the alley, staying close to the edge of the building, looking for cover. She ducked behind a set of empty kegs near a building that looked like it might have been a general store at some point, and judged the distance to the edge of town. Maybe I just run for it, she thought. I mean, I'm quick. I'm sneaky. If I can get into the woods I'll have more cover to hide.

This is a good plan.

No, this is a terrible plan, Eriko, she thought. This is the reason why you don't split the party. You're an idiot.

With another deep breath, she readied herself, and sprung into a flat-out sprint for the tree line. The entire way she expected to hear the scraping of long nails on the stone street behind her, but none came. With an undignified roll, she dove into the woods, ducking behind a tree.

She waited a few seconds, then a few more. Nothing pursued her.

Then she saw another creature, nearly identical to the one she'd killed, creep out into the street and make its way toward the center building where she'd murdered the other.

A few more seconds went by.

And then she heard a chilling cry, half-grief, half-warning, and what she definitely thought was a call to action, a high-pitched wail that no human could make.

Well screw this, Eriko thought, and started to run.

She avoided the road, which was both a smart decision and stupid one as she stumbled and tripped several times in the dark, ran full-speed headlong into a narrow tree she couldn't make out in the shadows so had she knocked the wind out of herself, and caught her cloak on a branch so bad she almost choked herself hard enough to vomit.

I will never split the party again, she thought, I promise I will never split the party again as long as we are in this world. This was a bad life choice, Eriko. Don't make bad life choices—

And that was when she slammed into someone so hard her vision went white in the darkness. The darkened figure let out a very familiar, very angry grunt, and she knew exactly who it was.

"Jack!" she said, clambering to her feet and offering him a hand up. "Jack, we gotta go."

But before she could explain, the sky went very bright for just a moment, and instantly faded back to pre-dawn darkness.

"That looks like one of…" Eriko said

"Morgan's spells," Jack said.

"Well, shit," Eriko said.

Chapter 7: Thoughts on the divine

Morgan couldn't get the sound out of his head. A woman's voice, pulling him from sleep, warning him his friends were in danger.

Wake up.

That voice. He knew who it was, though he struggled to truly believe it was her and not just a dream. But she'd already spoken to him once, the goddess Theana. As clear as glass, like a conversation over coffee, he'd heard her voice before. He knew she was real here, some divine creature who granted him his abilities in exchange for... in exchange for what? Morgan thought. These games often had vengeful, fanciful gods, more like the Greek or Norse pantheons than a modern monotheistic belief system, and clearly this was a fictional world where those divine beings took a direct hand in the affairs of mortals.

But why would something that powerful take the time to... nudge him awake to save him? Surely, she had followers everywhere. He'd been her cleric for all of a hot minute.

"You look like you're thinking big thoughts," Cordelia said. It still threw him off, even weeks after being trapped here, to see his friend's face with her half-orc features, the small tusks, the green-tinged skin. She walked beside him as they made their way back toward the abandoned town, sticking to the road to have a better field of vision in case the monster from their camp tried to attack them. Cordelia wasn't taking any chances, the beautifully crafted axe she'd taken from Ingo when he died casually swinging from her hand.

"Thinking thoughts, yeah. Not sure how big I'd call them," Morgan said.

He hesitated to bring up the conundrum of being a priest in a fantasy world with Cordelia. Well, with any of them, really. Morgan was relatively religious himself—absolutely not as religious as his grandma or his father wanted him to be, but then again, who was—but he had enough faith of his own that being an emissary for a made-up goddess made him slightly uncomfortable. He'd never had trouble with it when they played an RPG, but that was just play, after all. It was fun. The gods involved in tabletop role-playing games didn't talk back to you when you prayed. But it was hard to figure out who to talk to about his concerns. Cordelia came from a religious family, but she seemed to be fairly casual about it herself. Jack grew up Irish Catholic but hadn't considered himself religious in years, and Eriko was a devout atheist. Any or all of them could offer him their thoughts, but somehow, Morgan thought this was something he had to figure out on his own—it was, he thought with a laugh, his cross to bear.

He shot a side-eye at Tobias and almost laughed. Now there's the person to talk to, he thought. Tobias belonged to the Church of Tobias. He'd have no preconceived notions or judgments, and despite being a goofball and a prankster, was a shockingly astute observer. I'll have to pull him aside when things quiet down, he thought, cursing Eriko's curiosity streak silently.

"What do you think that thing was?" Tamsin said. The twins were bringing up the rear as the group walked two-by-two, staying close.

"Nosferatu," Tobias said.

"It wasn't a vampire," Morgan said.

"How do you know?" Tobias said.

"I just didn't get a vampire vibe off it," Morgan said.

"I think it's a ghoul," Cordelia said.

Morgan nodded, thinking about all the things he'd read about ghouls in different games, in H.P. Lovecraft stories, in folklore. They'd fought something they thought was a ghoul back in Moderate Expectations, but it had been a mindless thing, not speaking, eating the dead from their caskets in a local graveyard.

"It seemed pretty chatty for a ghoul," Morgan said.

"Something like it, then," Cordelia said. "Clearly it was undead the way it reacted to your spell."

"I still think it was a nosferatu," Tobias said.

A new voice spoke from the darkness so unexpectedly Morgan felt goosebumps rise across his entire body.

"We're not vampires, and frankly, it's a little offensive to call us ghouls," the voice of the creature from the camp said. "We prefer to call ourselves the eaters of the dead."

"Ah, shit," Cordelia said.

Morgan hefted his hammer and readied himself, thinking about what spells he knew he could call upon against creatures of the night. He saw a flare of light as Tamsin prepared a fireball spell. The four adventurers instinctually put their backs to each other so they could see in all directions.

"Where's the voice coming from," Tamsin said.

"Hey creeper!" Tobias said. "You do this often? Just… whispering dramatically from the darkness? You're not impressing anyone, y'know. It's… It's actually really disconcerting."

"Then maybe I'll step into the light," the voice said, and Morgan saw a pair of red points in the darkness, eyes staring at them. And then another pair. And another. And another.

"We're surrounded," Morgan said.

"No problem," Cordelia said. "We're only down two party members. I mean technically, we've got the core four here, right?"

"Core four?" Tamsin said. "Also tell me which way to shoot this fireball, please."

"Tank, healer, damage, and… well," Cordelia said, giving

Tobias a look.

"That's the beauty of the bard, darling," Tobias said. "We can do it all. Watch this."

And Tobias began to sing. Morgan gritted his teeth—it was one of the most obnoxious earworms of the past five years, the sort of song that latched onto your brain and wouldn't let go. Why, why would he do this?

The creature spoke again, still not emerging from the shadows.

"Save your charm spells for the living, minstrel," he said. "They're no use to you on the dead."

Tobias shrugged casually.

"Well, that's what I got, guys," he said. "Sorry. Anyone else?"

"Screw this," Tamsin said, and with a flick of her wrist, she sent a fireball splashing into the fire where a cluster of the bright red eyes watched.

And then the road turned into a battlefield.

Inhuman screeches squealed from the spot where Tamsin's fireball exploded, branches and underbrush catching flame, illuminating desiccated, spindly silhouettes in the darkness as the creatures scattered. Something leapt out of the brush on the other side of the road, and without thinking, Morgan swung his hammer upward, connecting hard with a meaty thud. The monster collapsed on the ground several yards away and then, like a video running in fast forward, skittered back into the forest to hide. Cordelia took a creature's arm off at the shoulder and then split it from hip to throat with her axe. Even Tobias got in on the violence, as always displaying an unexpected proficiency with the elegant sabre he wielded.

"See? We got this," Tobias said, smirking at the rest of the group.

And then he fell, his feet yanked out from under him.

"Tobias!" Tamsin cried out. Morgan watched in horror as Tobias was dragged by his ankles by two of the creatures, their pale, blue-tinged skin gleaming in the light of Tamsin's fire, eyes bright red dots. They hissed as Tobias kicked and tried to slash at them with his sword.

Morgan reared back to swing at one with his hammer and roared in frustration as another of the creatures grabbed hold of his weapon, preventing him from making the attack.

"Cordelia!" Morgan yelled, and the barbarian charged, only to be cut off by another of the ghoul-like things, bigger but almost comically thin. She nearly cut the undead monster in half as she fought to get to Tobias, but the creature didn't die—it reached out at her with long, bone-tipped fingers, forcing Cordelia to shove him away with her booted foot.

"Morgan, if you have any more cleric-y things up your sleeve, now is a good time," she said.

Morgan tried to call a spell to mind, anything, but he couldn't focus his thoughts as he shook the ghoul off his hammer. In frustration, he bashed its head, hearing bone crack and snap. Then the spell he wanted was there, as if written in golden letters before his eyes. He called out words—what am I saying, he thought, I don't know if I'm saying a prayer or magic words or something else—and the entire battle lit up like the sun. The monsters screeched like terrified animals. The shadowy silhouettes of the undead retreated into the forest like rats, fleeing from the divine energy of his spell.

As quickly as it appeared, the light began to fade. Morgan blinked away the afterimages, straining to focus his vision in the glittering, soft glow of the coming day.

"Are they gone?" he said. "Cordelia, I can't see. Did it work?"

Slowly, his vision returned to normal, revealing the road, the dying embers of Tamsin's spells. Cordelia stood in the middle of the path, her axe in hand, dripping with thick, black blood. Around them, pieces of the undead twitched and squirmed—arms, torsos, even a single head, removed from its body, still growling and baring its teeth.

"Morgan," Cordelia said, her body shaking with rage. "Morgan… the twins are gone."

Chapter 8: We're a delicacy

I have had better days, Tobias thought, listening to his lute clang pathetically behind him as the ghouls dragged him along behind them.

They'd tied his hands but hadn't blindfolded or gagged him, which told him they clearly didn't care if he saw where they were going or if he spoke to them. He glanced over at his sister, looking miserable and angry, her wizard's robes twisted and dirty from the trip.

Just us, he thought. Hopefully that means they couldn't capture the others and they can come rescue us and not something unthinkable. He almost laughed at the thought of these creatures trying to drag Cordelia in this undignified manner, but then a rock or root dug into his back and all humor went out of him.

We've got this, he thought. This is fine. We've been in worse situations before. Okay, maybe not worse situations, but between the two of us, we've got a lot of tricks up our sleeves. We can get out of this.

His view of shadowy treetops gave way to open sky, and it took just a quick glance around to see they'd returned to the abandoned town. Great, Tobias thought. We were coming back here anyway. They saved us the trouble.

They continued along the main road through the center of town before coming to a complete stop. Tobias tried to come up with a snappy one-liner, but before he could think of anything worth saying, he was hoisted up onto a ghoul's shoulder. And then he saw what they planned to do.

"Oh no," he said. "Can we not? I'd rather not."

He watched as two of the creatures skittered down the well in the center of town, almost spider-like in their movements. Next, the ghoul carrying him prepared to lower him down.

He stole a look at his feet, where his ankles were bound by old, filthy rope. Not, he thought, enough rope to lower him down a well with. Not at all.

"Maybe you could double up on the ropes?" he said. "Just in case? I mean safety first, guys, right?"

Not speaking, the creatures upended him, lowering him head-first down into the darkness.

Tobias began singing that sailor's song from *Jaws*, the one Quint sings when he thinks they're going to die.

"Toby!" Tamsin yelled, her voice echoing down the well as Tobias disappeared into the darkness. He'd felt strangely resigned to it all before he heard her voice, but the fear he heard there, fear for him and not for herself, spiked his heartbeat. He fought the urge to struggle against his bindings, knowing that even if he got free right now, he's just be plummeting toward a broken neck at the bottom of the well.

Eventually, the narrow vertical tunnel opened. Waiting for him at the bottom was the first of the creature they'd seen, the one by the campfire. He was bigger than the others—Tobias was tempted to use the word healthier, though that seemed weird to say about an undead creature—and his face, though monstrous, had more reason to it, less feral in nature than the lesser creatures around them.

"Hi," Tobias said. "Hello. Hail and well met, my good sir. Maybe we got off on the wrong foot. I'm Tobias, but folks call me Oberon the Blue."

The creature smiled at him with a mixture of amusement and, Tobias thought uncomfortably, a hint of hunger.

"Minstrel," the undead monster said. When he wasn't trying to spook them by a campfire, the ghoul's voice had a nice tone to it, Tobias thought. He sounds like a TV announcer. "You talk quite a bit. I suppose that's to be expected."

"I sing, too," Tobias said. "Play the lute... I mean if you didn't break my lute—did you have to drag it? If it's not broken, I can play that too. I'm a versatile performer."

"Good to know," the creature said.

"So that's it then?" Tobias said. "I tell you my name, rattle off my resume, and I don't even get a name?"

"I am Urfang," the creature said.

"Stop talking," Tamsin, who had just been lowered down the well beside Tobias, said in a stage whisper. Tobias ignored her.

"What do you do around here, Urfang?"

"I am the Champion of Shadows," the creature said.

"Are you the man in charge around here?" Tobias said.

Urfang laughed.

"I am my master's right hand, his eyes and his claws," Urfang said. "No, I am not the man in charge. But you'll meet my master soon."

"Is he as devilishly handsome as you are?" Tobias asked.

"I suppose that depends on your taste in aesthetics," Urfang said. He motioned for his unspeaking companions to move, and the others hoisted Tobias and Tamsin up like luggage.

"So, what's the nature of our visit?" Tobias asked. "Are we here to sing for our supper? My rates really are reasonable for appearances. I would've been happy to work a gig for a discounted rate if I'd known you'd go through all this trouble."

"I swear, Tobias, if you don't shut up..." Tamsin said, her voice pinched by how the ghouls were carrying her.

They made their way deeper into the water system, the ground damp below them. The tunnels were lit by sporadic torches, an almost ridiculously civilized touch in such an eerie place.

"We don't come across many of your kind in our travels," Urfang said. "My lord has a taste for elven flesh. We bring you to him as a gift. An offering."

"Our kind?" Tobias said. Urfang touched the tip of his ear with his clawed finger. The gesture was almost delicate.

"Few elves come to this region," the ghoul said. "You taste like spring."

"We're a delicacy," Tamsin muttered. "Just once, just once, I want to meet an evil creature in this world that doesn't want to eat people."

"That's just a rumor," Tobias said. "Really elf-meat is pretty gamey. I mean look at us. Barely any meat on the bones. We're like pheasants."

"We know what elf tastes like, minstrel," Urfang said. He traced that same hooked finger along the bard's cheek, drawing blood. Urfang brought his fingertip to his mouth and licked it with a horrifically long, forked tongue. "Mm. Sunshine and fresh fruit. My master will be pleased."

"Tam? I think he just drank some of me," Tobias said.

"We are in so much trouble," Tamsin said.

Chapter 9: The hunt master

"Kids, Jack," Eriko said as they ran toward the sounds of battle. "The house has kids in it!"

Jack readied his bow as he sprinted, anime-style, through the brush. Back home, Eriko's risk-taking had been entertaining and occasionally annoying, but he was really struggling to not be angry with her right now. The risk she'd put their group in by taking off bothered him more than he wanted to admit out loud.

"What if they were monster kids?" Jack said, readying his bow. As he ran his hand across the wood, he noticed an alarmingly distinct crack that hadn't been there before Eriko smashed into him. Great, he thought. This thing's going to need to be repaired, too. I'm a ranger with no bow.

"They were regular people, Jack," Eriko said. The sounds of combat were dying down. Jack hoped that meant their friends had won and not the opposite. "We have to help them."

"Let's help our people first," Jack said as they exploded out of the brush and onto the road. Embers from a fire were slowly tapering out, and body parts, some still twitching and grasping, lay scattered around. Standing in the midst of the carnage were Morgan and Cordelia, the latter covered in blackish blood that clearly was not her own. They both instinctually raised their weapons as Jack and Eriko crashed out of the woods, but while Morgan automatically dropped his hammer to a resting position, Cordelia stormed toward them, her axe still in hand.

"What happened?" Eriko said. "Where's Tobias and—"

Eriko was cut off as Cordelia, displaying the strength of the orcish form this game gave her, grabbed the rogue by the front of her jerkin and lifted her into the air one-handed.

"This is your fault," Cordelia said. "If you hadn't run off alone, this wouldn't have happened."

Jack started toward Cordelia, but Morgan waved him off and shook his head.

"Cordelia," Jack said. The barbarian ignored him, so Jack repeated himself. "Cordelia, what happened."

"The creatures. The ghouls. They took Tamsin and Tobias," Cordelia said. "Dragged them off into the woods. Are you happy now? Did you get your curiosity fix, Eriko?"

"How long," Jack said, watching as Eriko's face turned redder and redder. Her hands clutched at Cordelia's wrist for purchase, but her legs hung limp, as if not even bothering to fight.

"Minutes ago," Morgan said. "I thought we had them on the run, but…"

Jack looked at Silence, and the wolf started back at him knowingly. The ranger pointed at the ground, and Silence began sniffing, looking for a scent. Jack scanned the ground as well.

"We'll track them. Follow them back to wherever they took them. We'll save them," Jack said. "It's not too late. They took them alive, yeah?"

"I think so," Morgan said. "There were a lot of ghouls. I didn't see them take them."

Cordelia dropped Eriko, who collapsed to the ground rather than land on her feet. Eriko coughed and wheezed, rubbing her neck.

"Let's move. Maybe we can catch them on the road," she said.

"You won't," a new voice said. The voice was deep, and spoke slowly, with an old, gravelly tone. Jack whipped around in the direction the voice came from, drawing back his bow, which cracked and snapped in half in his grip, part of the bow spinning off until it hit the end of the bowstring and clattered to the ground.

"Shit!" Jack said. He threw the bow aside and pulled out the two short swords from his belt. "Who's out there?"

The last thing any of them wanted to see walked out of the shadows. Whip-thin and unassuming in height, the being had grayish white skin, piercing red eyes, a mouth full of pointed teeth. He wore dark clothes, studded leather armor covering his torso, with a cloak of such a dark green it was nearly black over his shoulders. He had a bow in one hand, another slung on his back alongside an intricate quiver, a sword at his hip.

"You're one of them," Morgan said.

Eriko staggered to her feet, backing away. Cordelia hefted her axe and adopted a fighting pose, but held back.

"They are my kin, that's true," the being said. "But I wouldn't call myself one of them. My name is Murtok."

"I don't care what your name is," Cordelia said, but Morgan stepped forward, holding out a calming hand to her.

"What do you mean, kin," Morgan said.

"You see me," Murtok said. "I have the same curse. No doubt you've spoken to the champion, Urfang. The clever one."

"There was one who spoke," Morgan said. "We didn't get his name."

"They are my tribe," Murtok said.

"Ghouls," Cordelia said.

Murtok seemed to consider the term, turning it over in his mind.

"You're not the first to call us that," he said. "We're a bit more than textbook carrion eaters. We've been around longer."

"What do you call yourselves, then," Jack said.

"Those of us who are not... new to undeath call ourselves the gaunts," Murtok said. "Creative, I know. But ghouls are feral things, clever in their own way, but more beast than man. The gaunts are..."

"You remember who you are," Jack said.

Murtok looked at him, surprised.

"You're not wrong, ranger," Murtok said. "And some of us… are not happy with what we've become."

"But not all of you," Eriko said, still kneeling on the ground, a hand at her throat.

"Most of us are quite happy with damnation," Murtok said. "I can't say I've ever met someone like me. The kin move from place to place, eating the dead, killing the living to make more meat. A gray plague. I follow them. I do what I can. It isn't much. I think the only reason the patriarch hasn't ordered Urfang to kill me is because…"

"Because?" Morgan said, coaxing.

"The patriarch knew me in life," Murtok said. "He may enjoy this damned afterlife, but he isn't without sentiment. I think I'm the last person who remembers him before he fell."

"Why help us," Eriko said, staggering to her feet. "You have the same curse. They're your 'kin.'"

"They need to be culled," Murtok said. "I've watched my old friend build up his tribe, his little army of the dead. I won't lie to you. I'm a sentimental monster. I don't want him gone. But they wiped out an entire village."

"Not yet," Eriko said. "They've got a building full of children in there."

She shot a wretched look at Cordelia.

"Yeah. That's what my fucking curiosity got me, Cordie," Eriko said. "That building you guys wouldn't let me open is full of kids being held like veal. Happy now?"

Morgan shook his head.

"Our first priority is our friends," he said.

"Of course," Murtok said. "They'll be brought to the patriarch. Elves are… his favorite. You have time, if you move quickly."

"Great, they're hors d'oeuvres," Eriko said.

"Can you take us to them," Morgan said.

"Can we trust this guy?" Cordelia interjected.

Jack kicked his broken bow aside petulantly.

"I don't care. You'll take us to Tamsin and Tobias. Our mage and bard. The elves," he said. "That was really specific. Sorry."

"I know exactly where they're going," he said. "All I ask is you put down as many of the mindless ones as you can."

"The ones who didn't speak," Morgan asked.

"Yes. They aren't gaunts yet. Don't feel pity for them—they have no memory of who they are. They simply hunger," Murtok said. "They're locusts. The world is better without them. Put their spirits to rest."

"What about you," Cordelia asked. "Don't you want your spirit to rest?"

Murtok gave the half-orc a sad, quiet smile.

"I've been here a long time," he said. "I am very tired. But you're adventurers. I see that in you. You know a world like this cannot exist without monsters. I don't get to rest until the world doesn't need monsters anymore."

He looked at Jack for a moment, and then slipped his extra bow from his back and handed it to him. Jack hesitated before accepting, but finally took the weapon. He turned it over in his hands. Beautifully crafted, with swirls and carvings on the haft made to look like dragon skin. As he examined it, he saw that, along the center, a band of dark metal ran through it, ending at each end in a vicious bladed tip.

"This is... this is a beautiful weapon," Jack said.

"Its name is Dragon's Breath," Murtok said. "It's enchanted, imbuing the arrows you release from it with arcane energy. And it is made to be used in melee if you're caught up close. It's built to be swung like a bladed staff. You won't break it."

"I... I don't know if I can accept this," Jack said. "A named bow?"

"I sense that you lost your weapon because I didn't find you fast enough," Murtok said. "And I'm asking you to hunt the walking dead. You'll need it. And I'm very old, ranger. That's one of many magical bows I can put my hands on when I need one. I can spare it."

Jack lifted the bow and, without nocking an arrow, pulled back the bowstring. He felt it grow hot beneath his fingertips.

"Huh," he said. The gaunt nodded to him, and Jack returned the gesture.

"Unless you have any other fancy weapons to hand out, we should save our friends," Cordelia said.

Murtok nodded, lifting his hood up to cover his hairless head.

"This way, then," he said. "Follow me."

Chapter 10: Points in sleight of hand

Tamsin wasn't afraid. And that worried her.

She was a worrier back in the real world. Not easily scared, but easily worried. About everything. Worrying was her thing, so to speak. And yet here, stuck in a makeshift cell in the subterranean lair of undead cannibals, she was just sort of mildly distressed.

I really should be afraid, she thought.

But like a lot of things in this game world they were trapped in, the reality part took some time to sink in. It worked in her favor, usually—not being afraid of an ogre charging at her let her call to mind the right spell instead of dropping into the fetal position and having a meltdown, for one. But right now?

This is a worrisome situation, she thought.

Her brother was up to something on the other side of the cell. It looked like he might be butt-dancing, honestly, and it was more than a little disconcerting.

"What are you doing over there?" she finally asked, tired of watching Tobias squirm.

"Remember how I realized early on that I—that my character—could do sleight of hand tricks?" he said.

"Yeah. You kept trying to steal shit. Which was really upsetting, by the way," Tamsin said.

"Well I'm almost out of my bindings," Tobias said. "I've been working on this knot for like two hours. I nearly have it."

"Great. So, we'll still be stuck in a cage, but you won't have your hands tied behind your back," she said.

"Baby steps, Tam," Tobias said.

"And what are you going to do when you get your hands free?" she asked.

"We'll figure that out when we get there," he said. "What spells do you have handy?"

Tamsin ran down the list of spells she had memorized.

"Fireball. Lightning bolt. Arcane shield. Detect and dismiss magic. Invisibility," she said.

"When did you learn invisibility?"

"It was in that book we found, at the ogre camp. Remember how I scared you at the tavern?"

"Oh! Right. Forgot about that. You have to teach me that spell," he said.

"If we get out of this, I will," she said.

Tobias continued to worm away at his bindings, banging his head accidentally against the bars.

"Ow," he said. "So, how many people can you turn invisible at one time?"

"Just one," Tamsin said. "Why? Wait. No. No, I'm not doing that."

"Yes, you are," Tobias said. "If you see an opportunity, you go invisible and you run, sis."

"I'm not leaving you here," she said.

"Come on now, I can talk my way out of anything," he said. "I'll distract them and you go for help."

"They're going to eat you," Tamsin said.

"I think they plan on eating both of us," Tobias said, grinning at her. "I think I convince them I'm more use alive."

Tamsin started to argue, but then they both cut the conversation short as the eerie sound of claws on stone approached. Soon, two of the feral ghouls appeared, flanking

Urfang, the leader.

"Hello, little elves," Urfang said, smiling at them with a deathly grin.

"Hey," Tobias said. "Great place you have here. Is it Zagat rated?"

The creature ignored him, casting his eyes back and forth between the twins, glimmering like a cat's in the dark.

"My lord has asked for you, minstrel," he said, looking at Tobias.

"No," Tamsin said.

"All I ask is that you don't over-season me," Tobias said. "I don't want to be a bad meal as my final act in life."

"Actually, I believe my lord has other plans," Urfang said. "I told him we had an elven bard, and he asked to speak with you before he decides if you're a meal or not."

"Well, that's an interesting turn of events," Tobias said. "Am I singing to *not* become supper?"

"I have no idea, minstrel," Urfang said. "I'm just here to deliver you to him."

"Well, then," Tobias said, standing up. "I'll need my lute."

"You'll have it, if my lord says you should," Urfang said. He unlocked the cage. Tobias staged a pratfall that Tamsin knew was fake, but the ghouls didn't seem to notice. What they did notice was that his hands came flying out from behind his back as he used them to catch himself.

"Man, I thought elves could see in the dark, but that is *not* true, guys," Tobias said, grabbing onto Urfang to steady himself. The undead creature shoved him back as if repulsed by the very touch of the elf. Before Tobias could speak again, Urfang roughly grabbed him and dragged him out of the cage, slamming the door behind him.

"If you hurt him, I will burn this entire cavern to the ground," Tamsin said.

"I've been alive hundreds of years, little elf," Urfang said. "I can spot an empty threat when I hear one."

"Chin up, sis," Tobias said as he was led roughly away. "I've always wanted to perform for royalty."

And with that, the ghouls hauled Tobias down the tunnel and out of sight.

Tamsin awkwardly climbed to her feet, her own hands still tied behind her back. She leaned against the cell's bars, trying to see which direction they took her brother. And as she pressed her head against the cell door… it creaked open.

They never re-locked it, Tamsin thought. Was her brother really capable of being so annoying he made them forget to lock the cell door? Was that what that stupid fall was for?

She took another step forward, and her foot struck something hard. On the ground just outside the cage, a short dagger, the sort a fighter might keep on his belt for utility purposes, lay forgotten. Tamsin slowly crouched down, picked up the knife without looking, and started fraying the ropes that bound her wrists. It took some effort, and she nicked herself several times, but after a few minutes, her hands were free. She tucked the knife into her belt and listened for footsteps. Hearing none, she muttered the arcane incantations required for her spell.

And in the blink of an eye, she disappeared from sight.

Chapter 11: Singing for my supper

Urfang dragged Tobias by the collar through the underground tunnels, the path lit by flickering torchlight. The nameless ghouls, the feral ones flanked them like an honor guard, snorting and growling to themselves, eyes alert but without much going on behind them.

"So how does one prepare elf meat?" Tobias asked. "Do you marinate it? Smoke it? I'm a pescetarian myself, so I'm not really sure what the best way to get the most out of elven rump roast is."

"Do you ever shut up?" Urfang said.

"Silence really isn't my thing, if I'm being totally honest," Tobias said. He fired the ghoul his best smile and got no reaction.

"Gods below, I hope we eat you first," Urfang said.

"Okay, serious question," Tobias said as Urfang shoved him harder down the corridor. "Gods below. Are there gods above? Are there gods on the... here, like neither above nor below? How does that all work?"

Urfang shot him a look that was almost but not quite inquiring. The big ghoul shrugged.

"Above, below, all around us, the gods are everywhere," Urfang said. "And they're all bastards. Doesn't matter what they're the god of."

"Fair enough," Tobias said. "At least I know that praying for a divine intervention right now won't be worth it."

"Praying for divine intervention is often even more costly than simply suffering your life's consequences," a new voice said as they turned a corner into a larger chamber. Male, deeper, distinguished, it sounded more like the narrator of a BBC nature film than an undead creature. Tobias blinked a few times, eyes adjusting to the darker setting, and his vision settled on a raised dais in the center of the room, dominated by a large, stone chair. Seated there was another ghoul, but as different from the others as Urfang was from the feral ones. His skin was darker, a deep blue-gray. He wore dark robes that might have once been elegant, but had fallen into disrepair, belted with a golden cord, tarnished and overused. The being stood up languidly and walked down the steps before him to stand in front of Tobias.

"The minstrel, my lord," Urfang said. "He talks too much."

"Talking too much is what bards do, Urfang," the elegant one said. He reached out with long, clawed fingers and took Tobias' chin in his hand. "Fresh elf blood. We haven't had that in so long, Urfang."

"No, my lord," the beefy ghoul said. He'd taken a step back to give the newcomer a chance to examine Tobias in peace.

"It's unfortunate, then, that I don't plan on eating this one," he said.

"What?" Tobias and Urfang said simultaneously.

The elegant ghoul laughed.

"You are Oberon the Blue, am I correct?" he said.

"That's one of the names I go by, yes," Tobias said.

"You've made a name for yourself, storyteller," the creature said.

"I try. The signal-to-noise factor out there is brutal, y'know?"

"But not too big a name for yourself. You are, what's the word I'm looking for? An up and comer. A rising star."

"Whose career was tragically cut short when he became elf steak," Tobias said.

"No, no, if you do as I say, Oberon the Blue, you have a long life awaiting you."

"A long life, or a long… undeath?" Tobias said.

"That really depends on what you do next," the creature said. "Do you know who I am?"

"I assume you're the boss," Tobias said. "But nobody's told me your name."

The dark gray ghoul returned to his seat at the top of the dais and sat down. He looks tired, Tobias thought. Do the undead get tired? Can they? I thought that was the whole point of being undead. You just kept going.

"My name is Constian," the ghoul said. "Do you know what we are, Oberon the Blue?"

"One of my friends said you were ghouls, but I get the feeling that's not entirely true," Tobias answered. He hooked his thumbs on his belt, not sure what to do with his hands.

Constian sighed and shrugged.

"That's not entirely inaccurate," he said. "We call ourselves eaters of the dead, or sometimes gaunts, but… you know, I used to be offended by that. But the fact of the matter is the gods are always particularly creative when they choose to punish mortal men. One undead grave robber isn't much different from another, I suppose."

"But if I'm reading between the lines correctly, all things being equal, 'ghoul' is not your preferred terminology."

"Not at all," Constian said.

"Noted," Tobias said. He opened his mouth to speak, inhaled, exhaled, bit his lip, then spoke. "So why are you asking me this? I've heard of playing with your food, but talking with your food's a new one to me."

Constian smiled at him. Despite the ghoulish face, despite the sharp teeth, Tobias could see that Constian was, in life, a beautiful man, elegant features still showing through in this harsh unliving state. Something of what once was remains under there, Tobias thought.

"We've existed this way for a thousand years, bard," Constian said. "And no one knows our story. And as much as I'd like to devour you, to butcher a rising teller of stories seems a waste of a rare and valuable resource."

"Oh," Tobias said. "So... I tell your story, I live?"

"That depends on how well you listen," Constian said. "Convince me you can tell our story to the world, and I'll let you go."

"Why would you... okay, I am super curious by nature and I'm legitimately fascinated to hear your story. I'm not even trying to flatter you here. I want to know," Tobias said. "But why would you want the world to know your story?"

"Because the gods are shit, and they would hate it if the mortal world knew about it," Constian said.

"Wow," Tobias said. "Okay, not really a religious guy here, totally can get behind this plan. One last question."

Constian made a gesture for him to continue speaking, a bemused look on his face.

"Why did you take my... um," Tobias said.

"We know she's your sister," Constian said. "You talk too much. And my men did take you because we enjoy a good meal of elf. But now we know she's valuable to you."

"Great. Cool. Okay. Why are you keeping her then, though?"

"Because if you refuse my offer, we'll eat her piece by piece until you comply," Constian said. "Believe me, it's difficult to not start already, but fair's fair. We want to give you a chance before then."

"Y'know, you could have just asked," Tobias said.

"A thousand years of undeath has taught me many things," Constian said. "And one of those things is asking rarely gets what you want, but bribery often does."

Tobias chewed on his lip again, then shrugged as nonchalantly as he could, wondering if Tamsin had been able to escape yet.

"Well then," he said. "How about we start at the beginning?"

Chapter 12: It would be a mercy

Cordelia couldn't stop herself from staring at the newcomer. He was grotesque in many ways, with his corpse-like skin, the pins of red glowing in his eyes. But he spoke to them like equals, and Cordelia had spent her whole life being alternately talked down to or condescended to, so she felt like she had a pretty good sense for when either was happening. Despite being a literal monster, this Murtok character really did seem to want to help them.

Still, she kept her axe in hand. You never know when the first time your instincts failing you would happen.

Jack and Murtok walked side by side at the front of the group, Silence acting as a shadowy outrider. Morgan hiked alongside Cordelia, his armor and hammer clearly growing heavier at this forced pace. Eriko, looking almost chastised by the entire thing, hung back alone.

"So, let me get this straight," Cordelia asked. "You're willing to lead us to the home of your… family, so we can kill a bunch of them and get our friends back."

Murtok glanced over his shoulder.

"Most of these mindless ones are not literally my kin," he said. "Yes, we share the same curse, but their patriarch, Constian, has been spreading the curse irresponsibly for decades now. He used to know better. He knew that this world will ignore monsters if they seem like myths, but once they become real, once they become... commonplace, then things don't end well for either side."

"Why not kill him, then?" Cordelia asked, unable to keep the annoyance out of her voice.

Murtok stopped walking. At first Cordelia thought she'd offended him, that he might attack. She tightened her grip on her axe. But the creature bowed his head, almost in shame.

"Because he's one of the last creatures in this world who remembers me for what I was before," Murtok said. "These feral creatures... it's not that I hate them. But they have no memory of the life before. That's the thing about the curse. You need to survive in this undead state for hundreds of years before your memories come back. And then you need to survive having those memories come flooding into your mind and realize that for entire generations, you've been the monster in the graveyard, desecrating the dead. There's a reason so few of us are like myself and Constian and Urfang. The memories of your past life blurring together with the memories of your undeath is more than most can bear. They're almost all mad, even the old ones. And the old ones who go mad... they're the worst. Mad, and hungry, and powerful. Killing the feral ones... it would be a mercy."

"But not your friend," Morgan said.

"This is why I need your help," Murtok said. "Because Constian... he and I did this job together. Maintaining the right population of ghouls and gaunts. For a very long time. I don't know what changed him."

"Maybe he's gone a bit mad himself," Cordelia said.

Murtok looked at her with his cigarette-ember eyes and nodded slowly.

"I worry that perhaps you are right," he said.

"In which case, we may need to put him down as well," Cordelia said.

Murtok shrugged. It was a simple gesture, but Cordelia saw an infinite weight in him as he did it, acknowledging that yes, killing his friend may be the only way.

"What about Urfang?" Jack asked. "He didn't seem... well, he didn't seem altogether sane, but neither did he seem completely mad."

Murtok grimaced.

"Urfang isn't as old as Constian. Constian found and groomed him," Murtok said. "He's always been like that. And Constian molded him into the tool he needed. An enforcer, a bodyguard, a spokesman. And..."

"And?" Cordelia said.

"And someone to help him with me if I ever turned on them," Murtok said.

"You don't seem like someone who is easily defeated," Jack said.

"I'm not without my skills," Murtok said, resuming their journey. The others followed. "But Constian and Urfang together are more than I can handle, and clearly, a creature like me does not easily find allies."

"We wouldn't be helping you if our friends hadn't been taken," Cordelia said. "Convenient."

Murtok shook his head.

"A fortunate coincidence for me, but not one I wished for," he said.

Eriko, silent until now, chimed in.

"We need to free the people in that building," she said.

"Our friends first," Cordelia said.

"There are children in that building, Cordie," Eriko said.

"And our friends, Eriko, are about to be eaten alive," Cordelia said. "I know it's cold, but I don't really give a shit about saving anyone else until Tamsin and Tobias are safe."

"Not now," Morgan hissed. "The two of you. Stop it."

As they hiked, the town became visible in the distance, the taller buildings rising above the treetops along the trail. Murtok stopped again.

"There are tunnels they use beneath the town. They use the well in the town center to come and go," he said.

"So, we go there," Cordelia said.

"One at a time, down a well," Jack said. "Sounds like we'd be feeding ourselves to them."

Murtok pointed a clawed finger at Jack in approval.

"There's another way in. They don't know about it," he said. "The feral ones are stupid and lazy. They don't plan. And they won't be watching the other entrance because there's no immediate benefit to it."

"Tell me the other entrance isn't some sort of sewerage runoff," Morgan said.

"The opposite," Murtok said. "Follow me. No talking, now— the feral ghouls are unintelligent, but they're perceptive as dogs."

He took them along the outskirts of the town, staying out of sight in the dense wooded area that surrounded the village. Cordelia resisted the urge to curse as she stumbled and tripped her way along. Morgan was less clumsy but noisier, his armor making a racket that sounded as if it could wake the dead.

Eventually, Murtok led them down a decline in the landscape, a steep, rocky hill. Jack and Silence all but danced their way down. Cordelia tried not to hate him for it. After all, it wasn't his fault he picked the character class that could be more graceful in this game world than he ever was in the real one.

Eventually, they came to the mouth of a lightless cave. A body of water—more than a stream, less than a river, thigh-deep and fast-moving, ran into the cave.

"The water supply for the town," Jack said.

"Exactly," Murtok said. "This will lead us into the underground tunnels."

"I hate this plan," Cordelia said.

Jack put out a hand as if to reassure her. Cordelia ignored it.

"How far in do we have to walk? Does the water get any deeper?" he asked.

"Not far," Murtok said. "I used this tunnel to come and go when Constian and his minions first came to this town. It never goes deeper than waist-deep. Tread carefully and we'll be inside soon."

Jack and Silence exchanged one of their weird, wordless looks that always made Cordelia incredibly uncomfortable.

"Patrol the perimeter of the town, Silence," Jack said. "Stay safe. Only fight if they catch you. We'll be back soon."

The wolf looked at the river with an almost human expression of relief. *He doesn't want to doggy-paddle down this stream any more than I do,* Cordelia realized, suddenly having more empathy with the wolf than she'd ever had since arriving here. Silence darted off into the woods, away from the town.

"Did your dog just abandon you?" Cordelia asked.

"He'll be back. Better than trying to piggy-back a wolf down two hundred feet of waist-deep water," Jack said. "Now let's go save our friends."

"Who are hopefully not already ghoul food," Cordelia said. She put one booted foot into the water and wrinkled her nose at the temperature. She sighed. "I'll go first, I guess."

Chapter 13: A story of hunger

The problem, Tobias thought as he listened to Constian unfurl his tale, is that he should be the one to tell this, not me.

The ghoul lord had a hypnotic voice, one that rose and fell with the story. The creature knew pacing, too, and the ebb and flow of story, how to weave history with anecdote, to make poetry from fact.

I don't know if I can do this justice, Tobias thought. He told the ghoul patriarch so.

"You'll have to do your best, bard," Constian said. "No mortal men would hear it from my mouth, and you know it."

"This is the worst rendition of Cyrano ever," Tobias said.

Constian ignored him, as the beings in this game world so often did when they had no point of reference for an anachronism. He gestured at Tobias.

"Come now, minstrel. Tell me my own story. Spin my tale for me," he said.

"I'll try," Tobias said. "Just hoping I can do well enough that you won't eat me."

And he began.

* * *

The seasons of Revery are unfair.

They follow a logical course, as in any world. Spring follows winter, autumn follows summer. But the seasons are unpredictable in their ferocity. It feels at times as if the gods themselves determine the cruelty of winter or the brutality of summer on a whim, to make for a better narrative, to put the mortals they allegedly watch over through some sort of dramatic challenge.

There are Great Winters when people starve, or freeze to death, and Hellish Summers when rivers run dry and crops wither, when livestock collapse in the heat. There are Relentless Springs, when those same rivers overflow, when whole villages are swept away by massive storms. And there are Hungry Autumns, when the chill comes too soon, when the harvests do not last, when the earth itself seems determined to cull the weak.

This not every year, of course, and that is part of the challenge. No almanac predicts the next Relentless Spring. No seers can see the next Hungry Autumn. There is no calendar to predict the next Great Winter, no divination to see a Hellish Summer on the horizon.

And so, we prepare, as best we can. But that's no way to live, and no amount of preparation can ever be enough. A generation might go by between one such season. No one alive, not among the shorter-lived races, of course, remember the last starvation or flood. They are caught unprepared.

Once upon a time, in a village not unlike this one, a Great Winter came.

We thought we were prepared. But the snow piled up to shoulder height. We could not protect the livestock, and so we butchered what we could, salted and cured their bodies, and hoped it would be enough to make it through until spring, and that when spring came we could find new livestock. That was a funny bit of optimism, of course, but we did not remember the last Great Winter. We assumed we would survive and worried about how we would rebuild. Not surviving, that was never a consideration.

At least not until the meat ran out. And the grains. It was too cold for rot, but the winter seemed to never end. Rats got into the grain, and we ate them too, because we had to. We had to melt ice in our mouths for water. Grown men froze to death crossing town to check on their neighbors.

We were hungry, and we were alone, miles upon miles from the nearest village, and we knew our neighbors would have nothing to spare, as we had none for them. The distance, in a way, was a blessing—we did not have to tell strangers we had no help to offer.

When the meat was gone, when our grain stores were gone, when the rats were gone… we prayed. We prayed before then, of course, asking the gods and goddesses to watch over us, but when the food ran out, those prayers became more direct. We beseeched them. We begged. End this winter. Send aid. Anything. Help us.

And we received no answer.

Some among us did what would, in less desperate times, have been unthinkable. They prayed to the darker gods. The ones who demanded souls as currency. And we offered our souls. We offered ourselves so that our families would survive. Some of us offered our families so that we might survive, though no one really talked about that.

Unlike the gods of light, the gods of darkness answered.

They laughed.

Your answer is before you, a voice from the darkness said. Which dark god spoke is lost in time. I'm sure he walks Revery still. Evil never fades. It simply hides.

Your answer is right in front of you. You know what to do.

When this voice spoke from the shadows, those of us who supplicated ourselves to the dark gods were in a place few wanted to spend time, where our dead were stacked like cordwood, because the ground was too frozen to bury them. It was so undignified, I remember. You'd sometimes catch a familiar face in the pile, someone you'd known your entire life, a friend or an uncle or some village elder who taught you how to shoe a horse or something memorable and simple like that. It was too cold for their bodies to rot. They were, for all purposes, meat.

The answer was right in front of us.

You might judge us. You weren't there, so I cannot blame you. I look back on the choices we made, and I feel shame sometimes. But that shame fades when I remember the anger. Have you ever seen a starving child? There is no crueler sight in this world or the next. There is nothing you won't do to save a starving child. You'll give your life. You'll sell your soul.

You'll eat your dead.

And that is how our village survived the Great Winter, a thousand years ago. Those piles of corpses fed us for the rest of that endless freeze. We stayed strong. We lived. And eventually, the cold lifted. The sky turned from gray to blue. Life returned to Revery. The world's undeserved punishment was over.

But ours was just beginning.

The gods who ignored us, the good and just gods, saw what we had done. Perhaps they saw all along. Perhaps this was part of some grand plan. I believe, in my darkest moments, that we were chosen for this. Because this is a world that needs monsters, and monsters are best when they deserve their fate. You can pluck a monster out of thin air, but when they are punished for a grotesque misdeed, doesn't that make for a greater villain, a darker nightmare, a better monster?

The gods were furious. They were disgusted. And they looked upon what remained of our village and said that if we want to be eaters of the dead, then eaters of the dead we shall be, for all of eternity. And they cursed us, every man, woman, and child who survived that winter. We became mindless things, carrion eaters. We were bedtime stories to scare children. We were pests to adventurers. Undead vermin, stupid and vicious when cornered, but cowardly and blind with hunger.

We have been hungry for a thousand years.

And eventually, some of us regained our minds and our memories. Suicide became common for those who could not live with what they'd done, or could not face what they'd become. But those among us who could face what they'd done, they became shepherds of the damned. We watch over our mindless kin. And most of all, we make sure they're fed.

We tell you this story not because we seek your pity. We know what we are, now, and we know there is no way back from damnation.

But know this, mortal men and women of Revery. Never forget the cruelty of the gods. For some day, they might cast those cruel eyes upon you.

* * *

The gaunt lord stared at Tobias for a long moment after he'd finished. The bard felt a bead of sweat run down his spine. He was uncomfortably aware of the ghouls all around him, awaiting their patriarch's orders.

"If you don't like it, I could set it to music," Tobias said.

The slightest smile graced Constian's toothy mouth.

"That won't be necessary, storyteller," the ghoul lord said. "I think you heard me well."

"I have one question, if I might," Tobias said. Constian gestured for him to go on. "What was your role in all of this? Were you the mayor? An elder?"

The patriarch shook his head.

"I was the village doctor," he said. "And I did not believe in the gods. But I was in the room when that dark god spoke. And it was my surgeon's hand that made the first cut."

"Do you regret it?"

"I have made peace with my sins, storyteller," Constian said. "But I might live another thousand years and never forget the face of the man who was our first meal. The mind and heart are capable of incredible dichotomies."

"I understand," Tobias said. "What happens now?"

Before he could answer, Urfang stormed into the chamber, a

long spear in hand.

"My lord," he said. "Murtok was spotted outside of town."

Hot anger flashed across Constian's face, replaced instantly by a profound weariness. His shoulders slumped.

"I apologize, bard. You'll have to stay a bit longer," he said. "But you've sung yourself out of becoming supper. Urfang, put our guest back in his cell. Gently."

"But—" was all Tobias could get out before being dragged away from the chamber. And his shock was rapidly replaced by a growing worry about what would happen when they got back to his cell and found Tamsin gone.

Chapter 14: One at a time isn't an option

Morgan watched from an alcove in the underground tunnels as one of the ghouls sniffed the air maybe thirty feet in front of him. It didn't seem to see him, which was good, but he also hadn't realized ghouls tracked by scent. Please let these tunnels stink badly enough to cover up the smell of my armor, Morgan thought. I knew he had spells that would take care of the creature easily enough, but apparently, all his undead-destroying magic was extremely flashy, and none of them wanted to bring the whole pack of ghouls down on top of them, not in these enclosed spaces.

From just out of sight, Morgan heard a hiss and snap as Jack released an arrow. The ghoul looked up, alerted to their presence by the sound, but before it could make a move, Morgan saw Jack's arrow flare, bursting into flames, and pass through ghoul's head, leaving the now truly deceased monster's head smoking, what little hair it had left on its scalp catching fire.

"Holy shit," Cordelia said beside him. "Can I multiclass into ranger and mug Jack for his bow? I want one."

Jack emerged from the shadows, Eriko behind him, still looking sullen. Murtok crept past them all, peering into the darkness for more ghouls.

"Well that worked," Jack said.

"It's inefficient, though," Morgan said. "Sniping at them is fine for now, but it's slow going. And we're screwed if we run into a bunch of them."

"We need to get moving," Cordelia said. "For all we know they're already having Tobias for dinner."

Jack nodded to her and, together with Murtok, took the lead, guiding them deeper into the tunnels, stepping over the twitching body of the ghoul. The ranger put an arrow through the eye of another ghoul a hundred paces into the tunnel, but then the cavern opened into a larger area, and Cordelia let out a whispered string of curses so vile Murtok looked back at her with an expression somewhere between horror and admiration.

"One at a time is not an option," Morgan said, taking stock of what the larger chamber contained.

The chamber was below them, down perhaps a dozen stone stairs. It was a hub of some kind, branching off on all four sides, with multiple doors in each direction. And it was teeming with ghouls.

"How many do you…" Morgan started to say, but Cordelia cut him off.

"Fifty-seven," she said.

"Holy hell," Jack said.

"I forgot that was your superpower," Morgan said.

"Counting audience members in community theater had to come in handy someday," Cordelia said. "Not that I thought it'd come in handy like *this*."

"Assuming I make a headshot every time, I can take out maybe a dozen of them pretty quickly," Jack said. He nodded at Murtok. "I assume you're good with that thing."

"Hundreds of years of practice, so I ought to be," the ghoul said.

"So that only leaves us with thirty-something ghouls to fight when they come crashing down on us," Cordelia said. "Not a problem."

"I can try that spell I used during their first attack," Morgan said. "But honestly, I've never used it before. I have no idea if I can do it a second time, or how many I'd take out with it."

"Still, that's about half," Cordelia said. "We can take half."

"Not to be Debbie Downer here, but we can only see the fifty-seven of them in this room," Jack said. He pointed toward the different doors below them. "Who knows how many are just out of sight but within earshot."

"I'm beginning to understand why you say the ghouls need to be culled," Morgan said to Murtok.

"I don't understand why he's done this," Murtok said. "Constian used to show more restraint. This is uncalled for. It's irresponsible."

Jack fiddled with his new bow and brushed his hood back away from his eyes.

"Maybe we can go around them," Jack said.

"There were no branching paths before this aside from the deep run where the river flows through," Murtok said. "It's how we made it this far so quietly. I'm not sure if my kin don't know this tunnel leads outside, or if they find it inconvenient, but they don't use this pathway."

"What if I charge in, berserker-style, and see how many I can get to chase me?" Cordelia said.

"That's a terrible idea," Morgan said.

"I know. I'm setting the bar low," she said. "Also, I'm not hearing any better ideas."

"This is awesome," Morgan said. "Our friends are going to be eaten like veal because we can't come up with a plan."

"Hey, Eriko, anything to contribute?" Jack said, looking over his shoulder.

At nothing. Eriko was gone.

"Are you goddamned kidding me," Jack said.

"Where did she go?" Morgan said.

"I'm going to kill her. I'm literally going to kill her," Cordelia said.

Murtok held up a hand, then pointed at the stone wall. Faintly, with the edge of a blade, a few words had been scratched into the stonework.

They read: "Idea. Need 10 min. Wait."

"I'll go get her," Jack said.

"No," Morgan said. "Give her the time. She's reckless but she's smart. We know this."

"She split the party again," Cordelia said.

"We're already split," Jack said. "This is more like asunder."

"So, what do we do?" Cordelia said.

"I think we wait and see what our rogue has up her sleeve," Morgan said.

Chapter 15: Bait

The sky had truly opened up by the time Eriko made her way back out of the tunnel, dumping a heavy rain down onto the town square. Pulling her hood up over her rain-flattened mohawk, she pulled the two short, curved daggers from her belt and walked silently, but almost brazenly, up the leaf-covered slope toward the town.

It was a short trek, and without working to stay hidden, she arrived quickly, the large central building where the prisoners were being kept rising more clearly under the gray near-light of day than it had been the night before. Everything about the town was gray, she thought. Gray mud, gray buildings, a hopeless gray mood draped like an ugly blanket over the whole place.

As she strode boldly into the street, she heard the distinctive half-crazed sound of a ghoul running her way. She sensed, in her supernaturally roguish way, exactly where the threat was coming from, and danced out of the way without ever looking at the creature, lashing out with one dagger to open its throat, planting the other into the ghoul's eye. She left the body on the street twitching in the mud.

She felt no fear. She couldn't tell if it was from knowing that most of the ghouls seemed to be gathering underground, possibly to hide from the growing light of day. Perhaps it was simply not caring about her own safety, the weight of knowing Tamsin and Tobias were in danger outweighing her self-preservation instincts. In either case, her pulse never even seemed to spike. Let them come, she thought. I'm here with a plan.

She heard more ghoulish heavy breathing and trotted out of the street to stand quietly against a nearby building. She traded one dagger for a throwing knife from her belt, and as soon as one of the creatures turned the corner, spotting the bleeding corpse of its pack mate, Eriko let the knife fly, embedding it in the ghoul's brain. Another undead beast, one Eriko hadn't detected previously, tore around the corner and ran right for her. The knife pierced the creature's skull but seemed to have no effect, comically sticking out of the ghoul's forehead as it charged at her. She readied herself and, just as the ghoul reached striking distance, she sidestepped him, horse-collared him and opened his neck ear to ear.

And that is how you play a DPS class, man, she thought, recovering her throwing knives and slipping them back into her belt. Rogue for the win.

She darted to the front door of the town hall and examined the way it had been barred shut. She used her dagger to pry open the first of several wooden planks that had been nailed on either side to keep the door closed, not particularly caring how much noise she made as the wood splinted and snapped. After yanking several planks free, letting them clatter to the ground loudly, she found what she suspected might be underneath—a clunky, but effective, metal lock sealing the door.

Rogue stuff, Eriko, you got this, she thought, drawing her lock-picking tools from the pouch where she kept them. She set to work, relying on feel and the faint sounds of metal on metal as she worked the rough, inelegant lock, looking over her shoulder for roaming ghouls while she tinkered. Finally, there was a soft click and the lock came loose in her hand. She threw it into the street angrily and yanked the door open.

Inside, there was nothing but darkness. The smell of frightened humanity was palpable, though, ugly and acrid in the silence.

"Hello?" Eriko said. "Who's in here?"

An older man, a long, matted gray beard framing his face, turned the corner, his eyes haunted.

"Who are you?" he said.

"It doesn't matter. You need to get out of here," she said.

The old man eyed her suspiciously. Eriko threw up her hands.

"Do I look undead? You gotta get out of here. There isn't much time," Eriko said.

The man looked as if he might speak, but then he disappeared back around the corner he'd emerged from. When he returned, he held the hand of the small girl Eriko had seen earlier. Behind them, several more children, a young woman around Eriko's age, and an older woman, haggard but sturdy, followed. More children followed, older ones carrying or leading the younger children. They all looked tired, terrified, and hungry, pale with bruise-colored bags under their eyes.

"Go on," Eriko said. 'Get out of here."

"What about you," the young woman asked.

Eriko tried to offer her a reassuring smile, but she couldn't bring one to her face. I could use a little bit of reassurance myself, she thought.

"I'm going to get the monsters' attention so you can escape," she said.

"There's too many," the older woman said.

"I have friends," Eriko thought. Not here, but… "Just go on. I'll be fine."

The group of survivors ran out the front door and headed into the forest nearby. Eriko waited until they were all out of sight before she started looking for what she needed.

Inside the town hall, she found several half-used lanterns, each with a bit of flammable fluid sloshing around inside. She smashed these on the front steps of the hall, took a deep breath, then ripped a bit of curtain from one window and drew her tinderbox from her belt pouch.

"This is so stupid," she thought as she sparked the flame and lit the curtain on fire.

She threw the burning fabric onto the front steps where the lantern fluid waited hungrily.

The fire came to life easily.

Eriko darted around into the alley between buildings and scampered up to the landing on the second floor where she'd first seen the little girl inside the window. Cupping her hands over her mouth, she started yelling.

"I stole your lunch, you stupid zombies!" she said. "What are you going to do about it?"

Ducking low, she waited, hoping the creatures would take the bait. It didn't take long until she heard their hissing voices growing closer.

A lot of them.

I think I just got myself killed, she thought. She tried to take comfort in knowing she'd set the town folk free, but she knew, in her heart of hearts, she had too much of a sense of self-preservation for that.

I don't want to die here, she thought. Come on, guys. Get our friends and get out. I'm gonna need you.

Chapter 16: Treasure trove

Tamsin was lost.

Really lost. This was like one of those levels in a video game where you had to remember which turns to take to get out or else you kept circling back to the same rooms. When she played those games, she'd look up a tutorial online and write down the instructions, not even bothering to try to figure out the puzzle herself. She hated those levels.

And now she was living in one.

Being lost was concern number one. Concern number two was that she could not remember how long her invisibility spell would last. Or did it last as long as she chose to maintain it? If it was the former, would it simply drop without warning? If so I guarantee it'll happen while I'm was sneaking past a group of ghouls, she thought.

And the third concern was that she had abandoned her brother to the ghouls, probably to be eaten, and she had no idea if she could find her friends fast enough to mount a rescue mission.

I should go back, she thought. Yes, the smart thing to do would be to go find the others. Together we might be able to stop these creatures from turning Tobias into veal cutlets. But I'm lost, and he's alone, and…

She turned a corner and entered an alcove that was nothing like she expected.

I think I found their treasure trove, she thought.

There were bags of gold coins, opened at the top to display their contents, the sacks as big as bags of grain. Sealed crates lined one wall with no indication what they might hold. Beautiful weapons were strewn about like toys. And in one corner, stacks of books.

Books, she thought.

Without thinking, she cast a spell that would identify magical properties in objects, and immediately, a dozen items in the room began to glow. Among them was one of the books, a leather-bound tome she immediately snatched up and tucked into her satchel, the runes on the cover glimmering with golden light as she picked it up. For good measure, she added two more books to her bag as well, even though they did not react to the spell the same way. A shield, leaning against the crates, glowed as well, its face adorned with a fanged beast. Tamsin found it almost too heavy to pick up, so she set it aside. A small leather pouch lit up, which she opened to peer inside of. It contained gems and a few pieces of jewelry, but she didn't have the time to figure out what was magical or what that magic did, so she simply tucked the pouch into a hidden pocket in her cloak.

A single dagger, jammed into the wooden frame of a box, glowed brightly, straight-edged with a sculpted bird's head for the hilt. She yanked it from the box and closed her eyes, trying to sense what sort of magic it offered. She knew instinctively it was a fighter's weapon, not a wizard's magical focus, but she slipped it into her belt anyway.

A few of the larger weapons she knew she couldn't wield effectively lit up as well, but she left them. Useless for herself, and who knew if she'd find Morgan or Cordelia soon enough to use them.

And then she noticed a small leather case gleaming from within.

Anxiously, she approached it, looking over her shoulder to see if any ghouls had noticed her ransacking their trove. Still alone, she took a breath and snapped open the case.

Within was a magic wand that looked like it had been made just for her. An elegant handle, hand-carved to have an almost scale-like quality and ending in what was clearly the pointed tooth of a huge reptilian creature. The shaft of the wand coiled like a tight spiral. It gave off a fiery reddish-gold light under her spell.

"Vine. Ten and three-quarters inches. Dragon heartstring," she said. "Okay, I'm just guessing, but that's what I'm going to tell myself it's made of."

She picked it up and gave it a few swings with a twitch of her wrist. Closing her eyes again, she tried to understand the magic it contained better, and this time she had more luck than she had with the dagger. Immediately she understood what it was for.

"My friends are going to think I'm a pyromaniac if this keeps up," she said, gripping her new wand tightly. "You're a wand of fire control, aren't you my new friend? Yes, you are."

Don't cuddle the wand, Tamsin, she thought. Do not hug your wand. No one at Hogwarts ever hugged their wand.

Okay, she thought. I have a wand of "burn this place to the ground," a magic knife, I'm invisible, and my brother's in trouble. Time to go get him. Steeling herself, she started to leave the alcove and head back to where she'd come from.

Something tackled her from behind, throwing a bag over her head and sending her into darkness.

Panicked, she felt her invisibility spell begin to slip, but she fought to maintain control. She threw an elbow at whatever it was that attacked her, but she hit only cloth. Rolling over, kicking her feet, she separated herself from her attacker and prepared a lightning bolt spell, stealth or no stealth.

Floating in the air in front of her was a sky-blue cloak with no wearer.

"Are you kidding me," Tamsin said, biting her tongue as she realized she'd spoken out loud.

The cloak leaped at her again. Tamsin bolted backward, but the cape was too fast. But this time, instead of covering her head, it wrapped itself around her shoulders, coiling like a particularly well-behaved cat.

"This is not acceptable," she told the cloak, but it remained. I swear it just purred, she thought. Great, I've found a knockoff of Doctor Strange's cloak, too. "Okay, look, cape. If you're going to hang out with me, you're going to have to pull your weight, okay?"

The cloak hummed as if to signal its approval.

"We're going to go save my brother. If you don't want to come with me, that's fine, but you better decide now, because I can't have you getting in the way or backing out later."

Again, a hum of approval.

"Can you do anything interesting? Cast spells? Banish ghouls to another dimension?"

No response.

"Okay, whatever. Just… you do your thing when I need you to, okay? We have a deal?"

The cloak rippled in a way that strangely seemed like a nod.

"Well then," Tamsin said, squaring her shoulders. "Now I just need to figure out where they took my brother."

The cloak, hearing this, lifted one corner of its fabric and pointed down the hall to Tamsin's left.

"That way?"

An affirmative ripple.

"Well, cape, you've already proven your worth, then," she said. "Lead on."

Chapter 17: Hungry for five hundred years

Morgan, Cordelia, Jack, and Murtok stood in a very awkward silence, waiting for some sign of what Eriko was up to. Cordelia's body language became more and more aggressive the longer the silence went on; twice Morgan reached out and grabbed Jack by the sleeve of his armor as the ranger tried to slink off to go find their friend.

"Don't," Morgan said. Why am I always the voice of reason around here? He thought. At some point one of these chuckleheads needs to step up. Particularly these two, Morgan thought angrily. Jack could be mostly counted upon except where his hero complex kicked in, like now, and Cordelia needed to rein in whatever anger issues becoming an orc barbarian has done to her mental state. Back home, she was always a voice of reason, but she'd become less and less reliable, at least when patience was involved, the longer they were trapped in the game.

Finally, Jack broke the silence.

"How did you do it?" he asked, whispering to Murtok.

The ghoul hunter seemed to be caught off guard, cocking his head at Jack curiously.

"Do what?" he said, also keeping his voice low so the creatures down the hallway wouldn't hear.

"I know that eventually you regained your consciousness, your human memories," Jack said. "But clearly the others still... y'know."

"Ate people," Murtok offered.

"I wasn't going to say it quite so bluntly, but yeah," Jack said.

Murtok took a moment to consider the question, his grayish brow furrowing.

"I have been hungry for five hundred years," he said.

"That legitimately sucks," Cordelia blurted out.

"You haven't eaten for five hundred years?" Morgan said, trying to keep the shock out of his voice and failing.

"No, I've eaten," Murtok said. "I hunt. Deer or elk. I fish. I try to sustain myself as I did in life. And it helps a little bit. This immortal body does take some sustenance from animal flesh. I can even eat bread, fruits and vegetables, just like I did in life. And it helps somewhat, briefly. But the curse has made it so my body is never satiated unless..."

"Unless you eat humans," Jack said.

"Sentient beings," Murtok said. "We don't discriminate. Elves, dwarves, orcs, gnomes, catfolk, anything that speaks and thinks as a human would will suffice, because they are beings we never would have consumed in life. It's the cruelty the curse requires. The disgust in ourselves."

"Wait, hang on—catfolk?" Cordelia asked.

"Is now really the time to ask for a zoology lesson, Cordie?" Morgan said.

"Talking cats, Morgan," Cordelia said. "You know how I feel about cats. A talking cat is my worst nightmare."

"They're really a nice people, on the whole," Murtok said, his casual tone almost comical. "They don't get along with the ratfolk, but..."

"Ratfolk?" Morgan said, his voice cracking at the end.

"Oh, I see how it is. You get to ask zoology questions and I don't," Cordelia said.

"You know I have a thing about rats," Morgan said, feeling his hair stand on end. "Seriously, ratfolk?"

"They're... not as nice," Murtok said. "Also, not as satisfying for ghouls to eat, but they'll do."

"But you've basically managed to fight the nature of your curse for half a millennium?" Jack said, pulling the conversation back on topic.

Murtok grimaced.

"It has not been easy, my friend," he said. "I am always hungry. Which, as you can imagine, means I am always in pain. But after a while... Well, after a few hundred years, if I'm being honest... I cannot imagine eating a sentient being ever again. I don't know that I could exist with myself if I did. I've regained enough of my humanity to know the repulsion I would feel. I don't know that I could physically do it."

"So, you'll live forever. Hungry. But mentally unable to allow yourself to do the thing that would end that pain," Jack said.

Murtok nodded.

"This is some Greek myth, punishment by the gods, eternal damnation shit right here," Jack said.

"I have no idea what half of what you just said means, but eternal damnation is very accurate," Murtok said.

Morgan put a hand on the ghoul's shoulder. He was shocked by how cold the creature's skin was beneath his palm.

"I am so sorry you have to live like this," Morgan said.

"Have you ever tried to... end it?" Cordelia said.

Morgan shot her a horrified look.

"Cordie!"

"What, I'm serious. If I were hungry for five hundred years I don't know if I could do it."

Murtok waved a hand at Morgan.

"It's fine. She's not wrong. I've thought about ending myself," Murtok said. "But I feel like... in life, I was the village hunter. I kept us fed. I kept us safe."

He looked at Jack and nodded at the bow in his hand.

"I was the outrider who watched over them. And when I...

came back, when I regained my mind, I tried to do that, still. I tried to guide the pack to where we would be safer. Where we would feast on… well, no one deserves to die at a ghoul's hand, but if I could lead them to bandit camps, or to a pack of raiders, or if I could draw a tribe of ogres toward us who might destroy a village like ours, then maybe I could… if not redeem us, at least limit the harm."

"You tried to be a shepherd," Morgan said.

"A bad one, but I did my best," Murtok said. "And I can't leave this world as long as some of my kind still roam it. I am the monster who watches over the other monsters."

"Your brother's keeper," Morgan said.

"Truly," Murtok said.

The all fell silent again, Jack studying his bow, Cordelia her axe, Morgan watching Murtok's face.

"It feels like an unfair punishment," Morgan said.

"We offended the gods," Murtok said. "Perhaps we deserved some sort of punishment."

"But not this," Morgan said.

"You'd have to talk to the gods about that," Murtok said.

You listening to this? Morgan said silently, wondering if the fictional goddess who had laid claim to him here in Revery could hear him. We have a deal, you and me. If I'm stuck here, I'll be your representative, I'll do good things in your name, because I am willing to believe you're one of the good ones. But are you? Was this you?

No response. Morgan waited patiently for a moment, wondering if this were prayer or just a conversation, if Theana was really listening or not.

And then:

We are not infallible.

Morgan looked to his companions to see if they reacted, but none of them appeared to have heard.

So, you did this, Morgan said silently.

Not me. These are not my children, Theana said in Morgan's head.

But I did not speak up. I am not a vindictive god, but I deferred to the others, and I let their anger determine their decisions. I did not disagree. Not then. But perhaps… Know this, Morgan, my Bastion. I do not know the gods of your world, but here, we are not perfect. Nothing should be perfect. I believe this to be true.

Nothing should be perfect, Morgan said. But everything can be better.

Theana did not respond immediately. Morgan wondered, briefly, if she considered the conversation ended. And then:

I chose you wisely, Morgan, my Bastion. You are wiser than you know.

And with that, Morgan knew, inherently, that Theana was gone and the conversation over. Talking to gods, Morgan thought. My grandma would kill me for this. But you do what you've got to do, I guess.

Morgan caught Murtok staring at him curiously.

"Does the divine have an opinion, priest?" Murtok said.

"Not the opinion I was expecting," Morgan said.

And then Jack put a hand up.

"Do you hear that?" he said.

"It is so creepy when you do that," Cordelia said.

Jack shushed her, and Cordelia shot him a look sharper than her battle axe. Ignoring her, Jack crept forward toward the large chamber at the end of the tunnel. The others followed.

Below them, the ghouls were inexplicably worked up. Pacing, growling, they seemed to sense something was wrong. Then, all at once, they looked toward one of the doorways—thankfully not the one the adventurers stood in—and, as a unified pack, ran toward some unseen goal.

"I think Eriko's got their attention," Cordelia said.

"We have to go get her," Jack said.

"She's smarter and sneakier than all of us," Morgan said. "Trust her judgment, Jack."

"Her judgment is what got us into this mess in the first place," Cordelia said. "I don't trust her judgement at all."

Morgan closed his eyes, begging himself to remain patient.

"Tamsin and Tobias. Let's get our friends first. Then we go ghoul hunting," Morgan said. He turned to Murtok. "No offense."

"None taken," the gaunt hunter said. "Your plan is sound."

And together, they ran the opposite direction of the ghoul pack, deeper into the tunnels.

Chapter 18: Con man

The feral ghouls smell like deli meat, Tobias thought as he was dragged back to his cell. The dragging part was a little annoying. He wasn't really putting up much of a fight. No fight at all, honestly. Maybe just walking a little slowly. In fact, he'd picked up his pace when he realized why the ghoul shoving him might smell like bologna.

Do… people smell like bologna? Tobias thought.

"You know, you really don't have to shove," Tobias said. "I'm seriously doing my best to cooperate here."

"Please don't talk," Urfang said from behind.

"I mean really, where am I going to go? You have my sister," Tobias said.

"Shut up, elf," Urfang said.

"Fine, be that way," Tobias said, and he began humming.

The feral ghoul to his left glared at him, but, incapable of speech, said nothing. The one on his right barely acknowledged his existence. Tobias wondered if Tamsin had enough time to get away. Out of the cage, certainly, but who knew how far underground they were? What if she got lost? Oh, no, of course she's lost, Tobias thought. Tamsin got lost in department stores. Regularly. I did not think this through.

He glanced back at Urfang, who seemed mildly annoyed at the singing, but also resigned to the fact that at least Tobias wasn't trying to make conversation, and so the ghoul champion let it pass. Tobias found his footsteps involuntarily matching the beat of the tune like percussion.

Somewhere in the cavern, Tobias heard the distant sounds of commotion—clawed ghoul feet running, the huffing and growling of angry undead. Something's up, he thought. He said so.

"You guys having a party?" he said, suddenly concerned that whatever the commotion was, it had something to do with his sister.

Urfang raised his hand, bringing the procession to an end. He pointed at the ghoul on he left.

"Go find out what that is," he said. Wordlessly, one ghoul bolted off to investigate.

"So, how'd you end up mixed up in all this?" Tobias asked.

"What?" Urfang said.

"Were you one of the villagers? Sign on later?" Tobias said.

Urfang seemed to consider the question.

"Constian raised me from the dead," he said. "He found me. Saw something in me. Turned me into his weapon. I was good at it, so I stayed."

"Did you volunteer?" Tobias said.

"No," the ghoul said. "I was dead and buried. No one asked my permission. Everything was dark, and then…"

Urfang spread his hands out before him.

"All of this splendor," Tobias said.

"I sense some sarcasm in your tone," Urfang said. "You think I'd rather be something else. But let me tell you, minstrel. A golden kingdom does not await most of us on the other side. Life as a monster is a vast improvement to oblivion."

"I can't tell if I'm developing Stockholm Syndrome, of if you lot are starting to grow on me," Tobias said. "And you're what, Constian's enforcer?"

Urfang nodded.

"His enforcer, his outrider, his spokesman. I am what is needed. Sometimes it's his dirty work. Sometimes it's his mercy."

"Sometimes you turn other people into ghouls?" Tobias said. The creature shook his head.

"Only by accident, which happens sometimes, when we go to battle," Urfang said. "My lord chooses his pack very specifically. Those he raises may never regain consciousness, but if they do, he chooses them for what they'll remember."

"I'm almost afraid to ask," Tobias said.

"Don't be," Urfang said, smirking. "Sometimes, yes, it's a punishment—he wants them to survive in undeath as punishment for who they were in life. But other times he pities them, or he thinks they deserved more time. Or, like me..."

"They're a weapon," Tobias said.

"We've yet to find someone worthy of becoming my second, but the search continues," Urfang said. "Maybe it will be you, elf."

"I'm way too lazy for that job," Tobias said.

They reached the cell where Tobias had last seen his sister. His heart started to pound. There was no way Urfang wouldn't notice an empty cage. Now or never, bard boy, Tobias thought to himself.

"What is this," Urfang said, unlocking the cage.

With one swift motion, Tobias unleashed the spell he'd been building with his song, a burst of spellcraft woven with his voice, waiting for a target. That target, of course, was Urfang. The ghoul champion began cursing and clutching his eyes.

"I'm blind!" he roared. "What did you do?"

With a movement so fluid Tobias shocked even himself, he pulled a long knife from Urfang's belt, booted Urfang in the rump, knocking him into the cage, and then drove the knife into the skull of the remaining feral ghoul. The wordless one never made a sound as it crumpled to the ground. Urfang, however, made enough noise for both of them.

"You little bastard!" Urfang yelled, claws scrabbling against the stone floor as he tried to find some sort of reference for where he'd fallen. With a dancer's grace, Tobias darted in, grabbed the keys from Urfang's belt, leapt over the gaunt's grasping fingers, and slammed the cell door shut, locking it.

"I'm sorry, Urfang," Tobias said. "I really do kind of like you, which is why I'm doing this instead of putting a knife in your skull. I know that's small consolation and you're going to want to eat my brains later, but really, just think it over before you go on a murderous rampage. I'm just trying to get back to my friends."

"I will eat you one digit at a time, elf," Urfang said. "And I'll keep you alive as I do, so you can watch your body slowly roast over a cooking fire..."

"See, you're making me regret not killing you," Tobias said. "Is it killing if you're undead? What's the opposite of undead? Unlife? I guess you're also unliving, too. Semantics, really. I hate semantics."

"I will destroy everything you ever loved, elf," Urfang said. "Even if I have to track you by scent."

"Oh, the blindness will wear off in ten minutes," Tobias said.

"What?"

"Yeah, I didn't permanently blind you, dude," Tobias said. "I should have told you that."

"It's not permanent?" Urfang said, genuinely confused.

"No, it'll wear off soon. But no offense, I don't want to be here when it wears off. Just... y'know, think pretty thoughts for nine more minutes and you'll be fine."

"I'm still going to kill you, minstrel," Urfang said.

"Well, I figured that was how this story ended no matter what," Tobias said. "At least this way I get a running start. Anyway. Good luck!"

Tobias took off at a full sprint, fast enough he could just barely make out the vile ways Urfang cursed him as he slammed his body against the cage door.

Now, Tobias thought—where did my invisible sister go?

Chapter 19: What I was put here to do

Jack put a flaming arrow through the brains of two more ghouls and found himself developing romantic feelings for his new bow.

"Are you sure this isn't offensive to you?" Jack asked Murtok. "I'm basically on a ghoul killing spree here."

The gaunt shook his head.

"These are mercy killings," he said. "I'm more concerned at the numbers we're seeing."

"Or not seeing," Cordelia said. "I know my attitude was originally, y'know, let Eriko handle it, she has a plan, but…"

"They are all up there," Jack said. "I'm in the single digits here. Morgan, I'm going to go up to the surface and help her."

Morgan locked eyes with Jack, and for the first time in a while, the ranger noticed how tired his friend looked. The rest of us all have our distractions, Jack realized. Eriko was enjoying the adventure, Cordelia working out her rage, the twins having a diabolically good time with roles that were essentially wish fulfilment. Even Jack himself, while not settled in or happy here, had the distraction of his scouting missions alone with his wolf to clear his head. And in the center of this storm of weirdos was Morgan, involuntarily being both rock and camp counselor, just like he was on the other side of the looking glass. Morgan always took on too much responsibility, but here, Jack could finally see it wearing him down.

"No, I'll go," Morgan said.

"Morgan, you're not…" Cordelia started to say, but the cleric cut her off.

"Can any of you do what I do?" Morgan said. "You missed it on the road, Jack. I can nuke these things. This is what I was put here to do. Yeah, I'm a healer, but just like in all these games, the guy who heals also has ways of destroying things that cheat death. No offense, Murtok."

"None taken," the gaunt said.

"I'm an undead killing machine. And they're all on the surface. Hopefully that means you two can find and free the twins."

"Constian won't be so easily fooled," Murtok said. "He's probably waiting for us down here."

"In which case, we have our berserker and our magic bow-carrying archer to take him out. Hopefully backed up by a magician and a bard," Morgan said. "I'm doing this. You're not dissuading me."

"I just want it noted for the record that I'm not crazy about two of my best friends going on suicide missions in the same night," Jack said.

"Yeah, because melodramatic self-sacrifice is your job, right?" Morgan said. "Don't look at me like that. I've been your DM enough times to remember how many PCs you've thrown in front of a dragon to save the group, you Freudian head case."

"Okay," Jack said. "This is how it's going, then."

"Yes, it is," Morgan said. Morgan stuck his hand out for a shake, but Jack hugged him instead. "I hate hugs, Jack."

"I know, Morgan," Jack said. "It's why I did it. Good luck."

"You too," Morgan said. To Murtok, he said, "Which way?"

Murtok pointed down an adjoining hallway.

"Down that corridor about forty paces, turn right, then straight on until you find a rope ladder. It'll lead you up through the well in the center of town. Your boots will get a little wet," the creature said.

"Worse things have happened," Morgan said. He took a deep breath and looked at his war hammer curiously. Holding his free hand over the metal head of the weapon, his palm began to glow with a bright golden light. The light drifted down off his hand like a slow-moving liquid, engulfing the hammer, which began to glow with the same light, intense but giving off no heat.

"Consecrated weapon," Murtok said.

"Didn't know I could do this," Morgan said. "We keep learning new things every fight."

"Luck, priest," Murtok said.

Morgan nodded. Cordelia punched him in the shoulder. The cleric laughed.

"See you all soon," Morgan said.

"You better," Jack said.

They watched him walk steadily into the darkness, disappearing around the corner.

"It's really just a question of how many of us get killed, isn't it," Cordelia said.

"Hey, on the bright side, if we have a TPK, maybe we get to start a new campaign," Jack said.

Chapter 20: I am a ninja

For roughly three minutes, Eriko thought she had the situation entirely under control.

The ghouls started appearing slowly at first, bubbling up from underground, creeping in from the forest edge. They knew something was up with the burning building, and entered one at a time. Eriko let them stalk around in the smoky darkness for a moment, and then would catch them unawares, jamming a dagger into an eye socket or through their spine. She killed—is that the right word? Maybe it's 'put down,' she thought—three or four easily before they ever knew she was there.

It was fun. I'm somewhere between *Assassins Creed* and Kevin in *Home Alone* right now, Eriko thought.

Two more entered the building, which she lured into a dark pantry area and dispatched deftly. Another three, and she was able to jump out of the shadows and dance among them until their heads were mostly separated from their bodies. It all felt so natural, so easy, that Eriko wondered if the class she'd taken on here in the game wasn't a rogue so much as an actual assassin.

"I am a ninja," she said, plunking a throwing knife into the throat of yet another ghoul.

The bodies were piling up on first floor, though, so she darted up to the second to lay in wait for them. They were more alert now, seeing the bodies of their compatriots, but they also didn't seem particularly bright, or at least not very interested in self-preservation, she thought.

She stole a second to glance out the window her stomach turned to acid. The streets were filled with ghouls, all that same drab grayish white, all with the same emaciated bodies and catlike ears, the bared yellow teeth and red eyes, looking for her.

"I messed up real bad," Eriko said. "This was a stupid plan. I'm not a ninja. What was I thinking?"

She heard more of the ghouls creeping ungracefully up the stairs. She caught one in the neck from behind, separating its spinal column, and another she almost brained, but the third proved too quick, blocking Eriko's vicious strike aimed at its eye, knocking her to the floor. She kicked it with both feet and the undead creature fell backwards and all the way down the entire flight of stairs, but she could already hear it scrambling to its feet.

The building was rapidly filling with smoke and flames. And ghouls, Eriko hoped. Come on in and burn, she thought. I'll just bail.

She yanked on the window pane, intending to crawl out onto the awning just outside the window.

The pane stuck.

She yanked again, putting her full, if not particularly significant, weight into it. Nope. Window was stuck. Totally stuck. She heard more ghoul claws exploring the house below and darted to the next window, which opened on the first try.

Okay, get them in the house, bar them inside, let them burn to death, or undeath, or whatever, and game over, I win, level up, get those sweet, sweet experience points…

Out in the street, there were simply too many ghouls to count.

This is exactly not the way I wanted to die, Eriko thought. A whole fictional world full of ways I could get myself killed and I end up on the roof of a burning building surrounded by dozens of flesh-eating undead. This sucks.

Matthew Phillion

And then she saw an impossible flash of light.

Striding down the street, swinging his glowing hammer with a grim, professional efficiency, Morgan easily put down ghoul after ghoul with ease. His hammer seemed to burn the undead energy out of them, leaving the bodies inert on the cobblestones. He was surrounded, though, as the creatures turned on him, the burning building no longer the focus of their attention. He's going to be swarmed, Eriko thought. Seeing the ghouls begin to turn their attention away from the house, she dropped down to the street below, letting out an undignified grunt as she landed, not on her feet, but in a sloppy barrel role, thumping her head off the stones as she tried to regain her balance. Popping back onto her feet, she slammed the door of the building shut, trapping whatever ghouls remained inside with the fire. Drawing both daggers, she prepared to run to Morgan's side, knowing the only reason he was here was to save her.

Why is he alone? She thought. Did things go that badly underground? What happened?

The ghouls overwhelmed Morgan, paying the rogue behind them no mind. Seeing her friend about to fall, Eriko leapt into action, stabbing two ghouls in the back simultaneously, which unfortunately then drew the attention of a half dozen more, who began to encroach upon her space slowly, like hunting predators.

I can't get to Morgan in time, she thought. I got my friend killed trying to help me. This is my fault.

She only had seconds for the guilt to sink in before she found herself surrounded as well, lashing out defensively as the ghouls reached for her. But her daggers weren't the right weapons for this kind of work, and she could find no cover, nowhere to run or hide...

One of the ghouls fell to the ground, smashing its face against the street, and then was yanked backward viciously. There as a growl, a roar, and the snapping of bone, and then a dark, furry shadow pounced on another ghoul.

Silence, Eriko thought. That stupid wolf is actually good for

272

something. This is unbelievable. She watched as Jack's oversized wolf companion tore another ghoul apart. The others began to focus their ire on him, but that just opened them up to Eriko's blades while they were distracted.

She took a split second to look for Morgan, and for a moment she thought he was gone, unable to see him in the crowd of undead.

And then a bomb of radiant light went off in the middle of the street.

Emanating from where she'd lost sight of the cleric, a glowing orb of gold and white appeared, like a bubble. It grew, and grew, expanding, but wavering, unstable and impermanent. Eriko shielded her eyes against the brightness, not unlike looking at the sun, and then a massive sound—not a boom, not a detonation, something else, like a voice crying out in the night—reverberated throughout the town center. Windows shattered. Glass fell from the sky.

And when the light faded, Morgan stood in the center of the street, surrounded by dozens of destroyed ghouls, covered in gore, his hammer still glowing bright.

The ghouls still standing began to scatter. Eriko destroyed one with another throwing knife; Silence took one down like he would a wounded deer. But the others ran in too many directions, too quickly to catch.

Eriko limped toward Morgan, only now realizing she'd turned her ankle jumping off the roof. Behind her, a desperate ghoul climbed out of the burning building, dropping like a piece of cooked meat on to the street from a second-story window. Silence casually ripped the ghoul's throat out and padded over to Eriko's side.

Morgan looked at her with eyes that no longer had pupils. They glowed with that same golden light his spells gave off. Eriko pretended not to notice as she saw the light begin to fade, his normal dark irises returning.

"Hey," she said.

"Can you please stop running off?" Morgan said. "I'd really like to make sure we all get home together."

"I'll try," Eriko said. "Where's everyone else?"

Morgan glanced at the well a few hundred feet back.

"Down there," he said.

"Then I guess we're headed down there too," Eriko said.

Together, they looked at Silence. The wolf stared back up at them expectantly.

"I don't know how we're getting a wolf down a well," Morgan said.

"I was really hoping you had an idea, because I don't," Eriko said.

"We'll figure something out."

Chapter 21: I come bearing gifts

"For the record," Cordelia said. "We didn't just split the party tonight, Jack. We divided it up into little pieces and put them all in different boxes and mailed those boxes in three different directions."

"Possibly four," Jack said. Cordelia considered punching him. Jack flinched like he read her mind and her intentions. "Sorry."

"What I want to know is," Cordelia said as they turned yet another corner in this ridiculous labyrinth. "Did the town build these tunnels, or were they always here?"

"I believe they are an ancient ruin," Murtok said. He and Jack both held their bows at the ready in a way so similar it made Cordelia's anxiety spike, as if watching this undead being was somehow a preview of a terrible future for her friend. "The townsfolk themselves never even seemed aware that it was here. And the glyphs and wards on the walls are not human."

Jack and Cordelia both stopped walking simultaneously, and, also simultaneously, blurted out: "Not human?"

Murtok seemed genuinely taken aback by the reaction.

"You're a half-orc," he said, his tone legitimately confused. "You know 'not human' is a relatively common feature in these parts, yes?"

"Sorry, where we come from it's…" Cordelia said, gesturing back and forth between herself and Jack.

"We're a little more homogeneous back home," Jack said.

Murtok shook his head as if he couldn't grasp what they were saying, but didn't particularly care to, which was the default reaction they always received when they talked about their lives before the game here.

"Old dark elven script," he said. "The dark elves weren't uncommon in these parts hundreds of years ago, though they've since migrated. The tunnels were abandoned. Perfect for a ghoul nest."

"Right. Exactly. Put out a few throw pillows, maybe some window treatments, and it's a perfect fixer-upper," Cordelia said.

"You grow stranger the longer we talk, warrior," Murtok said. "Perhaps we should focus on finding your friend."

"Perhaps we should," Cordelia said, giving Jack the side eye.

"Which friend are you looking for?" a familiar voice said.

"Tobias, you idiot, don't tell me you rescued yourself before we could rescue you," Cordelia said, her voice an awkward combination of relieved and legitimately angry.

"Ta-da!" Tobias said, striding out of the shadows, brushing his pale blue hair from his face. "Oh, shit. You're a ghoul!"

Murtok shrugged.

"You're an elf," he said.

"I'm a tasty treat," Tobias said. "I take it this one's on our side?"

"This is Murtok," Jack said. "We're helping him cut down on the ghoul population in exchange for finding you—Toby, where's your sister?"

"I was really hoping you knew," the bard said. "I helped her escape first, and I'm pretty sure she's walking around here with her invisibility spell up so we're never going to find her and that's really distressing. Also, I figure yelling her name in an echo-prone hall filled with the undead is a bad idea."

"Most of the undead are aboveground, trying to kill Eriko,"

Cordelia said.

"What?" Tobias said. "Where's Morgan?"

"Trying to save Eriko," Cordelia said.

"Could we split the party any worse?" Tobias said. "First rule of these stupid games! Don't split the party!"

"You're the one who got captured," Cordelia said. "You sort of started it."

"No, Eriko started it, and can we please find my sister and go save Eriko and Morgan? Because we love them, but also games like this are horrible if you don't have a rogue or a cleric in your party, so I'd rather not replace either of them if we can avoid it."

"Wait, hang on, so Tamsin is just walking around down here invisible?" Jack said.

"Unless she found her way out," Tobias said.

"I have never met anyone with a worse sense of direction than Tamsin," Cordelia said. "Remember that time she got lost in my grandmother's house? She's still down here."

"I wasn't going to say that out loud, but that was my main concern," Tobias said. "So, if we could—"

Before Tobias could finish, Cordelia caught a flash of metal out of the corner of her eye. She turned to see the larger ghoul, Urfang, taking aim at Tobias with a long polearm, wide and vicious enough that he could cut the bard in half if the blade connected. Cordelia tried to leap into action, but she was too far away. She knew she'd never make it. Visions of two halves of Tobias falling to the floor bubbled up into her mind's eye like a nightmare.

And then a pale blue cape wrapped itself around Tobias' head and slammed him to the floor.

The polearm passed over Tobias' body easily, whistling through the air with a sharp squeal. It crashed into the wall behind him, sending sparks and stone flying.

"I see you," Urfang said, once again raising his weapon for a killing blow.

This time Cordelia was ready for him, though—she caught the blade with her own, sparks flying again, metal on metal screeching and reverberating through the tunnels. She kicked the massive ghoul in the gut, staggering him back. He growled, swinging his huge weapon as if it weighed nothing. He attacked again, and Cordelia barely ducked out of the way. He's fast, she realized, superhumanly fast, and I don't know if I can take him. She waited for the whistle of one of Jack's or even Murtok's arrows, but she noticed that the ghoul champion had deliberately maneuvered himself to put Cordelia's back between himself and the archers— maybe they'd miss her, both being marksmen, but she knew Jack wouldn't risk hitting her with that magic bow and its catastrophic damage. I'm on my own, she thought.

The air in the tunnel grew intensely hot and Urfang went flying into the stone wall behind him. Cordelia fell backward to get away from the heat, shielding her eyes, but the furious explosion had one very specific target.

"Stop trying to kill my friends, jackass," Tamsin said, holding a wand out in front of her like a fencing sword.

Where the hell did she get a wand? Cordelia thought. But before she could ask, Tamsin flicked her wrist, and the air flashed hot again. Urfang was flung down the hallway, afire and smelling of burning flesh, bouncing along the stone floor like an unwanted package.

"Please tell me one of you knows how to get out of here," Tamsin said.

Tobias popped up into a sitting position, his face still obscured by the cloak, which seemed to have a life and a will all its own. It crawled around his shoulders like a particularly attentive housecat before settling onto his frame perfectly.

"Great. I find a magic cape and it likes you better," Tamsin said. "I come bearing gifts, by the way."

Wordlessly, Jack walked right up to Tamsin, slung his bow onto his shoulder, and threw his arms around her. Cordelia almost laughed as Tamsin went from mortified to concerned and then to realizing what was happening, planting a kiss on Jack's lips in return.

"Do we have to do this now?" Tobias said, still sitting on the floor. He tried to stand up, but before he could fully right himself, Cordelia watched as Tobias was slammed back onto the ground by an invisible force.

"We had a deal, bard," a new voice said. Cordelia gripped her axe and watched as another ghoul stepped out of the darkness, this one clear-eyed, like Murtok, rather than feral and out of control like the others. He had a regal way of walking and speaking, immediately authoritative, and he instantly reminded Cordelia of several people she couldn't stand back in the real world.

"And technically, I think we still do," Tobias said. "You know, I really was looking forward to telling the world your story, but the whole threatening my sister thing never really sat well with me. You could've just asked, y'know?"

The gaunt patriarch cast a quick spell, gesturing violently at Tobias with his hand. A wave of blue-black energy struck the bard, but turned to pale sparkles of light as it touched the cloak on his shoulders.

"Ha-ha! Magic cape! I have a magic cape!" Tobias said. "My sister gives the best presents."

"Technically that's a loaner," Tamsin said. "I want that back."

"Try me," Tobias said.

The ghoul lord hissed at both of them, then turned his ire on Murtok.

"You," he said. "You never leave well enough alone. I don't know why you haven't just killed yourself already with your insufferable guilt."

Murtok folded his arms and stared at his fellow ghoul calmly, almost passively.

"I don't get to leave until you do, Constian," he said.

"And are you here to kill me?" Constian said. "Traitor. I can hear my children dying up above. This is all your fault."

"They're not your children, they're your monsters," Murtok said. "You know you let it go too far. You know I only intervene when you let it get out of hand."

"This world deserves out of hand," Constian said. "You know as well as I do we have little time left. And this is how you spend it? Betraying your brother?"

"Time and time again, Constian, I've asked you not to do this. And time and time again, you fill the world with the damned," Murtok said. "I am so very tired."

"Then perhaps you need a hobby," Constian said. "A companion. A plaything of your own. Something to occupy your petty attention so you leave me to my work. Which one of these would you like to nanny for half a millennium until they regain their humanity?"

Constian pointed at each member of the group in turn.

"Perhaps a pet wizard who can't remember her spells. Or an orc barbarian stronger than you'll ever be. I'll even turn the bard, despite what I wanted of him. We remember everything when we come back. Perhaps a few centuries of raiding open graves for corpse meat will add gravitas to his song when he sings of us," Constian said.

"Seriously, big guy, I'm happy to start writing that song now," Tobias said. "There's no need to threaten. I'm practically already on your payroll."

Constian ignored him, continuing to lock eyes with Murtok.

"Oh, I know," Constian said. "I'll turn the ranger and give him our curse. Watch you spend the next five hundred years staring at a creature just like you, so you can be reminded of all the terrible things you did yourself before you regained your sense of shame."

Constian raised one clawed hand and began uttering an incantation. Before he could finish, a flash of firelight filled the hallway, and Constian cried out in pain. He clutched his wrist, staring at the palm of his hand, where one of Jack's arrows, still aflame from the enchanted bow, went straight through the palm, bursting out the back of Constian's hand.

"Monologuing?" Jack said. "Man, you guys were so much cooler before, and you've sunk to monologuing? That's so boring."

Constian began preparing another spell, but Jack interrupted him with a second arrow, this time through the opposing shoulder. The ghoul lord looked from Jack to Murtok.

"You gave him… that bow," Constian said. He smiled bitterly. "You really have betrayed us. Just finish it off, brother. I'm tired of this endless game."

"I can't, and I won't," Murtok said.

"I will if you give the word," Jack said.

"I think you should without the word," Cordelia chimed in.

Murtok held a hand up as if to ask them to wait.

"I blame you for many things, Constian, but I do not blame you for what we are," Murtok said.

The ghoul lord spat at him, then took a lurching step back.

"Coward," he said. He glanced around at the adventurers sourly. "You know I'll just make more, Murtok."

"I know," the undead ranger said.

Without another word, the lord's form became amorphous, fading into a black smoke. Seconds later, he was gone.

"I feel like that was a private conversation we weren't supposed to hear," Jack said.

Murtok shook his head.

"It's not the first time we've had it, it won't be the last, and you aren't the first to witness it," Murtok said.

"Not to ruin a dramatic moment, but we should go save our friends, guys," Cordelia said.

"Morgan and Eriko," Jack said, glancing to Murtok.

"We are terrible friends," Tobias said.

Chapter 22: I wish you well

Every part of Morgan's body hurt. His armor had taken the brunt of the scratches and blows from the ghouls, but the muscle beneath the chainmail had still taken a beating, and he felt it to his bones. A small trickle of blood ran down from his hairline, curving around his brow. His ears rang with a high-pitched whine.

Wiping the blood from his face, he set his hammer down, the weight of the weapon feeling exponentially greater. His shoulders burned from swinging it.

All around him, the bodies of ghouls lay motionless. The spell had done its job. He felt a twinge of guilt—they were monsters, yes, but they were people, once—and he tried desperately to fight off that sensation by silently repeating Murtok's words. It was a mercy killing. They were rabid, and even if they did regain sentience, they'd likely be driven mad by what they'd become. I sent them to whatever afterlife they were waiting for instead of this nightmare, Morgan thought. He needed to believe that.

"You okay, Morgan?" Eriko asked. She looked at him with an expression of concern, but with her soot-stained face, her mohawk flattened on one side and sticking straight out of the other, she looked as bad as he felt, if not worse. But where Morgan felt bone-tired Eriko looked almost manic, her eyes wide and wild, the terror of the battle still sending a river of adrenaline running through her veins.

"Just tired," he said, scratching Silence behind the ears. He gestured for Eriko to follow, and together, the trio approached the well in the center of town. "Let's figure out how we're going to..."

He looked over the edge and saw Jack staring up at him from the bottom. Caught off-guard, Morgan let lose a string of curses that were almost identically echoed by his friend at the bottom of the well.

"Holy shit, how long have you been standing there?" Morgan said.

"I almost shot you!" Jack said. "Don't ever do that again!"

"You're the one lurking at the bottom of a well!"

"I'm not lurking! I just got here! Lurking involves milling around!"

Morgan leaned exhaustedly on the edge of the well, scratching his head.

"I hope this means you have everyone with you," Morgan said.

"Yeah, I—" Jack began to say before being cut off by Tobias.

"Well, how do you do?" Tobias said. "You look well, Morgan! Well, really, you don't look so well. You look like you could use some well-wishing. I wish you well, you swell well-dweller."

"We should have let the ghouls eat him," Eriko said.

"Come on up," Morgan said, too tired to be annoyed with Tobias. "We killed most of 'em. The rest ran off."

The marching order up and out the well was a bit of an ordeal. Cordelia scaled the well first, less with skill than with brute strength. Morgan couldn't help laughing as he saw Cordelia get impatient watching Tamsin's sad attempt at climbing. The barbarian reached down to yank Tamsin's rope, hauling the wizard up the rest of the way. Cordelia picked Tamsin up like a kitten by the back of her robes and deposit her unceremoniously on her feet.

Tobias got much the same treatment, though Cordelia let the bard struggle a bit longer. Tobias was clearly looking for a way to ask for help without actually asking for help. Morgan tried to hide his surprise as Murtok followed next, the ghoul looking even more haunted and mournful than before. Jack emerged last, his fancy new bow slung over his shoulder. The ranger dropped to one knee and let Silence bump his head in greeting.

"How long were we down there? A few days?" Tobias said.

"Couple hours, give or take," Cordelia said. She turned her face toward the sun as it tried to burn through the morning mist, turning the sky into a creamy yellow haze.

"I don't like dungeon crawling," Tamsin said. "Just, y'know, for the record. This isn't going to be our entire career, right? Sometimes we can adventure above ground, I hope?"

"What you got there, kid?" Eriko said.

Tamsin followed Eriko's gaze to the wand at her belt.

"Oh. I found some stuff," Tamsin said. She pulled an ornate dagger from the back of her belt and handed it to Eriko. "This might be an improvement for you."

Eriko turned the blade over in her hand, flipped it, testing its weight.

"Might be," she said. "Thank you."

"Oh, unless... unless it's really yours?" Tamsin said to Murtok.

The gaunt waved his hand.

"Anything you found down there Constian or Urfang took from a dead body," he said. "Keep what you found. You need it."

"In that case, give me back my magic cloak, Tobias," Tamsin said.

The bard dramatically threw the sky-blue cloak he now wore over one shoulder.

"I can't. The cloak chose me."

"I found it. I saved it! It should be my cloak."

"This cloak clearly has a mind of its own, and it prefers me," Tobias said. The cloak rippled as if to agree with him.

"This is the Muffin incident all over again," Tamsin said.

"I'm almost afraid to ask," Cordelia said.

"Our family Shih Tzu, Muffin," Tamsin said. "She was supposed to be my dog, but nope, fell in love with Tobias at first sight, ignored me for fifteen years."

"I am friend to both man and beast, and now also sentient apparel," Tobias said. "It's not my fault I am charismatic as hell."

"I can't believe we worked this hard to save you," Tamsin said.

"What did they want you for, anyway?" Jack said.

"They wanted someone to tell the story of the ghouls," Tobias said. He turned to Murtok. "Which is a horrible origin story by the way. I'm sorry for, well, for everything."

Murtok gave the bard a half-hearted smile.

"Fate, chance, choices… none of it matters in the end, storyteller," Murtok said.

"Would Constian have lied to me?" Tobias said.

Murtok shook his head.

"If there's one thing Constian has always been, it's honest about where we come from," he said. "If he told you our story, he would have told you true. The bad, the ugly, the unfair, and everything in between."

"He called you brother," Jack said. "Was he being literal, or…?"

Murtok nodded grimly.

"We are brothers, both in our curse, and in our blood," Murtok said. "And that is why I can't end him. I'll fight him until this world has its final nightfall, and hope someday he finds redemption or peace. But I can't destroy him. He's the only being who remembers who I was before all this, and I him."

"Where will you go from here?" Morgan asked.

"He'll rebuild," Murtok said. "I'll follow. Do what I can to inhibit that. Fortunately, I think he feels the same about me as I feel about him. He hates me, but he knows I'm the only one left who remembers him. He wants me to let him enjoy his delusions of grandeur, but he won't kill me."

"Family," Cordelia said.

"You could travel with us for a while," Jack said. "I… don't take this the wrong way, but you seem lonely."

The gaunt hunter let out a barking laugh. It was so sharp it made Morgan's hair stand on end.

"I'm sorry," Murtok said. "My friends, I am lonely in ways that defies description. That is my own curse, and one I've long learned to live with. But thank you for your offer. Even one night with adventurers by my side has been a balm to my loneliness."

Jack held out a hand, and the undead ranger took it. They shook. Morgan watched curiously. It wasn't like Jack to connect with strangers this way, but then again, even in the real world, Jack had a tendency toward profound loneliness. Maybe he saw something of himself in the creature. Morgan caught the others staring curiously as well, Tamsin with a look of concern, Eriko curiosity, Cordelia distrust.

"I should go. The sun... is hard on my kind," Murtok said.

"Good luck," Morgan said. The ghoul nodded to him, then disappeared back down the well.

"So, nobody died," Cordelia said. "Good on us."

"Where do we go from here?" Tamsin said.

Eriko raised her hand.

"I set a bunch of villagers free," she said. "I think we owe it to them to make sure they're okay."

"Are we lawful good?" Cordelia said. "I wouldn't have pegged us for lawful good."

"Is there a 'meh good' category in this game?" Tobias said.

"If not, we'll make one up," Morgan said. "Which way did your new friends go, Eriko?"

Chapter 23: What is dead cannot die

Urfang groaned in the darkness.

His skin cracked and split as he pushed himself to his feet, much of his body blackened with burns. The pain was indescribable, even in this undead body so impervious to pain and damage. His skin had cooked beneath the wizard's spell, and every movement was agony.

He roared with rage as he bumped into a stone wall, the nerves on his entire right side flaring up with the impact.

He breathed deeply, cleared his vision, and staggered on.

This was not the first time some hero had tried to destroy Urfang. He'd survived worse than a fireball before. And he knew how to fix it.

Walking was difficult, as his eyes had been damaged by the flames—blinded twice in one day, he thought resentfully. He found the nearest ghoul corpse, dropped carefully to his knees, and began to devour the flesh of his kin.

Eat, the black heart in the center of his being commanded him. Eat, and all will be restored.

He gorged himself on his dead companion and crawled on, seeking another. It would not end here. He would need to consume a dozen or more bodies over weeks, or months, but this was the nature of his curse—to eat was to live forever.

Yes, he's survived worse. And this time, he had a target for his rage.

I will kill that bard and his sister if it's the last thing I do in this world, Urfang thought. I will set them on fire and roast them alive while they scream, and then I will tear them limb from limb. I will…

Urfang's vision swam as his undead body struggled to stay conscious. He could already feel his damaged muscles and skin beginning to knit back together. Slowly, methodically, he dragged himself down the stone corridor in search of another corpse.

The bard will have the worst death, Urfang thought. I may even bring him back again just to kill him a second time. No one does this to me without feeling my wrath.

I'm coming for you, little elves. Scream for me.

Chapter 24: The good part about being a hero

It didn't take long to find the survivors. Two old people, a young woman, and a dozen children weren't going to get far on their own but they did manage to flee almost a mile before giving up. Jack had no trouble following the trail of damaged foliage and broken branches they left behind. The group sat around a clearing not far outside of town, the older children wrangling the younger, the old man acting as a sort of desperate conductor to keep them from wandering off. The old woman held a toddler in her arms who could not stop crying. The inconsolable sobs gave their position away long before the tracks did. The younger woman held a sleeping infant, who looked far too peaceful for what they had been through, Eriko thought to herself.

The adventurers stepped out of the forest just a little too quietly, startling the villagers, who began to panic and run before realizing the group was not a pack of ghouls.

"You survived," the old man said. His eyes were shadowed and haunted. Eriko wondered what the man had experienced, being left for last among his peers.

"And the ghouls are dead. Mostly," Eriko said.

"We drove them off," Morgan said. "But I know that's no real consolation for what you've lost."

The old man put a hand on Morgan's shoulder, the cleric nearly a full head taller than him.

"You did what you could," he said. "You could have kept going, but you fought for us. You're the reason any of these children are alive. I'm Grahom, for what it's worth. This is my wife, Mila. And…"

He trailed off looking at the young woman.

"It's okay, Grahom," she said. "He hesitates because we were just neighbors before all this happened. We're not family. Not any more than those who share the same village are. I'm Jin. The children… well, they belonged to everyone and to no one now. They're all orphans."

"Why did they spare you?" Tamsin asked. Jack held out his hands and Jin, smiling, handed him the sleeping infant. Jack placed the baby's head on his shoulder and swayed automatically.

"I don't know that spared is the right word," Jin said.

"They were saving the children for last," Mila said. "We're no strangers to the stories of ghouls in this country. We never saw them in person ourselves, but the tales are not unheard of. They save the young for last, and as merciless as it sounds, I think they just kept the few of us as caretakers until they didn't need us anymore."

"It would make sense," Cordelia said. "How long did they have you in that building?"

"Maybe a week," Grahom said. "They began picking off our people a month ago. A farmer here, a trader there. A young couple who snuck off in the night. And then one evening, as the sun set, they came boiling up out of the town well like a nightmare."

He looked over his shoulder to see if any of the children were listening, but most seemed to be studiously looking away.

"I don't know what we're going to do with them all," Grahom said.

"There's not enough of you to go back to the village, is there," Tamsin said.

Grahom gestured to himself, his shaking limbs and tattered

body.

"Maybe others would come and rebuild with us, but alone… at best we'll starve. At worst, bandits come through and finish what the monsters started."

"My kin would take us in," Mila said. She smirked as Cordelia took the infant from Jack and, with a gentleness her size and strength made seem impossible, rocked the child in her arms. "I was born in a town not far from here. A day or two by horse if the ghouls haven't killed all of ours. A bit longer by foot since we'll need the little ones to walk."

"I saw horse tracks," Jack said. "Give me a little time, I'll find the ones who got away. I know there were still functional carts or wagons I saw in town."

"We'll get you there," Eriko said. Morgan raised an eyebrow at her, which she actively ignored. "You're sure they'll take you in?"

"My husband may find some of my cousins annoying, but if we show up with a story of monsters and a wagon full of orphans, they will open their doors to us," Mila said. "The whole town will. I wouldn't want to try to make the journey on our own with all of these little ones, but if you'll help…"

"We'll help," Eriko said. "No question. You can count on us."

Morgan put a hand on Eriko's shoulder and kissed the top of her head affectionately. She shrugged him off.

"I'm proud of you, party-splitter," Morgan said.

"Cut it out, dude. You're embarrassing me," she said.

Morgan laughed that melodious, infectious laugh of his and walked away.

"Jack, why don't you try to find those horses," he said.

Jack tilted his chin at Cordelia.

"Want to lend a hand?"

"I love horses," Cordelia said, handing the baby to Tobias, who looked the infant like Cordelia had just placed chewed bubblegum in his hands before handing the baby immediately to his sister.

"We'll be back," Jack said as he, Cordelia, and Silence wandered off into the forest and quickly disappeared out of sight.

"Why don't we get you back to the town," Morgan said. "See if we can't find one of those wagons our ranger saw."

Grahom nodded.

"It may be traumatic for the children to see…"

"They've seen worse," Mila said. "And if the town is littered with dead monsters, then they'll see that there's nothing left to fear. Because while monsters are real, so are heroes."

The old woman beamed a radiant smile at Morgan, who returned the favor.

As Grahom and Mila began gathering up the children, assigning older ones to watch over younger ones, Jin pulled Eriko aside.

"I know you're the one who came back for us," she said. "I remember seeing you in the window. I thought maybe you'd be scared off and not return, but…"

"I, um… I just went to get more help," Eriko said. "Y'know. My friends. I couldn't do it alone."

"Well, I just wanted to thank you. I don't think we had much time left before… the end. You saved us just in time."

Eriko felt her face flushing. She tried to imitate Morgan's casually heroic smile, but could only muster an awkward smirk.

"Hey, it's… Y'know, what heroes do, right?" Eriko said

Jin squeezed Eriko's hand.

"None of us will ever forget you," she said, and then, almost laughing: "I like your hair."

Jin turned quickly and walked away, scooping up a stray little boy who wasn't obeying the older child assigned to him. Eriko ran her hands through her hair nervously, then saw Tobias staring at her.

"Shut up, Toby," Eriko said.

Tobias' smirk grew wider.

"I will cut your hair in your sleep if you say anything at all about this," Eriko said.

Tobias bit his tongue at her, shrugged, then fixed his new cloak and walked off. Eriko caught him singing a cutesy pop song as he strolled away.

"Jackass," Eriko said. She looked down at her hand, remembering Jin's touch. We've been here so long I was starting to forget what that felt like, she thought.

She smiled quietly to herself, and, her heart a little lighter than it was before, trotted off to help guide the orphans to safety.

Chapter 25: Dragon country

Jack and Cordelia scared up a few unhappy but uninjured horses roaming the countryside outside of town, including several draft horses who would be perfect for pulling a wagon full of kids. The hodgepodge of horses were as weird and inconsistent as the party itself, but that almost seemed like part of the charm, Jack thought.

The survivors packed up a few things, making very brief forays into the town while guarded by different members of the party just in case any lingering ghouls made an appearance, but trouble never reared its ugly head. Jin raided a few homes for toys and clothes for the children, while Mila knew where dry goods and other food were stored, and Grahom led them to a few storefronts where they could find tools or trade goods so they didn't arrive in the next town empty handed.

In the end, they loaded up two carts, a larger one for the children, which Grahom drove, and a smaller one filled with what little they could scrounge from the town, which Jin guided. Jack smiled as he watched Eriko turn down a horse to ride in favor of sitting with Jin in the cart, but he stayed out of earshot, letting the two have their private conversation.

Tamsin, who had been observing Grahom unsuccessfully explain to Morgan and Cordelia how to hitch the wagons to the horses and finally just giving up to and doing it himself, caught Jack watching Eriko. She put a hand lightly on his shoulder.

"That's unexpected," she said.

"What part?" Jack said.

"That Eriko... how do I put this. That Eriko is letting this place feel real enough to let that happen," Tamsin said.

"I think it's starting to feel real to all of us," Jack said. He checked the saddle on the horse he'd chosen for himself, laughing at how, like using a bow or tracking people through the wilderness, he just knew how to saddle and care for a horse, wondering what game skills Morgan and Cordelia's characters didn't have that was causing them to critically fail hitching a wagon. "I'm happy to see it, though. Eriko's... she's not inclined to be happy."

"I don't know anyone else like that," Tamsin said.

"I know you mean me, but I think five out of the six of us are not inclined to be happy," Jack said.

"True enough," Tamsin said. She checked on her own horse and then looked at Jack. "You know something funny? I can tell that in-game, my character has no idea how to saddle a horse, but I really do know how from real life. I'm actually better at this than the rest of you. Who knew being a spoiled kid with riding lessons would come in handy as a wizard?"

"Did you help your brother with his?"

"I did," Tamsin said, looking guilty. "I was so tempted to saddle his horse wrong so he'd fall off so I could get back at him for stealing my magic cape, but it seemed..."

"Petty?"

"Like a waste of hit points," she said.

Jack laughed and ran a hand casually along his horse's neck.

"So. Jack. Are we a thing?" Tamsin said.

Jack peered around his horse to look at her.

"Do you want to be a thing?"

"Do *you* want to be a thing?" she asked back.

"I really think I do," Jack said. "I kind of feel like we're supposed to be a thing. Whatever world we're in."

"I think if we were back home reality wouldn't let us," Tamsin said.

"So, screw the real world," Jack said. "We're here now. We almost die on a daily basis. Let's be happy."

Tamsin nodded and laughed.

"Okay," she said. "Let's give it a shot."

They hopped on their horses, shared a laugh as Tobias overshot his target and slid right off the other side of his horse and had to try a second time as a wagon full of children laughed, and had a bit of a scare as Cordelia's horse seemed to look at her like she'd offended the it somehow and almost threw her off. But with a bit of work, they found themselves on the road.

Jack and Cordelia traded off taking the lead, Silence trotting along beside or between them as an extra pair of eyes scanning the forest. It was an uneventful trip, a welcome change, as none of them wanted to do battle with a wagon full of kids in tow. Eventually they came to another small town, this one pleasantly ordinary, with no undead infestation to deal with. They were welcomed warmly, if fearfully, until the adventurers told them about ending the ghoul threat.

They bartered for a few more horses and agreed to stay for a few days, offering to deal with a goblin problem in the hills beyond the town. Tobias performed at the local tavern, but he did not tell the tale of the ghouls. Not here, not so close to where so much tragedy had happened.

One afternoon, Morgan gathered the group together, and they walked a little bit outside of the village, sitting beside a strangely serene river that ended in a waterfall off a sort, rocky cliff. The trees cleared where the waterfall dropped off, and they could see mountains in the distance, and, even further, signs of a larger city.

"We need to figure out where we go from here," Morgan said, sitting down on a stone.

"That city looks interesting," Tobias said.

"I keep thinking we owe Moderate Expectations an ending," Cordelia said. "I don't like that we never went back."

"Eriko?" Tamsin said.

"I'll go where you go," the rogue said, though there was an unusual hesitation in her voice. "This place is pretty, but we'll all go mad here without some adventure."

Jack caught something in the air, just the slightest sound. He tilted his head to hear it better, and then walked away from the group to tune out the conversation.

"Jack?" Morgan said.

Jack held up a hand, and his heart caught in his throat as he spotted the source of the sound. In the distance, an impossible sight appeared. Flying on massive wings, scales gleaming blue and copper, a dragon sailed through the air lazily, its wings making the rhythmic noise that had caught Jack's attention initially. The group fell silent, watching as the dragon settled onto the tip of a mountaintop on the other side of the valley below. It let out an almost birdlike squawk, looked out over the landscape below it, and then took flight again, disappearing into the distance like a glittering jewel.

"We're in dragon country," Tobias said.

"Wow," Morgan said.

"So," Tobias said. "Let's not go in that direction. Sound good?"

Epilogue: Among the dead

Mordecai the Unholy was watching butterflies.

I'm allowed, thought Mordecai, who had been known as Leo in the real world. Just because I'm a necromancer doesn't mean I can't like to watch living things. Everyone's always expecting me to live in a bubble of gloom and death. Some of the nicest people I know are necromancers.

Okay, that last part is a lie, he thought. Most necromancers are mad at best, truly vile at worst. He didn't blame people for not wanting to associate with him.

Except the undead, of course. The undead never really had a problem with him.

He saw the ghoul ranger emerge from the forest and enter the butterfly-filled field, drawing his hood up to hide from the sun. He's early, Leo thought. Poor bastard. I would have waited until nightfall. Probably thinks I'm a horrible person asking to meet with him in a sunny field in broad daylight.

"Mordecai," the ghoul said.

"Murtok," Leo responded. "You're in one piece."

"And there are dozens fewer ghouls in the world, thanks to your suggestion," the ghoul said. "The group of adventurers were every bit as helpful as you said they'd be."

"Glad they helped, Murtok," Leo said. "Did they all survive?"

"Despite, honestly, their best attempt at getting themselves killed through terrible planning, none of them were killed fighting the ghouls," Murtok said. "I'm glad for it—they wouldn't have deserved an ignominious death like that."

"And your observations about them?" Leo said. "Are they… invested?"

"They're good people, Mordecai," Murtok said. "Even the most self-centered of them stepped up to fight. My brother… he told them our story."

Leo nodded thoughtfully.

"And how did they react?"

"With skeptical empathy," Murtok said. "Which is the best I could hope for. Too much sympathy and I'd fear they'd be sucked in by my brother's darkness. Not enough and who knows what would happen. But they listened. They felt something. They seemed to understand what was at stake. You chose your champions well."

"I didn't choose them," Leo said. "For better or for worse, they are what the gods have thrown us. We have to work with the tools given."

"Well, it could be worse," Murtok said. "Is there anything else you require?"

"No," Leo said. He withdrew a leather folder from within his robes and handed it to the ghoul. "The potions I promised. They should help with the pain."

Murtok accepted folder, staring at it but not opening it to look at the contents.

"Thank you, Mordecai," Murtok said. "There aren't many in this world who will help a suffering ghoul."

"Let me know when you need more," Leo said.

The ghoul looked at him with a glimmer of suspicion, but said nothing.

"Go on, old friend. I know the sunlight pains you. There's no reason to suffer needlessly."

Murtok nodded and turned to leave. Leo called out.

"Murtok, one last question."

The ghoul ranger turned back.

"Did you like them?" Leo asked. "You have a better heart than I do. I trust your judgment more than mine."

Murtok smiled a toothy grin.

"I think they are good people, Mordecai," Murtok said. "And we both know there are not enough of those in this world."

The necromancer bowed his head.

"Be safe, hunter," he said.

"You as well," Murtok said, disappearing back into the forest.

Leo, who was also Mordecai the Unholy, accidental master of the dead, let a butterfly land on his fingertips. He found himself hypnotized by the delicate beauty of its wings.

I hope good people are what we need, he thought. We've tried monsters and bastards and failed. And we don't have time to try again.

ABOUT THE AUTHOR

Matthew Phillion is a writer, actor, and film director based in Salem, Massachusetts and the author of the Indestructibles Young Adult superhero adventure series, the spinoff series Echo and the Sea and its sequels, and the pop fantasy Dungeon Crawlers adventure series.